SEDUCING DARKNESS

DARK SPELL SERIES BOOK 3

ISRA SRAVENHEART

DEDICATION

So, hey...
Here we go again.
It's been a wild ride. Just when we think we're being brought back down to
Earth, you come along and relight the fire.
With you, it's never ever boring, yet you always manage to keep me
grounded, a quality that is very difficult to possess. Not only do you excite
and motivate me, you also pick me up when it's all gone to shit—which is a
quality extremely difficult to find in anyone.
However, you have surpassed them all.

You don't completely believe in yourself right now, but you'll rise from the
ashes again. I just know you'll be greater than you ever envisioned.
That's kind of the point—to see it through.

1

Afair maiden with long, shimmery, golden hair that fell all the way down her back was getting ready to retire for the night. She walked earnestly up to the iron window frame in a thin, white lace nightdress and proceeded to draw the rich red velvet curtains so that her idyllic chateau was once again hidden from any prying eyes.

She was holed up in her isolated tower, away from all humankind, but honestly, she preferred it this way, just as it had been for a year now. Although she sometimes wondered why on Earth she wasn't off gallivanting with others, she remembered that the human condition was tragic at best.

Oh, how it repulsed Isra that people could go around with all these feelings and emotions, and still somehow manage to get through their day without losing their tiny, apathetic minds. It was unthinkable! Isra was disgusted by it, and she was brutally honest when she expressed how she truly felt about those endearing romantic notions that a lover bestowed unto his beloved. In fact, it might just succeed in making her vomit if she spent too long pondering it.

Oh, hell no. I won't be doing any of that. The human disease is absolutely vile. I must avoid it at all costs. No, I can't allow myself to be tainted with all that misery. Eww. Isra grimaced. The thought made her shudder.

She was nineteen years old but yet she'd been through many tribulations in her young life. At only seventeen, she handed her heart over to the darkness. Since it had been broken, she had no use for it anyhow and questioned what the point in it was.

You find a man. He dangles the illusion of love in front of you. You fall for him—hook, line and sinker—and then catastrophe beckons. He then toys with your feelings, knowing you'd do anything to keep that romantic connection forthcoming. No! I'll never get involved in that nonsense again. It's just not worth the energy, Isra cursed to herself vehemently, stamping on the reverie in hatred as she recalled her fateful dalliance with Jonathan.

He was a charming fellow she'd met when she'd been aimlessly waiting for her best friend, Everilda. They became acquainted, and Isra regretfully had a fondness for the buffoon, whom she found was deeply involved with Everilda from the outset. Suffice to say, Isra wasn't best pleased when she happened to witness none other than Jonathan and Everilda in a fiery spat. It turned out the two not-so star-crossed lovers had been quarrelling. Everilda taunted poor Jonathan, shouting out his failures for all and sundry to hear.

"Oh, he was a waste of a man. What did I ever see in him? I must have been walking around in a daze. Disoriented, blundering on about the fanciful love I believed we shared when it was just one big illusion. It's abhorrent. If it wasn't for Everilda, I'd still be in that frightening delusion now. It doesn't bear the thought of how many years of drudgery could have been ahead of me. However, we cannot live in the past. One has to continue moving forward or disappointment will surely become a burden," Isra said to herself, pausing to glance at the view from the window.

Shambre Fell was a distinguished citadel cloistered away from those whose eyes may be tempted to look in on the witch with the blackened soul. A flowing stream enveloped the cloister and its most meticulously kept secret. The cerulean-blue aquatics delicately melded with the soft greenery of Shambre Fell's adequately preserved gardens. Isra could often be seen tending to the scented amethyst and ruby-red rose bushes that cultivated alongside the access to Shambre Fell, but the extensive assortment of perennials and saplings took care of themselves. You could say that it was magic because Isra barely lifted a finger.

Isra mustered a smile and gazed up at the translucent sky. It was remarkably clear for a summer night. There were no clouds whatsoever but beyond the rich cobalt-blue, tiny stars shone brightly, their numbers in the thousands. It was peaceful knowing that even though Isra wasn't out to experience the beauty of nature, the stars reminded her that she wasn't alone.

She had little knowledge of the former occupant that dwelled here before. She recalled a nice young fellow with mousy brown hair that had shown her around the elegant tower of Shambre Fell before she'd taken up residency. He explained that the last tenant was a most formidable witch who perished in tragic circumstances. The irony was that Isra was indeed a witch—however, Isra was immortal, which was extremely exhilarating for a nineteen-year-old female who had barely begun living out her existence. In any case, it was doubtful the latter would happen to Isra.

Isra had her own set of circumstances that had resulted in her turning her heart to darkness. It was a rather sordid tale, but Isra fell for that Jonathan fellow, not knowing he was cavorting with none other than her best friend, Everilda Daughtry. It was the ultimate betrayal, in Isra's eyes. Both Everilda and Jonathan knew Isra was much entwined with both of them and yet they still conducted their shady business.

Suffice to say, Everilda and Isra parted ways since that rather embarrassing event. Everilda had also paid the piper when the prestigious Wingdom's Academy not only banished her but stripped her of all of her powers. Isra giving her heart up to the darkness was just the icing on the cake. As far as Isra was concerned, Everilda losing her powers was poetic justice for her treachery. But still, the two women remained at loggerheads.

However, Isra also caught the attention of light-bringer, Samuel Reynaldi, when her budding romance with Jonathan turned sour. Samuel was the Lord and Chief of Spirisity, the heavenly realm in which light beings lived. As it turned out, Samuel became aware of Isra shortly before she discovered Jonathan's betrayal.

Samuel sent his feathered friend, Astrid, to keep a close eye on Isra, as he was greatly invested in Isra's case despite the fact she had not completely turned over to the dark side at that point in time. But Astrid developed a fondness for the budding young witch, and so he'd gone against all of Samuel's protocols, not only transforming himself into a magnificently handsome human but later, the two lost souls formed an alliance, which riled Samuel even more. The light-bringer was disappointed. Astrid was a trusted confidant, and so Samuel had to intervene.

Isra and Astrid were about to unleash dark magics unto the world. Samuel couldn't allow that, so he made sure Isra was kept in Shambre Fell where she could never lay eyes on another human soul again. Of course, Samuel cleverly wiped all of Isra's memories clean. She had no recollection of ever meeting Samuel or Astrid, much to Astrid's defeat.

Strangely enough, as Isra turned her attention back to the window frame, her piercing lime-green eyes happened to fall upon a jet-black raven preening his feathers while casually flashing his golden-yellow eyes back at her ominously.

Oh, my. She's seen me. I'm not prepared for this at all. Whatever will I do? Astrid fumbled around awkwardly, trying to maintain eye contact, as it would be ignorant if he turned away now.

"Why, hello, my beauty. Aren't you a sight to behold! I could have sworn for a moment you seemed familiar, but my brain does like to play tricks on me!" Isra mumbled.

Astrid was apprehensive about whether he should respond. He felt so flimsy about it. It was the fact of Isra not knowing him. Then there was him being banished, therefore forbidding him from engaging with her. It made him feel conflicted. But as luck would have it, Isra turned away from the window and stifled a yawn.

Isra quickly disregarded the notion of familiarity, grabbed the black iron bolt, and latched it onto the window so that it was left ajar, which was promising for Astrid. He hadn't been shut out. He watched as she disappeared behind those rich ruby-red curtains. Presumably, she was clambering into bed, laying her head on the soft white pillows, retiring for the night.

"Well, at least I am not excluded from looking in on her this evening. I guess I'll sit here for a while and wonder what she's thinking," Astrid mumbled to himself, carefully spreading one of his wings so that he could preen the other.

You see, Astrid the raven had never *really* left Isra's side. Did those good and kindly folks at Spirisity honestly think that would be the end of it all? That Isra would be none the wiser and Astrid would simply shack up with another raven? No, of course not. Don't be ridiculous!

Astrid was a rebellious soul at heart, and he knew deep in his gut he and Isra would soon meet again. He wasn't going to give up now. Of course, he had to master the art of subtlety when he kept watch on Isra due to his banishment, but he was an elusive bastard. The way he figured, Samuel and James would have a difficult task ahead of them if they attempted to keep tabs on his comings and goings.

"It could always be worse. They could have completely destroyed us by turning me into something revolting. I could have been a horned toad or something that slinks. So, I'm going to count my blessings. It's all about perception. When the time is right, I will indeed make my entrance," Astrid marvelled to himself with delicious enthusiasm.

2

———

Isra opened her eyes immediately, waking suddenly from a dream. She rubbed the palms of her hands across her eyes, although she felt dazed. She'd had a most splendid dream, one where she was sitting against a large oak tree. The robust trunk provided support for her back as she idly chilled out in a luscious green forest.

The sun was peering over her, shimmering a little as noon dragged on. A stranger was watching her from a distance. Isra assumed it was a man. She'd seen him before somewhere, though she couldn't recall where...

And then everything had gone blank. Her memory was just as bemused as ever as she lay in her bed.

Isra shifted up against the mahogany bed frame, sitting against a soft white pillow. The sun was just creeping in, bringing out the harshness of day. Something caught her eye—a strange black shadow. It was odd, but Isra thought for a split second that she'd caught sight of a black raven peeking through the tiny slit between the window and the plush red velvet curtains. But it was impossible.

Perhaps I simply dreamed it. My imagination is merely playing tricks on me. Why would one of those charming, magnificent beings come and visit me of all souls? It's silly. No matter. One cannot lay about all morning. We must press on, Isra thought, shaking the notion from her mind.

ASTRID TRIED to hold his breath as his claws made an eerie sound from being perched on the window ledge. He was almost reeling from how close he'd come to being caught. He made a sharp effort at ambling away from the window at lightning speed and attempted to compose himself.

"Shit, you almost got caught again, didn't you? This isn't very stealthy, Astrid, is it? Damn. I've got to make adjustments!" he said to himself.

Astrid cursed sullenly and swiftly veered around the corner of the window ledge. He was trying his utmost to not get spotted by Isra but it was proving to be somewhat challenging. Astrid knew he simply couldn't just fly away. He had to keep visiting her, if only to get a glimpse of all he had lost.

The pain of losing someone you love is immeasurable. You never get over it. You may well be able to accept the situation for what it is, but you never truly heal. Instead, you paper over the cracks in the hope that, over time, the pain becomes more manageable.

"I keep returning here, knowing there's virtually no chance of us ever being anything like what we were before, and yet I still come back, reliving it all again. Every day... Seeing her. Watching her brush that long, golden, shimmery, fair hair with ringlets dropping past her shoulders. Yet despite it all, I know it's inevitable for us to never become friends again, never mind the latter. I always come back, holding this wretched pain inside myself, every single day," Astrid muttered sadly.

He was angry with Samuel for all the trickery enacted, and more so, Astrid was aggrieved with himself. He continued revisiting his eternal torment without a moment's pause. It had only been a month since Samuel had cruelly taken away Isra's memories so she'd have no knowledge of ever knowing Astrid, but he remembered it like it was yesterday, the second when he noticed Samuel's sky-blue eyes staring out at him mysteriously and he'd interjected, "So James squealed then?"

Astrid remembered standing there nervously, awaiting the reply even though the answer was obvious. Samuel retorted, "Yes, and a good thing he did, too. You're about to unleash Armageddon with our little spitfire!"

The rest of it Astrid didn't want to think about. It resided far too heavily inside his mind. It would have been easier if he could just block it out. Maybe it would have been better if he'd lost his memories, too. But Samuel would never have done that. He would always want Astrid to remember every single second of that fateful day in Nefaria Sands. In some twisted way, Samuel probably regarded it as a necessary means to remind Astrid of what one's fate is when they shy away from the light path and manoeuvred towards darkness. It was as if Astrid crossed the penultimate enemy line and there was no way of coming back from the breach.

"Well, we can't go back, can we? There isn't anything I can do to change that outcome. Dwelling on it won't make much difference either. But I wonder—"

Astrid paused momentarily. He eyed Isra's bedroom window with scrutiny. It surely wouldn't do any harm if he had a tiny look at her, would it? It couldn't damage the situation any further than it already was if he let himself into her bedroom for a split second. After all, he'd already had the tragedy of her never knowing him. How could it possibly become any worse?

"I could just slip in. She's out cold in there. If I'm really quiet and methodical enough, she won't know I was ever in her presence. I just want a decent look at her. It will surely satisfy my curiosity."

He pondered in earnest, questioning whether he'd slip through the gap where the window had been left ajar. He was perched on the side of it and knew Isra had fixed the bolt on the window from the inside. If he was going to get in, he'd have to squeeze through.

"She won't have any inclination I was ever here. What could possibly go wrong?" Astrid blustered as he edged away from the window, perusing the land below, which, he had to admit, didn't look inviting. There was a significant drop from Isra's bedroom to the ground. "Hmm. I may as well just have a little look and then I can be on my way."

Astrid felt as if he was being a little intrusive. On many occasions, he was reprimanded for stalking Isra, but this was a whole new set of circumstances whereby he couldn't be discovered for doing so.

"Now, if I just grasp how I'm going to get myself in this cramped gap, then we'll be away," Astrid meandered to himself.

He knew crawling into Isra's bedroom was badgering improper, but the way he saw it, it was innocuous. He'd be in and out before anyone saw anything at all, Isra included and Samuel none the wiser. It would be Astrid's little secret.

Astrid ambled over to the window, conscientiously eyeing up what he was up against. Discreetly pushing himself through the tiny crevice, he managed to get through effortlessly. It was a much easier task when he moved past the rich ruby-red velvet curtains, but alas, it was dark, so he bungled around clumsily until he landed aimlessly on the cold stone floor.

Astrid proceeded to shake the inconvenience off and shrugged. "Oh, well. These things cannot be helped. One must learn to steer better when there's no glare of daylight to shine the way. Still, I've never been here before. I must admit, it does have a certain allure to it," he remarked as he inspected the exquisite, vivid colours overshadowing Isra's bedroom.

The four-poster bed was the centrepiece. It was beautifully donned in ruby-red velvet curtains around the bed itself while the bedding consisted of brilliant white pillows that matched marvellously in comparison to the blood-red bed covering and the curtains by the window.

Astrid sneakily deployed himself onto the foot of Isra's overstated bed, where he was able to see her altogether. Her long, soft, shimmery, fair hair descending past her bosom practically melded in with her lustrous white nightdress. He edged closer to her, noticing that something looked peculiar. She looked a little off-colour, like something had been drastically abrogated from her admirable being.

"Of course, this has all been deftly done. Samuel has executed a masterful job of establishing an astonishing climactic world constructed to beguile Isra's soul. And he hasn't stopped at the internal enrichments. She's an adumbration of her former self," Astrid observed as he watched Isra sleeping from his deliberately chosen spot. "Well, I've seen her. What more else is there for me to do? Samuel didn't just take her memories away. He's totally overhauled her, down to her essence. I wonder if there is anything left behind."

Astrid's consciousness took him back to that momentous day...

3

~ One Year Ago ~

Astrid could only stare, as Isra had vanished before him. Just like that, she'd disappeared in a golden, shimmery light. Who knows what Samuel was planning to do with her, but one thing was for certain—things were going to be very different from now on.

Samuel turned to Astrid in earnest. The light-bringer had a furrowed brow. Clearly, this situation had been plaguing him greatly.

He looked worn underneath the eyes. It was doubtful Samuel had been sleeping properly. The heavy, drooping bags under his eyes signified it had most definitely been several weeks since Samuel had managed to get a full night's rest. But who needs sleep when you're an almighty, powerful light-bringer that manages to tear down those accosted to the dark with a simple flash of your hand?

Samuel had also been knocking back the Irish whiskey to extremities, so his heavy alcohol consumption was also a strong contender in kicking him off his game. It went without saying that Samuel was struggling in his role recently, and it showed when the old man tried to force a half-smile in Astrid's direction. His brow was weathered and covered in small, wiggly lines due to constant frowning. It's true that those who are ascended are still victims of that mighty fiend, ageing. There is no escaping that inevitable fate.

"I am not the enemy here, Astrid," Samuel began in a formal tone.

Yet he paused, seemingly having difficulty finding the exact words. Now, how do you find the correct way to deploy in a situation where you have to do the thing you'll be hated for? He shook his head and straightened himself before continuing.

"But you and Isra have been cavorting with one another for aeons, and not to mention against *my* orders." Samuel scolded Astrid with a fierce glare. However, he softened his gaze a little. "This is for the best. I understand you feel things have all got out of hand and quite possibly you could be right. In any event, it is my job to ensure the safety of the realm. You have to understand, boy, you can't just hand a forceful sorceress like Isra the keys to obscurity and then expect me to sit back and let you all get on with it! Sure, I could have let you both run ragged, but sadly, I am doomed to protect this apathetic, disastrous world, and simply put, I cannot allow it, my son!"

Samuel finished curtly, although he did muster some compassion as he emitted, "Again, it's for the best. She won't remember who you are, and hopefully, we can all recover from this situation, refreshed and ready to hightail the next dark soul."

Wait, I'm not being punished? Are you kidding me? I thought I was truly done for, but if he's saying I can go back to business as if nothing has happened, well, he's got another thing coming if he thinks I'll just go along with his suggestion. The audacity of it! Isra's been magically hijacked, and I am expected to move on! You have to be fucking joking, Astrid ranted to himself, trying to establish just what was occurring.

If he wasn't to be banished, why hadn't Samuel done anything further?

Samuel stared out at the golden ray of light shining brightly on the soft pastel yellow sands of Nefaria. At first glimpse, nobody would be able to decipher what the light truly concealed. However, the blazing rays of the sun came streaming across the aquamarine skies, and then, with a subtle wave of Samuel's hand, he harnessed the magic within him to bring the gold illumination back to life.

That bright, golden hair with delicate ringlets that came past her shoulders stuck out amongst her brilliant white lace dress. Even though those infamous piercing lime-green eyes of hers remained shut, you could just about make out that tiny green glow from outside their sockets.

"Of course, I appreciate that you find this deeply distressing, but the reason I haven't sent you hightailing back to Spirisity with your tail between your legs is I want you to understand the severity of what you've done. Sure, you felt that returning Isra's devilish magic to her was justified. But there is always a consequence when one dabbles in the dark arts. Isra had her glowing orb taken from her and thus also her memories of ever knowing you. My reasoning is you two were in way too far over your heads. I truly can't even begin to fathom just what you thought you were doing, having Damien Daughtry's other half transform you into a man, but it stops now, boy. He's been taken care of. And Isra? Well, I am about to demonstrate..."

Samuel paused, concentrating on Isra standing erect for all to see. Astrid could only look on in terror, having no inclination of what Samuel was about to do, but it didn't feel as if it would be pleasant. Samuel had masterfully put Isra on display like she was a child, vulnerable and restrained yet unable to feel a single sensation or comprehend what was happening to her.

Astrid witnessed something like this before—quite an old legend, one he'd heard from a long time ago before ever seeing it for himself. It was known as the Sleeping Beauty spell, a curse designed to put one in a deep sleep. However, unlike the fairy-tale you've been led to believe so willingly, the participant is still very much in a daze long after they've awakened. They barely remember anything and constantly search for the missing piece until the day they perish.

Of course, Samuel wants to unleash the Sleeping Beauty curse on Isra. He believes she should be fated to suffer. In his eyes, she's the villainess, the one that can send his not-so-love-and-light realm crashing down into despondency if she ever regains her power. He must know somewhere deep inside himself that if she comes back from this, knowing what he's done, he's in for quite the nasty surprise, Astrid thought to himself anxiously, curiously staring up at Isra from where he was perched on the soft yellow sand.

However, he was suddenly hit by a fleeting notion that made him smile. *What if she returns one day, not only recapturing the brightness inside of her that he took but also becoming what he fears she'll always be? It is possible. She can still become Lady Isra of the Dark. It has indeed been foretold, and we all know how obsessed Samuel is about these pragmatic prophecies. Perhaps the real reason he sees fit to seize control of her is that he is deeply threatened by Isra.*

Astrid looked at Samuel one last time, eyeing the light-bringer carefully. His reasoning, all his irrational logic, became crystal clear. Astrid wracked his brains, trying to recall the day he'd seen that writing imprinted on the wall regarding Isra. He couldn't quite remember the exact wording, but it was profoundly astute in suggesting she would become a mighty sorceress. That was the long and short of it. So even after Samuel going to such desperate lengths to attempt to placate Isra in an ethereal stronghold, Samuel could indeed live to regret this.

Astrid watched quietly as Samuel muttered some words under his breath while standing behind Isra so that he was almost parallel to her. Then, Samuel cautiously closed his eyes, and although he still maintained a warm smile, he got to work envisioning Isra's fate.

White, cloudy energy descended from the weary heavens, completely covering Isra's form. Tiny, white glowing embers began sizzling away as the cloudy energy travelled down to Isra's feet. The small white sparkles dissipated, and several harsh white lightning bolts struck Isra, ruthlessly embedding themselves into her as they singed and howled into the atmosphere. Crying out in anguished screeching, they finally became reduced to nothing, leaving Isra's lifeless body illuminated in pure white before it completely vanished from view.

Astrid was about to assume the worst. It was painful for him to witness. He couldn't bear it any longer. There she was, erected for the whole world to see, and had been completely obliterated. At least, that was how it appeared to him. Astrid wasn't entirely sure just what effect Samuel's white light ritual had on Isra, but he was damned sure it wasn't anything good.

Just imagine Astrid's disbelief when a voice began chortling away eerily inside his mind:

"Oh, there she goes, and now she has gone. The light has won. Our dark witch will no longer penetrate the sun because, with this implication, she has no ruling over our legislation. Her memories are tattered. The realisation will never be spoken and thus our spell can never be broken. But if she awakens before the spell is truly done, then, my dear friend, those love and lighters better run!"

That is most intriguing, Astrid silently responded to the voice in his head. He was about to respond with something further when Samuel jolted him out of his reverie with a sharp bang.

"Come on, boy. The show is over. Let's get home," Samuel instructed. He patted his left shoulder for Astrid to hop on. "Perhaps after this haughty day, some strong coffee is in order, eh? I think it would be pleasing."

Astrid said nothing. He didn't know what to say. He wanted to remain angry at Samuel but something inside him suggested there would be a better alternative. Astrid had to be patient, but for now, he'd be able to sit tight and wait for a reckoning.

~ One Hour Later ~

SAMUEL STRAIGHTENED HIMSELF, arching his back to get more comfortable in his favourite red velvet armchair while a steaming hot mug of coffee was situated next to him on his solid wood desk.

Astrid could only glance upwards at the light bringer from where he was perched a couple of feet away on one of the idle chairs positioned parallel to Samuel's desk. Those chairs gave a grand view of the world outside, showcasing Spirisity proudly while also displaying the other beautiful facets of the land. Despite the view, Astrid was sore in his heart, having lost Isra when Samuel intervened only an hour ago. And now was the dreaded talk, the one where he and Samuel would come face to face and finally discuss all that had been bothering Astrid. It was the conversation that would also establish why Astrid rebelled against Samuel's wishes, though honestly, Astrid didn't want to have it.

He'd had enough; feeling defeated at having to watch Samuel take Isra's precious memories from her, making Astrid a stranger as he swept her head clean of everything.

Meeting Astrid... The moment Astrid detailed the prophecy surrounding her... Even the final moment they had together where Astrid handed Isra some of the greatest power she could ever hope to own. All of that was gone, courtesy of Samuel. So it was only natural that Astrid harboured some resentment toward Samuel, but Samuel didn't care for that.

"Astrid," Samuel finally mouthed after what seemed like centuries of Astrid being alone, secluded in his gathering thoughts regarding the events of that day.

"Samuel," Astrid replied.

His tone was musty yet formal, for he showed no emotion—just a blank canvas, as though this was a business meeting of sorts. Astrid wasn't about to show just how downtrodden he felt.

Samuel narrowed his eyes carefully before he remarked in an earnest tone, "I know you are probably very irked by me right now, but I had no choice, boy. You and Isra were in far too deep. I had to step in."

Samuel turned to the window that showed the paradise of Spirisity in all its glory. Acres of green grassy land surrounded by soft green hills amongst a crystal-clear blue sky stood out like a painting. Samuel couldn't help but admire the view.

"Astrid, you know, in the scheme of things, I knew you were going to end up with her. I just hadn't realised how far you'd gone down.

You used to be so much more. You had a passion for the work we did in bringing those who were darkened back to the light, but with this girl—woman, or whatever she was—you were besotted from the start, and I knew you would only plunder further until it was at such a point neither of you could return."

Samuel waited for a reply, but when none came, he continued.

"Honestly, boy. I knew there were destructive traits in you and perhaps it's my fault since I disregarded them, but I've always been good to you, always taken care of you, ensuring you understood the matters at hand and that there was no indifference. Still, you going to Damien Daughtry and getting transformed into a human was never on my radar. I had so many hopes for you. I guess in the end, you disappointed me, but I always knew in the back of my mind you would, so I can't scold you too much for that," Samuel retorted candidly.

Astrid said nothing. He didn't know what he could say that would change anything. He could only meet Samuel's blue, glinting eyes with his yellow ones and feel the harsh branding coming down upon him. Samuel continued, turning his gaze back to the window and onto the majestic land.

"I feel there is nothing left here for you, Astrid. I have done all I can to be a strong, fatherly figure to you and it's simply not been enough."

Astrid still wasn't sure what he should say and so he dropped his head to his claws before agreeing with Samuel.

"You are right, master. But I'd do it again. I know you don't understand my reasoning as to why. I was so drawn to Isra from the moment I heard her name and even her wretched origins. I was delighted by the glow in her eyes, even when she was weeping beside me. She was unlike anything I had ever known. I'd risk it all over and over again just to get a glimpse of her," Astrid blurted out, realising he'd admitted his feelings for her unknowingly.

Samuel took his focus from the glorious sights outside, turning to Astrid with a furrowed brow as though something was troubling him.

It was clear to Astrid there was something that sounded final in Samuel's voice—a culmination between them both.

"It's not what I wanted to hear, Astrid, but thank you for your honesty. Perhaps we can let the matter settle for a few days and then attempt to get back to normality. Whatever that may be," Samuel concurred.

"And Isra?" Astrid piped up.

He didn't want to sound too eager, but he was desperate to know what had become of her, even though he doubted he'd ever see her again.

"She's safe. Out of harm's way. But she will always be watched by the closeness of Spirisity. You could say she's still our little pet project but it doesn't change anything, Astrid. She has no memory of knowing you. I know that must sting but it is for the better end of both of you, even if you cannot see beyond that for now. You two were too dangerous to exist together as one. Someone had to put an end to it. People don't understand that sometimes love can be our worst enemy because two souls are sometimes so well matched for each other that all their dark and evil characteristics only clash in a fiery blaze amongst the good. It is that way, even if we choose to overlook that tiny detail," Samuel mustered before he turned away again to the window, having had no more to say to Astrid.

As far as Samuel was concerned, this was it.

4

A tear fell from Astrid's eye as the memory of that day came full circle in his mind. Samuel had done everything he saw fit in a bid to stop Isra from becoming anything other than what she was, but Astrid saw a glimmer of hope in the form of that cryptic lyric he heard while witnessing Isra being encased in Samuel's white light spell.

"Thank goodness it's over. I never want to relive that as long as I live."

Astrid gasped, overcome with emotion. If he was human, he'd have been able to wipe his tears, but alas, there was no such ability for a raven.

"I best leave this place forthwith," he muttered, trying to regain his focus. He looked over lovingly at Isra one last time as she lay sleeping. "I'll be back," he told her.

He lifted his wings above his head, arching his back as he prepared to take flight. In one swift motion, he flew over to the window ledge, gently squeezing himself through the tiny gap once more, and vacated into the murky, midnight-blue skies before anyone could see him.

~

Samuel quivered, staring impatiently at his steaming hot coffee. He figured that with the masterful invention of a kettle to brew his favourite beverage, somebody would have managed to conjure up something that could magically make the coffee immediately ready for consumption. However, such a remarkable innovation had yet to be discovered.

He scowled as he eyed the steaming hot mug evilly. "I do hope some buffoon gets off his idle backside one day and makes my life so much more convenient. It simply isn't practical for a man of my talents to have to wait to drink his coffee. Eurgh!"

Samuel strode over to the window, hoping that perhaps it would give him a moment of clarity. He looked out onto the realm of Spirisity in earnest. It was a quiet, sombre morning and although there had been a bout of torrential rain in the early hours, the delicate, soft, yellow crocuses still stuck out among the mass of greenery. Samuel couldn't help but chuckle; the violets managed to withstand their grip in the soil despite the horrific downpour whereas the bluebells hadn't been quite so fortunate. Their heads drooped by their sides as they clung frantically to their robust green stems.

"Everything withers away eventually," Samuel mused quietly while still eyeballing the prestigious land he was the proud owner of.

As the light-bringer and Lord and Chief of Spirisity, this grand monastery of a home and the magnificent gardens belonged to him so long as he remained in his post. As long as he continued being the big, influential source of power in the fight against light versus dark, he was allowed to reside here.

"I'll likely never see the day where I am forced to say goodbye to this eccentric place. It's been home to me longer than I care to remember. I'll never have anywhere else with quite as much character," Samuel marvelled to himself.

He was indeed pondering the notion that he might sit outside with his coffee if the weather fared slightly better. *It's a shame it's such a dreary day, otherwise, I'd park myself on those grey steps, sipping my lovely caffeine. Enjoy the morning glory, but alas, the elements don't share my vision.*

Samuel's office door unexpectedly flew open, bringing his reverie to a grand holt. James strode in. His mousy brown hair was a little unkempt, but he seemed his usual bright, cheery self. He sat in the chair opposite Samuel's desk without care.

"Good heavens, James! Don't you bloody well knock?" Samuel called out as he steered his attention away from the window immediately.

"No. And anyway, you looked like you were having a moment there," James interjected. He didn't care for the fact he'd made Samuel shamelessly jolt out of his vivid reverie.

"Yes, I was. However, I would appreciate it if you'd knock, dear boy," Samuel snapped. He sat on his comfortable red velvet armchair, proceeding to take a large sip of his lukewarm coffee. "Well, at least it's cooled down. There has been some improvement to this day!" he muttered earnestly.

James raised an eyebrow suspiciously in Samuel's direction. "You know, I can't see the necessity for all this nervousness. Astrid is banished. We took care of him and Isra, so chill out, man. The worst is over."

Samuel looked up at James with a stern glare but softened it a little as he mustered amicably, "While I appreciate the sentiment of what you are implying, James, I'm far from being able to relax. I'd much rather be tense. Just because Isra is safely implicated in the stronghold I placed her in doesn't mean all is well. She could strike back at any time and plunge herself right back into that darkness."

"Right. I understand your meaning, but she can't remember she ever enacted anything. She has no comprehension of who you or Astrid are. I doubt she would recognise me either. So really, I cannot fathom why you are so concerned."

Samuel stared awkwardly at James for a moment and took another gulp of his coffee, which had become room temperature and therefore was not fit for consumption. Samuel attempted to muster some kind of decorum and staggered out, "I don't think you understand the magnitude of what we're dealing with. There hasn't been a situation like this for almost a millennium. Yes, Isra has been taken down; however, there are complications of which you're not aware of." Samuel paused and then blurted out, "You see, I made a big show of things down in Nefaria but mainly for the benefit of Astrid. Isra had a powerful glowing green orb in her possession—"

"Yes, and you destroyed it. Therefore, it is no longer problematic," James responded swiftly.

Samuel's face dropped as he fumbled for the words. His pupils became increasingly large and he knew his fibbing was about to come full circle.

"Ah, yes. About that... I never obliterated Isra's magic. I just made an illusion alluding to the idea that I had." Samuel was red, flush with embarrassment as he confessed his sin.

"And why didn't you?" James pressed with a wide-eyed stare.

He was shocked Samuel would have done something so underhand. It wasn't very light bringer-like.

If he didn't destroy her forceful magic, why on Earth would he keep it under wraps this entire time, making out like he had? There's something amiss here. He's been jumping out of his skin from the moment I walked in, James blundered in thought, trying to fathom exactly what was going down.

"The magic Isra conjured up is extremely unique. Yes, it comes from darkness, for she is rooted in it to the very core of her being, but push that aside. It is valuable, and one day, having power like that lying around could indeed be rather resourceful," Samuel explained. "In normal circumstances, I would have seized it up and crushed it into smithereens but after the shenanigans Isra and Astrid played... Well, I feel as though that day may come sooner than we delude ourselves into believing."

"I see," James responded. "Well, I don't pretend to completely understand your reasoning, but I trust your judgment." But James wasn't entirely certain as to whether Samuel had made the right call. *It's a bizarre thing for a light-bringer to do. Any true light being would have quashed Isra's magic in a heartbeat. But here he is, saving it for a rainy day! Oh, my.*

"I know you have your reservations, James, but trust me. I understand the lineage that somebody like Isra comes from. I am trying to do my utmost to please the warring witch families. I know that doesn't sound very light bringer-ish but believe me, there's more to this job than handing out harsh punishments for those that go against the code," Samuel uttered in a serious tone.

"Warring witch families? Am I missing something? We don't deal with that," James countered in an abrasive tone.

"Actually, we do. I do, anyhow. I know you've not been in the business as long as I have, but there are things that the light are responsible for. However, we don't shout it all around the realm. It's quiet for a reason. If you think of it this way, the stratagem is pure genius if nothing else. I keep tabs on the warring witch families, and we may have one less soul that tumbles down to darkness."

"Then we'd all be out of a job," James shot back.

"Not necessarily. You see, it's all rather muddled behind the scenes. Those dim-witted mortals think of us as sweet, angelic beings floating around on shimmery white clouds. I mean, really. The stereotype is quite fucked up. But it is no matter because while they presume they know what we are and what we do, we will be out stopping darkness from escalating."

Samuel paused, realising he wasn't completely transparent with James, especially about a certain witch.

"I never told you this, but Isra's lineage isn't strictly human. She was born to be a fine sorceress and one day, she may well be so. But I have to please her relatives although she has no comprehension whatsoever of her origins," Samuel admonished carefully.

James's eyes narrowed at Samuel sceptically upon hearing his outburst of well-chosen words. "Hang on a moment, Samuel. Do you mean to tell me that Isra is connected to some of our most powerful witches? I mean, I don't follow the heritage but from my understanding, there are some frightening foes out there. But thankfully, I'll never have to lay my eyes on any of them."

James then scoffed, much to Samuel's disdain. He knew then he would have to go into more detail to make James understand the severity of things.

"I should have been straight with you from the beginning, but I must warn you that this conversation cannot go any further than this very room," Samuel elaborated. "Isra is the illegitimate daughter of Damien Daughtry."

"Oh, wow," James quipped. "Dare I even ask how you came to own such knowledge?"

"I became aware when I met Isra's very unfortunate mother, Gwendolyn Passe. She was troubled over Isra's behaviour. Gwendolyn couldn't handle Isra making things spark up out of nowhere and setting things alight. It's the same reason I named her 'firecracker.' Anyhow, when Gwendolyn met me to discuss the way forward, Damien Daughtry showed up along with her. Now, he was a very desperate man, extremely wary of whoever happened to be lurking around, for he was trapped in a mortal marriage with the dear old Damaris—a God-fearing woman if I'd ever seen one. Damien didn't want the news of this child getting into places whereby he'd have no power to silence the news."

James cocked his head, seemingly confused. Samuel nodded and then continued.

"Let us not forget, this was only a couple of years after he'd been famously kicked out of Wingdom's Academy because of his association with Rhiannon, a demoness. His mother, Marie, forced the marriage upon him, so Damien had been playing away. Gwendolyn was the poor peasant that had found herself in his grasp. Goodness knows why because she was not magical in any sense of the word, but they came to me, desperate for a solution."

James was hanging on the edge of his seat, carefully soaking up every word Samuel enunciated. He was more shocked than appalled, but still, the news was something that should have been disclosed from the outset. Of course, James understood why it hadn't been broadcast.

"And what was the solution you proposed?" James asked with curiosity.

"That Isra be signed over to me. I would be her guardian, watch over her, and ensure she had a good life, raised in the most proper manner I could see fit. The only thing I insisted upon was that Isra's true parentage remained a secret. They'd have no further contact with her. And that would be that. Of course, I did my utmost to entrust her with a good family but evidently, I lost sight of her for a while until the very day 'on high' brought it to my attention that Isra was headed straight for darkness almost two years ago."

"I see," James responded. "You knew who she was from the beginning then? You know, Samuel, I may be missing something here, but you did your utmost to keep Isra and Astrid apart. Does he have some mystical link to her also?"

James then wondered in provocative thought, *None of this makes any damn sense. I've been working for Samuel for as long as I can remember and all of this, well, it's baffling, to say the least. He knew Isra the entire time but yet said nothing. Surely, he had to have known about the prophecy pertaining to Isra also?*

James managed to compose himself slightly but he remained suspicious as he mentioned, "I mean, it doesn't quite make sense that you'd know who she is and Astrid happened to stumble into Spirisity one day. It all seems to be knitting together in ways it shouldn't."

"You're exactly right. I didn't know who Astrid would be at the time or even that it was him. I only knew the poor simpering sod as a raven but when I left Damien and Gwendolyn to gather my focus, I had a vision of Isra and it was Astrid standing with her as clear as day in the present timeline. But I didn't know who he was when I first became aware of her destiny," Samuel admitted.

He did seem quite conflicted about it all, but James couldn't work out if Samuel was telling the truth or whether he was conjuring up convincing stories that sounded appetising. Regardless, he knew there was more to this tale.

"The vision of Isra was extremely clear. She was deemed to be with a man. I now know this plucky soul was indeed Astrid, but they were deemed to bring about darkness and destruction. If their hearts aligned, they'd be dangerous to the realm. It kept on shouting this nonsensical word in my ear: 'twinflames, twinflames.' I didn't know what the hell it was. I'd never even heard the term and had no idea of what it meant. I honestly found it bemusing. Nonetheless, it stated very clearly that Isra and her counterpart would be connected as two souls destined to be together. Of course, let's skip the fluffy love stuff but it went along like this:

'They are destined to unite in the physical realm but be cautious because their coming together is also fated by great darkness. It will be one path towards the light or it shall be fated towards the other. Either way, Lady Isra is set to become a predominant figure in darkness.'

"Now I didn't fully understand it, even back then, but I knew Isra could not be situated with Daughtry or Passe. Efforts had to be doubled. I had no idea who the lucky male would be, so I couldn't rule anything out on that end. Besides, Isra was a mere baby. She couldn't adopt this role for years. I did my utmost to keep watch on her over the years. However, time is a funny thing; before you know, it escapes you, leaving it difficult to recapture what flew by so fast," Samuel finished thoughtfully.

"I understand," James mouthed apologetically. He felt extremely awkward now. This wasn't just a revelation but a mighty bombshell that could indeed lead to chaos. *Can you imagine what might commence if Isra became aware that she is directly related to Everilda? Her arch-nemesis. It doesn't bear thinking about. Oh, my goodness.*

"Apparently, you didn't do a very good job," Astrid retorted sarcastically from where he'd been sitting on the window ledge the entire time, idly taking in Samuel and James's conversation with much interest.

Although he was rather bemused at what he'd overheard about Isra, Astrid didn't have much in the way of an opinion on it. But then again, Samuel was no stranger to harbouring ghastly secrets relating to dark souls he was in charge of.

So my Isra is Damien's daughter? Well, now. Who could ever say they saw that coming? Oh, my! I am surprised he didn't react at all when I mentioned Isra to him by name unless, of course, Samuel magically fucked with his memories, too. I must get on. I am getting rather exhausted by these torrid revelations, Astrid thought, feeling a pang in his stomach.

Well, he'd done all he could and still managed to find another sordid secret the light folk were trying to hide, and so now it was time for him to go and seek out a delicious, juicy worm.

Everilda hung her head, desperate not to be spotted while taking in the beautiful blue seas of Seclera. She fathomed in the back of her mind that this place was as good as any to have some peace. Everilda hadn't been doing too well since she reunited with her father, Damien Daughtry and her demoness mother, Rhiannon.

It wasn't that Rhiannon was horrible to Everilda. In fact, it was quite the opposite. Rhiannon was so warm to her daughter that Everilda struggled to come to terms with it. With her Christian mother, Damaris, she received nothing but criticism. Her mother would often snap at Everilda, declaring just how wrong she had done something whereas Rhiannon was extremely encouraging to her wayward daughter. In any event, Everilda needed a moment to herself in an attempt to wrap her head around all this.

"At least I'll get some time to process my feelings, all while I figure out what the heck I'm doing with my life!" Everilda commented as she stared at the rough cobalt-blue ocean guarding Seclera.

"Oh, dear," a sneering, harsh voice piped up. "Are things not going your way? Oh, my! Well, that is most delicious indeed!"

Isra was standing inches away from Everilda, adorned in the most fanciful, rich purple lace dress with beautiful embroidery at the edge of the long sleeves. Isra's long, shimmery, golden-white hair hung down her shoulders, swaying gently in the morning breeze.

"Isra..." Everilda returned, sounding somewhat embarrassed at being found by somebody when she had chosen to conceal herself.

"Everilda!" Isra snapped back. "My, my, dear girl. You are a sight for sore eyes. Look at the state of you!"

Isra looked her foe up and down with a sly laugh, mocking her callously. Everilda was dressed in a soft powder-blue linen dress that gently enveloped her slim yet curvaceous form but didn't do much to enhance her figure. She had also become rather plump around her middle, which made her bosom stand out a little more. Perhaps it was all the rich dinners drenched in fattening sauces that had helped her to accumulate the extra weight. In any case, she looked distinctly different compared to Isra's slender form.

"Yes, well, I'm going through a transgression in my life, so if you don't mind, I would appreciate the gesture if you could leave me be," Everilda wailed, sounding deeply distressed; surely the sight of Isra was enough to make her feel even more terrible.

"Ha, girl, I just got here. Why, I think I'll stay awhile. You know, I haven't seen the wonders of Seclera in almost a year. I used to come here to meet Jonathan on our rendezvous," Isra muttered before taking a pause to venomously add, "or at least I did before you ceremoniously fucked that up for me!"

"Please. I don't wish to rake over the old coals," Everilda pleaded. "You have everything you've ever wanted—supreme power that allows you to do whatever you like. You're no longer tied down by the restraints of Wingdom's Academy because they are so freaking terrified of you. So how about you just leave me to wallow?"

"Well, I would depart but it's more fun if I hang around," Isra mused with a snide smile plastered across her face.

While the two women engaged in their rapturous confrontation, Astrid was soaring over the warm, sunlit skies. He spotted the two maidens down below, instantly recognising one of them as Isra. You couldn't miss her with her bright lime-green eyes, but it took him a second to work out that the other was Everilda.

Oh, my goodness. That can't be good. I should go down there and check if all is alright, Astrid thought, and with that, his idea of seeking out breakfast was quickly disregarded. He'd have to snatch himself some fat, delectable worms later.

Astrid proceeded to head downward, zooming right in front of Everilda and Isra and leaving them both rather bemused. They couldn't figure out why this raven was hovering mid-air in their midst. However, Astrid made his position clear, as he wanted to eradicate any confusion when he asked calmly, "Ladies, what's all the hubbub about? Why do you both look like you're about to rip the other's head off?"

"Ha, she started it!" Everilda spat. "I came here for a quiet moment to myself." She sardonically let out a huff.

"I didn't expect to find you here, dear. It's not like you've got any momentous abilities to let us know you'll be in our presence anymore," Isra jibed with a sarcastic glare.

"Yes, but do you need to keep reminding me of how I lost my powers? I mean, is that honestly necessary?" Everilda pressed before she turned back to Astrid, looking seething with rage. "And how is this any business of yours anyway?" She cornered him while still sounding very angry.

"I heard the kerfuffle between you two ladies while I was preparing to seek out some lovely, juicy worms. I couldn't help but hear the tragic hysteria," Astrid retorted dryly.

"Well, my fine friend, that is all well and good, but *she* is far from a lady. At least not one you'd expect to be exceptionally well dressed. She smells like excrement," Isra remarked, hinting at the fact that Everilda's downtrodden status as a mortal meant she often reeked of horse manure from residing in the filthiest hovels.

"Oh, dear! This is really quite the pickle between you," Astrid marvelled sardonically. "Isra, why don't you go back to Shambre Fell? There's nothing here for you in Seclera anyhow. Leave your old foe to her misery while you reign supreme in the darkest depths of immoral hatred, hmm?" Astrid suggested, but he sounded as though he was ordering her around.

Isra raised an eyebrow sceptically at the raven. She didn't take kindly to folks telling her what to do, especially when she had no inclination as to who they were. A stranger, albeit an animal, instructing her on how to behave was rather unorthodox to her, to say the least.

Who is this raven? He thinks he can place demands on my eccentric self. Hmm. It certainly intrigues me. He must have a very bold heart to address a shadowed being like myself in this manner when we have not made yet acquaintance, Isra murmured to herself in thought as she stared up at Astrid with sheer fascination.

"I find it most endearing how you believe you can place instructions upon me. Please tell me why I should pay you any mind," Isra retorted candidly. However, there was a hint of callousness in her voice.

Everilda looked vexed, glaring at both Isra and Astrid with rage as she seethed, "What do you mean, leave me to my misery? It was *her* that made all of this doddery commence in the first instance!"

"Yes, well, I'm sure you played a significant part in it also." Astrid quickly disregarded Everilda, placing his full attention on Isra.

Isra couldn't help but burst into a fit of giggles at Astrid's blunt yet blatant remark. She cackled with a hint of glee. "Oh, my! Why, I like you already, even if you do insist on bossing me around!"

Astrid lowered his eyes at Isra carefully, meeting hers with his golden-yellow ones in a warm gesture. He vastly remembered why he'd been drawn to her in the first place. There was something so reminiscently beautiful about the way that eerie light green beamed out of her eye sockets. It was enchanting the way they shimmered and shone but also looked like a dark, dense void if you happened to get close enough to her. Of course, the darkness didn't bother Astrid. He found it incredibly exhilarating and thus that was how his attraction to Isra manifested.

"If I told you what my reasoning was, you'd never go along with it. Trust me. I know that's hard for you to undertake, but please go back to Shambre Fell. I will meet you there shortly—"

Astrid stopped mid-sentence. He found himself admiring Isra. She had grown miraculously during the last year, and he had to admit that he was impressed with how she mastered her immense power, although as of yet, she had no idea what she was really capable of.

"All right. I shall, but only because you mocked dear old Evie. I relish every second of her defeat," Isra gushed wickedly.

But all good things will happen in time. We cannot force the magical beauty of her essence, for it is inside her, you see. The darkness... it swirls around her, dancing with her rhythm as she allows herself to be seduced by the mesmerising, forceful agility gravitating alongside her soul ever so wonderfully, Astrid thought, marvelling and simultaneously knowing he would have to begin planning the next steps.

Come to think of it, he hadn't expected to be back in the thick of it so early, but he was pleased he'd just managed to accomplish the unlikely—stop Isra and Everilda fighting in their tracks, at least for the time being.

The paternity of Isra was sure to ruffle feathers if either Isra or Everilda, perhaps even both, managed to discover the truth. This would not be a situation where all parties would remain civil and behave amicably. You can bet your life that all hell would break loose.

And I've just recently almost unleashed hell with her myself. I'd much rather it was me that was centre stage rather than having to diffuse two angered souls; one very powerful witch whereas the other, a desolate mortal. I don't perceive the odds to be in Everilda's favour, Astrid concurred earnestly, looking back at Isra one last time before he launched himself into the beautifully clear powder-blue skies and proceeded to fly off, heading towards Shambre Fell.

"Ha, fantastic, my girl! Little do you know, but we are making strides towards vast improvement already! Bravo, firecracker," Astrid called out after her.

Isra was left bemused, wondering exactly what he was referring to.

She mumbled apologetically, "Well, I haven't got the foggiest on what he's jabbering about." She then paused, licked her lips, and turned her gaze on Everilda. "But I must say, I am extremely impressed at how he dismissed you, my dear. Perhaps you'd best vamoose immediately. This is no place for the downtrodden."

Isra chuckled with a larger-than-life evil grin.

~

ASTRID HAD JUST ARRIVED back home after having the most eventful day interacting with Isra and Everilda. It was late in the night now, but things were developing at a rapid rate. He occupied a nice, warm dwelling located inside the hollow crevice of a cedar tree. He'd cleverly spotted this domicile while soaring around Shambre Fell one crisp winter morning and having taken interest in the clearing that Isra had adored so much, he'd found himself staring up at this mighty cedar tree. His lodgings weren't exactly ideal but would suffice for now.

The tree was strong and robust, elongating at around thirty metres tall. It was so high that if you managed to get to the top after navigating all those blackish-brown hairy twigs, you could probably see the clouds. But Astrid had no desire to go that far. He was quite content dwelling in this hollow crevice at the base. It was roughly ten feet away from the ground so he was safe from any unwanted visitors. Not that he'd be on the receiving end of any bother; ravens could very easily take care of themselves.

Well, that went rather well, I must say. There is some concern she may reject my advances but one cannot be pessimistic at this juncture. I will do my utmost to advise her to the best of my abilities. But let us only hope she will be receptive to what I have to relay, hmm, Astrid thought to himself.

Things had indeed escalated with Isra. He had to be honest with himself—he never prepared for one moment that he'd be returning to her life so soon. At least not in a way whereby he wasn't able to be by her side in his rightful place as her lover but yet still supporting her in some capacity. It was euphoric to be able to be in her presence after such a harsh separation.

Of course, he'd have to be diligent because, under Samuel's law, Astrid was still forbidden from going within arm's length of Isra. But, then again, those light-bringers weren't exactly smart when it came to retaining knowledge on the comings and goings of their dark souls.

Astrid could be flighty and reckless at times but he was also wholly smart, a highly intelligent being that could engineer anything if he was strategic enough.

"Isra doesn't have any knowledge of who I am but that's all right. I'll just get to know her again. Our relationship will be reborn anew," Astrid muttered happily.

He was beginning to realise just where this fantastic occurrence of bumping into Isra and Everilda had taken him. He still hadn't managed to find the time to snack on some fanciful worms, but there was more than enough time to listen to the wailing cries of his stomach later. For now, he would plan his journey to Shambre Fell. It was late, almost approaching midnight, and he figured Isra would be preparing herself for slumber. He'd have to get right to it tomorrow.

5

Isra awoke at the crack of dawn, just as the sun gently peeked out from behind the soft, fluffy, inanimate white clouds. It looked set to be a cheery day full of wonder and excitement. The skies were a beautiful, pristine blue. It seemed a delightful morning to spend some time gallivanting around this beautifully serene area she found herself in.

Perhaps she'd go and pick berries. It was the height of summer and so the blueberries, strawberries, and raspberries would all be plump, ripe, and bursting with flavour if she happened to lay her hands on some.

Summer wasn't Isra's favourite season, though she had to admit, it did have some advantages where nature was concerned, so her hatred towards it softened in recent years. She wasn't quite as fazed by it as she had been a long time ago. Although there wasn't much she found pleasing about the hot days and sweltering nights whereby you could wear very little clothing in a bid to keep yourself cool, it did have some good sides. Isra learned to adapt. Her fateful romance with Jonathan had commenced during July and so perhaps that was her reasoning for having a lack of benevolence towards the heat.

Since it was predicted to be a warm day, Isra dressed carefully in a long, flowing, deep violet lace dress, cut at the chest so there were no sleeves or straps. But it was generously forgiving on her slim frame. The fabric clung to her hips. The purple matched brilliantly with her shiny lime-green eyes that sometimes were aglow in the night. Isra wasn't entirely sure where today's escapades would take her so she made sure to pack a flask of steaming hot blackberry tea that had the tiniest hint of strawberry, a classic addition that beautifully complimented the vibe of summer.

Still, it was barely seven o'clock in the morning, but Isra had already made her decision to venture out. She assumed that nobody would be around to see her as it was far too early for all the non-magical folk. So, she placed her flask of blackberry tea inside a woven oak basket she found cleverly hidden in the kitchenette cupboard before pulling on a luxurious black velvet cloak. She made her way down the grey stone spindling staircase that led down to the lower floor of Shambre Fell and carefully turned the handle of the grand ornate oak door to reveal the glorious gardens of Shambre Fell outside.

Isra hadn't seen much of the grounds except she'd remembered admiring the deep purple and ruby roses growing just outside of the doorway along the windows. Adjacent to the roses was an enormous apple tree that was just about to bear fruit, hiding shyly in the corner. It was the most favourable attraction of Shambre Fell for Isra. Just like her, it was almost ready to blossom, having grown and been through so much. There was plenty of time for her to soak up her blissful paradise situated on her doorstep.

Isra strode on ahead, finding herself in a strange, darkened clearing surrounded by a mass of tall pine trees. She seemed to find it familiar but yet couldn't recall a time she'd seen this before. The ground below her feet was a light ochre colour, also met by soft murky green grassland that looked like it needed severe love and attention. Evidently, this place was very neglected and had been for a considerable number of years.

But, still, she persevered, wandering through the effervescent dark pine greenery. She came to the end of the sheltered clearing whereby a majestic oak tree stood serenely by a crystal-clear blue lake. As much as Isra wanted to stay here a little longer, she knew it was best to carry on, for there was so much more for her to explore in this unknown terrain.

She continued walking for just over an hour. Her feet were beginning to hurt. The skin in her heels burned as she touched each blade of grass with her black lace-up boots. The heat was sweltering but somehow, she managed to withstand the harsh climate.

Isra made haste in looking straight ahead. She didn't recognise the area at all. It must have been a remote region that was hidden among all the mass amounts of woodland dotted around here, there, and everywhere. Isra knew the borders of Seclera very well, having attended Wingdom's Academy that was just practically next door to it. Nonetheless, she never pictured anything nearby to look like this.

Just overhead appeared a gloriously brilliant orange sun with golden yellow shards glowing vividly from where Isra stood. It was so prominent among the rich cerulean-blue skies that it was impossible not to notice it; however, there was the impending notion residing in Isra's mind that she'd somehow been here before.

An improbable thought, as she had no recollection of ever physically seeing the place, but Isra had the faintest aroma of *déjà vu*. There was simply something about the way the dark and brazen orange called out to her. It seemed ludicrous. It was roughly just after eight in the morning, but some entity was surely luring her with its immaculate majesty.

"I guess it won't do me any harm. If I stray from the borders of Seclera, I can always make my way back to familiar territory," Isra mused quietly to herself, transfixed by the idea of going towards this wonderfully bright and shiny dystopia.

She stepped forward, bracing herself for the inevitable. Suddenly, the light blue skies turned a cold shade of royal blue.

"All right, so nothing is what it seems here," Isra muttered cautiously as she ventured on.

Isra saw, very clearly, an idyllic island. Tall, green grass blades saturated the land around the deep pooling midnight-blue lake that shone so brightly in the sun that you could spot silvery-white sparks emitting off it. Isra persevered on, noting there was an isolated rustic wooden bench positioned by the mass of green grass. Waves of hot fuchsia emerged, colliding with the vibrant orange and sunshine-yellow.

Isra walked over to the bench earnestly, her feet very sore from all the walking she had done. Planting herself upon the warm wooden seat, she breathed a sigh of relief as she stared up at the perpetual splendour of neon orange, golden-yellow, and luminous pink. It was calming in a way, although it was garish with all the gorgeous flaming colours. Isra's attention soon was elsewhere, her eyes focused on a serene white farmhouse that had magically appeared on the other side of the enormous body of water. It was bizarre; Isra was certain she hadn't noticed it a few moments ago.

"That's strange; I didn't see a house when I first came over here! How did this transpire? It's so unnerving," Isra murmured nervously.

She glanced at the house awkwardly. She became stiff as a log as she sat there waiting whatever was about to emerge from the wickedly glorious farmhouse that had appeared out of nowhere.

"Oh, now what do we have here?" a male voice chuckled with intrigue.

Isra spun in vain. The voice troubled her! She presumed she was alone only to be greeted with two disturbingly provocative azure eyes staring back at her opposite from where she sat on the bench.

Isra gasped awkwardly. "That's funny. I was so sure nobody was here only seconds ago."

The stranger was intense and continued gawping at Isra with much fascination. "Oh, no. Really? Do you often wander off onto someone else's land?"

He narrowed his blue eyes at Isra sceptically, causing her to feel immensely intimidated by this bewildering individual who appeared in her midst. He towered over her at six foot two and had a well-mannered, robust look about him, standing proudly and donning a red silk shirt that had been buttoned to the top. He also had an affinity with the colour black; he donned a black velvet cloak to match the black suit trousers he wore. Bewildering, beautiful, bright blue eyes shined luminously. His darkened ash-blonde hair was almost hidden beneath the hood of his cloak.

He was a young fellow of eighteen years of age. He had that rather conspicuous young warlock look plastered all over him—cocky, overconfident, and overzealous. There was little empathy to be seen within this man, but he wielded a lot of power over the feminine entity.

"Well, actually, I was... um..." Isra stammered, realizing she didn't know why she had come here in the first instance.

She remembered passing through the vast woodland clearing just after leaving Shambre Fell but somehow, she must have been swayed. She couldn't recall entering the borders of Seclera, which was adjacent to Shambre Fell, so how could she have continued, not comprehending where she was going?

That's so bewildering. I can't recall finding the location which led me here. Oh, there's something most peculiar occurring here. I don't like this man. He speaks so formally yet there is an antagonising edge about him. Hmm.

Isra mulled this over with care. She didn't feel at all comfortable in his presence but he seemed to be able to burn into her with his penetrating glare.

The male, whose name was Alan, stopped looking down at Isra upon sensing her increasing fear of him, smiling as he renounced formally, "Oh, but it's no matter to us. We often get foreign witches in our realm, but you are a witch of a special calibre. How very rude of me. I should have introduced myself. My name is Alan, and you are most welcome to Immortal Yonder."

Isra stopped in trance, never expecting to find herself among other witches, except maybe when she'd had a brief dalliance at the eccentric school for those training to hone their craft, Wingdom's

Academy. However, she didn't think there would be actual realms whereby witches resided solely above other beings.

"I'm afraid I've not heard of it. I am from a small village named Shambre Fell. Forgive me, but how do you know what I am?" Isra pressed with a forewarning glance, although she was deeply interested in this gentleman despite how disconcerting he was towards her.

"Ah, so you were the one the light folk placated in that monastery. I have to say, I'm honoured. You must have conducted some stellar accomplishment to have the love and light brigade chasing after you like some long-lost dream," Alan recited confidently.

His outburst was most thought-provoking for Isra, who had no inclination of what he was talking about.

"The love and light brigade placated me? Huh. I don't recall such an event taking place. Please, do ensure you are being wholly correct, as you might have the wrong identity." Isra paused solemnly, but Alan said nothing. "It could be mighty awkward for the poor tragic soul that was castrated by those good and kindly folk. I personally haven't had any dealings with them myself."

Alan seemed taken aback. *I am sure it was her. Father said it was a witch who had tumbled over to our side. The famous light-bringer magically disarmed her. It has to be this fine maiden who has appeared in our domain. Otherwise, who the hell is she? She hasn't stumbled into our lands on false pretences, has she?*

Alan was indeed puzzled by Isra's bemused response but thought it better to disarm the conversation.

"Oh, I am so sorry. Please forgive me. I believed there was a witch from our neighbouring lands that was placed in a stronghold by those who reign supreme in the light," Alan uttered calmly.

However, he was suspicious because his father had elaborated that there was only one witch who had been pulled down from the depths of her own destruction.

"Perhaps you are indeed mistaken. I am as dark as they come. Oh, but some people would rather put that out of their petrified little minds! I am Isra," she articulated formally. She was civil with Alan, but she wasn't about to drop her guard just yet.

"Well, Isra, may I say welcome to the dark side! Here in Immortal Yonder, I can only assure you that you will be accepted and approved of. Nobody dares tread this way if they have any of that 'light energy' in them. My father has spent most of his life eradicating the whole miserable lot of them. In fact, the current Light Bringer in Chief has had a torrential time trying to stop us warring witch families from ascending to our true greatness," Alan announced proudly with a grin, hinting that there was more to the dwellers of Immortal Yonder than he originally let on.

"You know, I'd like to hear about your journey to our side. Maybe you could come over to my farmhouse someday? I make the most delicious chocolate chip cookies that you will have ever tasted! Honestly, you'll want more. They are so scrumptious."

He offered his invitation to Isra very casually, although his tone sounded rather flirtatious, as if he was suggesting Isra might desire far more than just cookies. In any event, Alan was keenly scanning Isra up and down but most of all he was checking out those lime-green piercing eyes. Alan perceived that if there was going to be any shred of a clue as to whom or what Isra was, it would be lurking behind those beautiful eyes glowing spectacularly in the sunlight like emeralds.

Alan stared deep into Isra's cold eyes that flashed him a rather unprovoked death stare... however, there it was, a tiny glimmer peeking out from her eyeballs. A green, serene glow of pure darkness. The type of bright, illuminated gleam that could only be found in someone who had turned their back on everything they once believed in.

Oh, come on. It has to be her, Alan thought to himself in frustration.

Isra had a glint in her eyes. She had the look of being forced to grow up far too young, the look one only displays when they have to overhaul everything they ever had faith in as it came crashing down around them.

I swear on all the good graces on Earth that this is her! But how in the hemisphere does she not recall it? I know that Mr Reynaldi did a magnificent job on the girl but to mess with her mind? I mean, it's unthinkable. Here we have a witch and not just any, but the finest in her calibre. So she got wounded by love and turned to the shadowy terrains of life; haven't we all? But to snuff out her potential like that is unfounded, Alan conferred to himself sullenly in thought.

He knew Samuel Reynaldi was a powerful and remarkable man. He was able to perform the most challenging tasks concerning dark souls that inevitably crossed over to the point of no return. That is when dark dealings became his jurisdiction. But Alan also knew there was something deeply amiss with Isra.

"I would very much be gratified by such an invitation," Isra responded.

Alan still found himself distracted by his thorough analysis of her but said. "Excellent. That pleases me more than you know."

There came a sudden pause as he realised there was a major flaw in his plan. "Oh, darn! Father said I couldn't have anyone over tomorrow, but he's out of the house all of this evening. Maybe it would suit you to come over tonight?" Alan petitioned.

If I have the infamous dark enchantress who sold her heart to darkness in my home, well, that will give the light-bringer something to whine about, Alan chortled to himself, sounding amused.

"I didn't have anything planned," Isra answered promptly, becoming stiff and awkward; something about Alan's presence caused an internal chain reaction in her. Unexpectedly, she added, "Oh, wait... the raven said he would be coming to see but I guess he will have to wait until I am available."

"The raven?" Alan questioned.

He didn't say anything of great importance, but he wanted Isra all to himself; any unwanted guests would certainly not be welcomed at his humble abode.

"Ah, yes, but he's nobody, really. Just a raven. I don't even know him,' Isra returned.

Alan eyeballed Isra with suspicion, staring into her bewildering, piercing green eyes, as though he was trying to fathom if she was being creative with the truth.

Hmm. Good. The last thing I want is some bothersome, cawing raven catching a glimpse at my dinner guest. Not that we will be having a meal, but the sentiment is there, he thought with self-importance.

"Fantastic. Well, then, it will not matter if for some reason you just so happen not to be at the destination you agreed to meet this, er, raven. I don't like the blighters, personally. Horrid things. They gnaw away at corpses! If you're not careful, a raven will peck your eyeballs out in seconds. You can never trust such a venomous creature!" Alan elaborated carefully, trying to raise concern in Isra but at the same time, he didn't want her skedaddling away from him either.

"I shall take great heed to bear that in mind," Isra said cordially as she stood, revealing her floor-length violet dress. It trailed behind her as she proceeded to walk away. Isra had already clutched her woven basket tightly in her dominant hand.

"Don't be a stranger," Alan called out!

"Oh, I won't," Isra responded as she slowly dissipated from his sight, walking straight through the same invisible magical gateway that brought her here.

6

"Goodness me. She is a nightmare unto herself," James mumbled as he trailed behind Isra.

He'd been following her for quite some time but wasn't brave enough to admit he'd forced his way into Immortal Yonder, which was strictly witch territory. But still, he'd witnessed Isra in an entrancing conversation with one of the warring witch families' sons. He wasn't entirely sure which one it was, but that hardly mattered. The point was that Isra was getting close and personal in areas she deftly shouldn't.

She's only recently been placed under duress. Samuel was certain she wouldn't be able to get up to anything even remotely obscure for quite some time. It seems he was gravely wrong. I'm the bastard that is going to have to report back on this horrific charade. He doesn't like things like this. I hope he's not in one of his foul moods. I could do without being chastised this afternoon, James thought to himself.

He was slightly annoyed. Isra was difficult to keep up with, unpredictable as she strode along, practically at the speed of lightning. Nevertheless, James had to try and keep up with her.

Isra headed towards Shambre Fell, and James noticed those green glorious hills. With him being on the edge of Seclera, it was time to take a left to Spirisity. He'd have plenty to report back to Samuel.

~

JAMES EXCUSED HIMSELF, pushing past the plush royal blue velvet curtain. He hoped Samuel was in a somewhat pleasant state of mind, although it was unlikely. He didn't wait to be invited in as he usually did and instead shoved open the door to Samuel's office. It hadn't changed much. It was the same old office but now there was a large oak-stained bookshelf about ten feet tall positioned against the back wall of the room.

Samuel was sitting on his favourite blood-red armchair, aimlessly holding a steaming cup of coffee in his right hand. He wasn't expecting anything terribly interesting on this fine late afternoon. In any event, he was about to hear something that would awaken one of his foul, musty moods.

James's entrance completely jolted him out of his absent-minded staring. Reeling from the interruption, he called out, "James, good heavens! Don't you bloody well knock?!" He hastily wiped up some spilt coffee with a clean white handkerchief he'd stowed away in his desk drawer.

"I would have. Anyway, everything is quiet, so why so serious? You should just chill out, man! Astrid had his ass whooped. Well, in the verbal sense. There's nothing to worry about. Relax already!" James chided with a scowl.

Samuel clutched his coffee mug with his dominant hand, glugging the contents nonchalantly before uttering, "I don't want to relax. I prefer to remain tense. And now you should have something to tell me. How is our irksome little witch?"

Oh, how he wanted to be kept abreast of Isra. The heat was pretty much off by now but still, she was very much attuned to the darkness and could still unleash goodness-knows-what. The fact that Astrid was safely out of the arena was reassuring to Samuel since he could focus more on the love and light business again, but the concern of

Isra relapsing into familiar dark territory was more than Samuel could bear.

"Ah, well, get on with it then!" Samuel cursed solemnly, barely taking notice of James as he reached over to his trusty whiskey decanter sitting idly on the shelf opposite him before grabbing a glass tumbler. "I trust it has been a pleasing expedition for you."

Of course, Samuel was referring to James spying on Isra. Now that Astrid had been given his marching orders, this intriguing yet haphazard duty had been pushed onto James, much to his amusement; he truly struggled to keep up with the feisty enchantress.

James groaned as he sat back against one of the chairs adjacent to Samuel's desk. "I am not sure *that* is the right word for it. 'Enthralling' might be more suited to this afternoon's antics. In any event, I am sure to need a nap at any given moment."

"Well, let us not waste any time, boy. Have at it. What's our little witch been up to, hmm?"

Samuel motioned for James to speak and then reached over for a tin of ginger nut biscuits. Samuel was quite partial to the spicy yet sweet treat. He found them rather appeasing with a steaming hot caffeinated beverage. He offered one to James, who wrinkled his nose at the treats.

"No, thank you." James waved his hand awkwardly at the gingersnaps, and then said curtly, "She's still in her idyllic tower, unaware of ever knowing the raven."

James was trying to remain polite despite noticing that Samuel was about to drink himself into a stupor again. He thought, *I cannot see the problem here. Astrid is gone. Isra is placated under one of the finest strongholds that's ever existed. So, although her true nature is dark, she does not know how to retrieve it. Why is he getting intoxicated over something meaningless? You'd think he'd maintain his integrity by attempting to keep a cool head.*

"Excellent," Samuel replied, then added in, "I hope it stays that way," and he swiftly poured himself another stiff Irish whiskey before proceeding to take a large gulp of the satisfying, sickly sweet liquid.

"Yes, but..." James began.

Oh, no! Samuel's eyes narrowed at James immediately. He'd said the immortal word, "but." That could only mean one thing.

Oh, goodness knows, I hate that dreaded forsaken word. It means something I didn't plan for is coming. "Do not fucking say the word because I don't want to hear it," Samuel reprimanded James sharply with a glare.

"There's a new development. There's this, erm, warlock in very close vicinity. A young, boisterous male that's become very much acquainted with Isra. I saw it with my very own eyes," James said, petitioning Samuel to take him seriously.

"No, no, no!" Samuel squealed with frustration. "No. I don't want to hear anything like that."

Samuel eagerly swallowed the rest of the sinful brown concoction before flashing James an apologetic stare. "Don't misunderstand my meaning. It is just, we've only just got her under duress. If she's making merry with a warlock, that is the last thing we need. More temptations come from falling in love with another witch than anywhere else," Samuel mustered carefully.

"Well, we can't just bury our heads in the sand. Just because Astrid has vamoosed doesn't mean everything is hunky-dory," James retorted sardonically, as if to implore to the light-bringer that perhaps the matter was worth investigating, although it appeared to fall on deaf ears with Samuel.

"Please, for the love of my sanity, do not tempt the mighty forces in such a way! So she's getting close to a warlock, fine. Let her get on with it. It's not Astrid. And I'm trying not to have a nervous breakdown," Samuel admonished gravely. His tone was very sour, as if he had been sucking on lemons. He didn't seem to be best pleased with this news at all.

"Right, but that's not all. This could be extremely problematic, as the fellow is young Alan Grimsbane." James grimaced awkwardly. "He's taken quite the fancy to Isra."

"Aww, the little shit must be all grown up then! You know, I used to catch him in the bluebells. The bastard was always tearing around here when he was about ten years old. I'd often scold him for ripping the flowers from their precious stems. It used to amuse me how he'd threaten to turn the other mortal boys into tiny fairies if they happened to like the same girl he did. Oh, those were the days! I also dealt with his father, Nathaniel, back in the day when he was kicking around with Damien Daughtry. It certainly is a small world!" Samuel casually muttered.

"So his charming, wayward son, Alan, has set his sights on our Isra, hmm? That is most endearing. I'd like to meet Alan personally. I think it would be privy to introduce myself. Can you arrange that?" He narrowed his bewildering, deep sky-blue eyes in James's direction.

"I can, but I was hoping we'd discuss the situation at hand first," James blundered with a nervous expression.

Samuel rolled his eyes quizzically and waved his hands in the air. "What in goodness knows do you mean by 'the situation,' hmm? There isn't one, as far as I am aware. Unless you've had a bunch of satirical goblins whispering in your ear, knock it off. Let's not create a predicament when there isn't one, shall we?" Samuel insisted firmly.

You could tell by the way his normally sky-blue crystalline eyes were turning red that he was getting increasingly irate by the second. Just the thought of James suggesting that a certain raven was lingering around Isra caused Samuel to throw a hissy fit.

"Right... Well, I feel a little timid saying this, but when I was listening to Isra talk openly with Alan, she mentioned something about a raven speaking to her," James blustered.

He fumbled with a loose cotton strand on his white tailored shirt. He knew telling Samuel anything like this was almost guaranteed to make him lose his mind in the sense that he'd go into a fit of rage, lashing out at anyone or anything that just so happened to be in his path at the time.

"Oh? And I suppose you believe this raven to be Astrid? But how could that be? We fucking banished him, remember? Or is your memory experiencing a slight case of demented brain cell disorder?! Hmm? How about next time, you properly go off and analyse the facts instead of toddling along based on hearsay!" Samuel spat out angrily before pausing for a moment, trying to regain his composure.

He ran his hands through his slicked-back hair, his irritation and frustration becoming very apparent.

Samuel was still intensely angered when he insisted that there was to be no further discussion on the matter. "Astrid is gone. He's never coming back. Now let that be an end to it all," he cursed sullenly before he turned his focus back to his empty white coffee mug.

"Eurgh! Why isn't there any efficient service around here? James, you will fetch me a fresh mug of coffee immediately. I feel like I'm going insane. I need caffeine. *Now!* And after you've delivered my caffeinated beverage, you can get your lazy backside into gear and arrange a meeting between Alan Grimsbane and myself!" Samuel ordered.

James reluctantly got up from his seat and headed straight for the blue curtain, being adept at taking a swift exit as fast as he could. He groaned tirelessly, feeling as though he had more than his fair share of the Astrid and Isra saga.

I was trying to tell him I'd heard it directly from the horse's mouth but seemingly Samuel is not ready to hear it. He'll love it when it comes back secondhand that Astrid is back in the vicinity. I can't imagine another raven making its acquaintance with Isra. Of course, it's Astrid, and there is no doubt he has a single care of being caught. Yet again, the very same charade is playing out.

Meanwhile, Samuel was caught in his conflicting train of thought, attempting to resolve his puzzlement. *Honestly, where is his head at? If Astrid is back in tow with Isra... no, it's ridiculous. He wouldn't be that inferior to start conversing with her after all I said to him. Astrid knows what his banishment entails. As for James, some people just don't understand common courtesy these days. I wonder what it will take for me to get a decent cup of coffee around these parts. I must say I am bloody parched. My mouth is as dry as a bone.*

He shifted on the armchair and placed a diligent finger to his lips in anticipation. Then Samuel concurred quietly, "So Alan wants to court Isra? That's fine. I do not see why this union cannot occur. Damn, I'll even give the boy my blessing but first, he must hear my reasoning. That is imperative if we are to be in any way successful. Astrid is gone. I don't know why James felt it absolutely necessary to bring him up in the conversation. He's a strange one. I don't think he's fully coped with being pulled up to the front of the stage. He's not a very adept showman."

A swift chuckle could be heard from the other side of the room. Samuel's window was slightly ajar, and Astrid was perched on the edge of the window ledge, eagerly listening to every word. He looked extremely amused.

"Oh, I'm gone, am I? We'll see about that. Like they think banishing me would stop me from going back there? Ha! And a new man is hovering around Isra, is there? Right. Looks like I'm about to pay our little dark witch a visit, as she seems to have escaped me earlier," Astrid marvelled with delight.

7

Alan stared over at the wooden grandfather clock in anticipation. The big hand had just struck twelve while the little hand hovered on seven, causing Alan to tap nervously on the enormous mahogany table he was seated at. He'd gone to a lot of trouble for just tea and biscuits.

A beautifully layered pastel pink and white silk cloth was laid on top of the table whilst a shiny silver tea set with a kettle and milk pot sat in the centre of it. Two soft white and baby pink porcelain cups were positioned at either side of the large table. It was almost as though Alan was preparing for an interrogation of sorts rather than an elaborate tryst.

"She should be arriving at any moment," Alan expressed casually, although he couldn't help but feel dissatisfaction at the fact that it was now two minutes past seven.

Where was Isra?

Isra was just about to pass through the veil into Immortal Yonder when she noticed a black raven staring down at her from the tall mass of pine trees she'd just walked past. His golden eyes glared at her from above. She glanced around apprehensively and then reciprocated his wide-eyed stare. Isra suddenly felt very exposed. She looked over at him, feeling perturbed at having no idea what to say.

"It is quite ignorant to make an arrangement with somebody and then not fulfil your end of it," Astrid grumbled, a hint of annoyance evident in his voice.

"Ah, yes. I do apologise. I became distracted. I am sorry you felt ignored. I didn't mean for that to occur. It's just that Alan... Well, he came about so bizarrely. I am about to meet him for cookies and tea," Isra blurted out nervously.

She wasn't intending to inform anyone of her dalliance with Alan or even that it might be considered anything more than a simple conversation between two magically inclined souls.

"Yes. I know of him; Alan Grimsbane. He's the son of a warlock. Bit of an odd character, but his protégée is quite the looker, or at least so I hear," Astrid mentioned.

However, he felt a little out of sorts. He didn't want to create an awkward atmosphere between himself and Isra. He was most certain this conversation would most likely be heading towards a romance.

So, she's presumably attracted to Alan and this leads me to the conclusion that their rendezvous is most definitely the start of a courtship. I don't want to be rude, but I do have my misgivings. He's a horrendous bastard from what I can recall. He treats the female sex as though they are a plaything and nothing more. Isra would be vulnerable to that. I fear the worst if she was to become too close to him. But of course, I cannot elaborate on why I feel that way. Oh, my. This is perplexing. What should I say? If I cannot be her lover, can I at least attempt to be her friend? Surely any romance she has with the Grimsbane boy will be short-lived, and much to her devastation when he tragically crucifies her heart as he has with each of his other ill-fated romances, Astrid thought.

He tried to find the right words to say to Isra. She was invested in Alan, and it was going to prove difficult for Astrid to sweep in. He was still only able to communicate with her in his raven form, but needless to say, the idea of seeing Isra form a connection with another man was simply too much for him to bear.

"A looker? What do you mean by that?" Isra asked as she threw him a perplexed look.

"Ah, my apologies. I meant simply that he is attractive. He has what the ladies find desirable, and that is what has them practically throwing their underwear at him. Quite literally, as a matter of fact."

Astrid blurted this out sardonically, although he quickly realised Isra didn't grasp the comedic notion.

"Well, I do not know about discarding my undergarments and throwing them in his direction, but I guess I will bear in mind what others before myself have done," Isra mouthed bluntly.

"Yes, well, I know this is awkward. It is for me also, but perhaps I can meet you at Shambre Fell after your date? That is if he's not keeping you entertained until the wee small hours," Astrid proposed with a smile.

Isra agreed, although she was trying to maintain her sense of formality. "All right, but I am due to meet him at any moment now. I am afraid I'm already dragging my heels and therefore I am rather late! My tardiness will hopefully be excused on this occasion."

Astrid dropped his head sombrely, trying not to show the emotion he felt because Isra had her attention placed elsewhere. The rejection was sore. He had to admit it but of course, he wasn't going to. He couldn't—Isra still had no clue as to who he was.

I guess she will be occupied for a while but maybe we can have a more joyous conversation later. I still haven't explained what it is I have to speak to her about but maybe I can use that as an excuse so we can converse. I doubt she even cares about her spat with Everilda now, Astrid thought.

At least he'd reached an agreement with Isra about meeting him. It was progress, even if he didn't believe it to be so.

"This evening it is. I hope I can explain more elaborately for you exactly what all of this pertains to. Enjoy your night!" he announced abruptly as he soared into the skies before Isra could utter another word.

"Wow, he went off in a hurry. Never mind. Perhaps I will discover what has irked him in time," Isra recited to herself as she bravely strode forward into the veil of Immortal Yonder.

You see, the first time she came here had been an accidental occurrence. She had been hot and sweaty and hadn't realised she'd stepped through an invisible gateway, but now she saw it clear as day. A large, thriving elder tree stood proudly to the side of the veil with bright ochre-green leaves shaped like ovals whereas white blossoms discarded themselves due to the intense heat. Isra realised that when she put her right foot into the veil, the magnificent sunset reappeared but if she took her foot out, it vanished within seconds. It was so simple and yet she'd managed to easily miss it because she had been distracted at the time.

The orange became more prominent, and the skies were awash with a luminous pink glow. Just beyond this eloquent beauty was Alan's perfectly situated farmhouse, although it didn't appear to be as white now. It had a more rustic look to it. Weathered, light brown hardwood beams stuck out among white concrete walls that were elegantly fashioned with white stone slabs. Isra barely noticed the farmhouse's reflection in the dark, aquamarine lake water, but she somehow knew something about this place seemed way murkier than it had before.

That's funny; I could have sworn it was a gleaming white that shone back at me relentlessly in the cerulean reflection. But it is no matter, for I am here now. Still, I don't feel at all comfortable in this terrain. It has a sinister vibe, one that I don't care for. But hope will fly away, I suppose, Isra formulated in her mind.

Isra might have spent some more time pondering this but suddenly, she was jolted out of her reverie when a voice called to her, "Hey, don't be lingering now. Come on in. I don't bite unless I am politely requested to. But usually, I decline," Alan expressed in a slightly vexed tone; it had just struck seventeen minutes past seven o'clock, which meant Isra was severely late.

"Oh, I am so sorry. I became distracted. That is happening a lot to me today!" Isra mouthed cautiously. She bent her head in an apologetic stance.

Alan gave no indication he was unimpressed by her belated arrival but chided in a cheerful tone, "It's no skin off my nose. How about we go inside, hmm? I'll have to put on a fresh pot of water, but it doesn't matter."

"That would be most pleasurable, I am sure," Isra announced softly.

Alan led her over to the farmhouse and Isra took care to soak in her surroundings as she walked around the breathtaking blue lake. She found herself greeted with the brilliant white walls that made everything seem surreal. The sheen from them was bright indeed.

"I could have sworn all of this had been so different before..."

Isra gasped as she stepped through the white wooden door, noticing the three luminous silver window panes that all looked mirrored, as if you could stare right into them. There was also an odd feeling, like somebody watching from the other side.

"Hahahaha!" Alan guffawed. "Oh, girl! Your mind is playing tricks on you. This place does tend to move but it hasn't in many moons. Trust me, you'd know if it did. Immortal Yonder is not known for the art of subtlety. Come on," he urged, leading by the hand through the house and into his dining area.

Isra's eyes fell onto the table with its shimmery white tablecloth, but her attention was mostly focused on the pastel pink and white cups. They looked adorable, like large marshmallows that had swelled up. Even the wall behind from where Isra was seated had a lovely apple green colouring to it.

"Well, I must say, I hope this tea is as enthralling as you make it sound," Isra said as Alan got work on heating a kettle of water he'd gathered together minutes before Isra made her appearance.

"Oh, it sure will be. Do you take your tea with sugar or are you more of a gooey coated honey kind of girl?" Alan asked sweetly, fumbling around in his kitchen cupboards and then bringing out a tiny white China sugar pot followed by a small jar of honey alongside a silver teaspoon.

"I'm usually more inclined towards sugar. Honey is rather sickly for me," Isra answered in a stalwart tone.

"Ah, most women do. Honey is more of an acquired taste. However, it is also used in a lot of the traditional spells, so I guess that is why there is always a steady supply of it," Alan confessed.

Wow. He is surely involved in some deep methodology if he's got plenty of surplus materials on hand to use in spells. I am tempted to inquire as to which magics he fancies himself an expert but maybe I shouldn't let my curiosity get the better of me. I've never found myself up close and personal with a warlock before. But I have to admit, I'm intrigued by him greatly, Isra thought.

She tried to imagine what Alan would look like when he was standing erect by a large black cauldron, mumbling away some barely decipherable ancient language while tossing certain key ingredients into the bubbling pot.

Oooh, I bet he's so dark and mysterious. If only I could get a glimpse of him when he's toying with the forces, mmm.

Isra drooled away to herself in thought, not realising she'd completely ignored Alan. He, on the other hand, witnessed her little trance whereby her mind was elsewhere.

"Something amusing you, love?" Alan called over to her as he placed a steaming hot cup of tea next to her on the table.

"Oh, no. I just saw a bird or something out of the corner of my eye," Isra excused herself swiftly.

She gently picked up the hot white and pink cup, expecting to taste tea. Normally she'd find it robust and somewhat sweet. However, when she lifted the mug to her lips, she was astonished to find a caramelised pecan taste with delicate hints of fragrant white chocolate. Oh, it was scrumptious indeed, but how could tea possibly taste so unbelievably heavenly? Isra had no idea of how this was feasible.

"Of course, you did!" Alan humoured her, not bothering to acknowledge her tiny white lie. He flashed her a cheeky smile that was also met with friendliness.

"I must say, I am enjoying this tea," Isra commentated heartily.

"Ha, I suspected you would. I mean, most of the ladies who find themselves in this place have pretty much come to the same conclusion. The tea is sweet and fine with fine tasting notes of candy-coated flavour," Alan stated proudly, which brought Isra to an impudent conclusion.

Oh, so he has a lot of female visitors coming by for tea. Meanwhile, I haven't even been given the delectable cookies I was promised, Isra surmised as she wondered just who might have been entertained by Alan's hospitality. *It is never a good idea to let one's mind run away with itself. Who knows what fanciful debauchery has occurred here. It's not even a light dimension, so it's all untapped from those watching from higher up the food chain.*

Isra consoled herself candidly, stopping herself from suddenly thinking such things. The last thing she needed was for her curiosity to go into overdrive wondering what Alan might be doing when the night was young and maidens were in abundant supply.

"I am not the only feminine wonder to be bowled over by your wondrous yet satisfying tea then, eh?" Isra asked quizzically. Her eyes narrowed reproachfully as if she was scrutinising every single word he said.

"No. But the last one... well, we did more than just sip tea. She was my one and only. I thought I was truly in love with her, and then boom! My entire world came crashing down. I've not had one woman in this abode since that. That is until now, until you, Isra," Alan divulged.

"Oh, I am sorry for my approach," Isra atoned for her assumption about Alan before pausing to add, "I too have been burned by love. The last one consumed me. My best friend, no less, was also in love with the rascal. I've not been near a man since," she confessed weakly.

"Then we must make a great effort to change that," Alan concurred. He winked, which caused Isra to beam all over her face. Her entire being glowed at that very moment.

"I'd be very impressed to see exactly how you'd undertake that marvellous feat." She grinned before eliciting coyly, "But where are my cookies? You lured me here with pretences about biscuits and tea, but damn, you left out the cookies!" She giggled.

"Oh, I do apologise. I fucked up there, didn't I? It's no quandary. I'll fetch them from the pantry. I hope you deem them to be worth the wait," Alan murmured as he ran out of the dining room.

There was a peculiar rustling sound. Presumably, he was rummaging around somewhere, seeking out these extremely well-baked cookies he had so supremely promised to deliver unto Isra. When he came back into the kitchenette a moment later, Alan appeared quite flabbergasted. The cookies were on the silver platter exactly where he'd left them. However, instead of the original decadent dark chocolate he'd prepared to serve Isra, they were now delicious dark chocolate and sensual strawberry, the perfect aphrodisiac, one would be led to believe. But where the strawberries had emerged from, he had no clue.

It was mysterious. They'd just materialised from nowhere. He was certain that his oven was bewitched! He would have remembered going out into the local orchard to pick fruit just as well as he would also remember washing them and cutting them to size after he'd brought them home. Alas, this was not to be—they'd come out of nowhere.

Goodness knows what happened. I didn't put strawberries in my cookie batter. I can't fathom how they've gotten here but I do hope my guest finds them to her liking, Alan thought with a puzzled expression, one that didn't fade when he presented them to Isra, proceeding to lay the silver platter in the centre of the table.

Alan watched in nervous anticipation as Isra eagerly reached over to grab one before taking a bite into the chewy, soft cookie. Interestingly enough, the cocoa content, despite being dark, was just about right for Isra. She tasted the bitterness but yet it had that profound sweetness that made it so irresistible.

She commented on the strawberries sticking out of the chocolate cookie with enthusiasm. "Well, these are most gratifying, and the strawberries are so juicy. It's almost like I am back to my days of strawberry picking."

"I wish that all of the maidens I have encountered were as endearing as you," Alan gushed, causing Isra to blush as she swallowed the remnants of chocolate cookie inside her mouth.

"I understand your experiences have not been pleasant, but with Jonathan... oh, he was a scoundrel. He knew the entire time he was courting my best friend. Worst of all, she knew it also! They were as thick as thieves, I tell you! The only reason they exposed themselves was she was chastising him one night in full public view. Can you imagine the scandal?" Isra exclaimed, recalling the fateful night when Jonathan and Everilda's infidelity was revealed.

"My beau wasn't quite the same. She was remarkable in many ways. Beautiful, too. Honestly, she just had this elegance about her combined with her immense beauty, and, well, she was a sight to behold. But alas, she was not a virtuous soul. Neither was she cut out for the dark. Don't get me wrong, she had her shadow side but by golly, her jealousy was truly vile. Before I knew it, I was being accused of all sorts of unmentionable things. I told her, 'If you can't handle this, just get out. This pathway is not suited for all persons.'

"After that, she resented me. It's a sad story, but the short version is she's a shadow of her former self now. I don't wish to dwell on someone else's unfortunate occurrence, but goodness knows the fierce entity known as karma got her real good. If only it could have ended on a high note, but she brutally halted our relationship. The sexual relations we had were fantastic but when it came to its horrific climax, oh goodness, did I ever want my life to end right there!

"The bitterness in her voice when she told me we were no longer going to be together was seething. I could feel the venom inside her. Something took her over but, I'll never truly know what or whom," Alan disclosed with a painful glint in his usually gleaming blue eyes.

Isra said nothing for a few seconds. She found herself at a loss, incomprehensible at knowing what she could say. She'd finally found someone who had the exact tragic experience as her. Not that she had ever allowed that reckless love to overshadow her life. Nonetheless, it had led her onto the path she now tread upon.

"If it is any consolation, I have been in a very similar position. I cannot say that I empathise with ending my life, though I was willing to risk it all, sending my heart up to darkness. And, boy, did I do just that! I am told I was quite the force to be reckoned with. But my memory is hazy. I am sure it was spectacular," Isra consoled.

Alan straightened himself out of his downward stance, having had something dawn on him instantly. "You know, there are magics we can use to retrieve your memories. However, you may not like what you find. The truth can destroy you if you aren't ready to embrace it. Isra, may I say it has been an absolute pleasure to be in your company. Please have it upon my assurance that I am willing to do this again but would you do me the honour of accompanying me for one lonely night?" Alan requested with eager enthusiasm.

"I would most certainly be gratified to be in your presence once more," Isra answered with fast flair. "I am not completely clear on what the truth will be. I do know that I had this great path to darkness I solely travelled, but alas, I do not recall how I ended up here. I've learned a lot in my short tenure, walking these streets of obscurity, but one would presume if I had accomplished a mighty feat it would have made me widely renowned and I might at least be able to detail exactly what occurred."

Isra placed a finger to her lips. It was odd that she hadn't spent much time worrying about or even paying any great heed to how she had arrived, but she knew something was amiss. She'd managed to land herself this magnificent chateau; meanwhile, she hardly ever left it so she never went beyond that which she knew. And for someone capable of rapturous things and that had conquered the pathetic weasel, Jonathan, and her nemesis, Everilda... well, it was dumbfounded she knew nothing of it. Just knowing that she had done it, for Isra, that wasn't enough.

If I could remember, I'd dance along to dear old Evie's defeat because my conquest would have more majesty than ever before. But maybe I am not supposed to know. Alan is rather specialised in these matters. He understands darkness. He not only lives it, but he invites it into his life as though it is an old friend. I'd like to become more acquainted so that I may comprehend it while also wholly understanding myself.

Isra pondered the notion quietly, realizing that Alan was not only going to be someone who was very much interested in her but that there was a strong likelihood he'd be able to help her through this transition in her life.

8

Astrid perched himself on the window ledge of Shambre
Fell. He hadn't heard from Isra all evening but presumed
she had a most delicious evening and therefore was
otherwise occupied. But it didn't matter because he was here now
and he'd be able to finally converse with Isra, providing her with
some well-thought-out answers she was seeking. Astrid would have
to take due care; he'd come to Isra on the pretence that her quarrel
with Everilda wasn't worth her energy. Isra wholeheartedly agreed to
him visiting her again as he'd sorely mocked dear old Everilda, an act
that filled Isra with glee.

*She doesn't trust me. She has no inclination as to why I said she
shouldn't fight with Everilda. However, she's sure to have pressing questions
on why a poor doddering raven would be so invested in her. I did make her
smile by taking Everilda down a peg or two. That alone gives me
satisfaction. I feel that I have impressed her enough to be invited into her
life, albeit even if it happens to be short-lived.*

Astrid continued to motivate himself in thought as he hung
awkwardly around Shambre Fell. The sun was out in its full glory,
having draped its warm rays across the land. The heat was noticeable
in the air and Astrid felt the sun on the back of his feathers. It was

only just noon but Isra was not here. Astrid decided he would wait, for she wouldn't be straying too far.

She can't be anywhere else. Surely things with the Grimsbane chap haven't developed so fast that Isra is still being entertained at his humble abode? I shall await her return. There can't be much else for her to do around here. Shambre Fell is her domain, even if she doesn't fully comprehend just how true that is, Astrid conferred with himself in rampant thought.

He had to admit he was beginning to worry over the Alan debacle. The irony was this relationship was so fresh and new that it was ridiculous to imagine it would be anything more than a fleeting enterprise of two young minds getting to know each other.

"She has to be home by now. Last night was their joyous occasion, so one hopes it is all done for now," Astrid perused carefully.

Suddenly, he heard a loud clunk coming from downstairs. Isra slammed the ornate door behind her as she led Alan into the main area.

"It's rather grandiose. I do have this eccentric staircase. It isn't much, but I like the way it twists around so that when you look down from the top, it resembles a spiral."

"It's nice. I happen to love that which is outlandish. People mistake it for being unrefined but in actuality, it is the weird ones, the mystics, and the dreamers that make us all question whether we are truly living," Alan remarked in good humour.

Astrid's ears pricked upon hearing Alan's voice. *Oh, so this must be the famous Alan? He doesn't sound very warlock-like but I guess appearances can be deceiving. Things must be progressing sooner than I anticipated if she's brought him home,* Astrid worried, veering closer to the window ledge in the hope he'd get a decent look at what was going on in Isra's living room.

Astrid manoeuvred himself so that he was lurking right by the window itself, perched on the ledge so he was as close as he could get. He keenly listened to the conversation being exchanged between Isra and Alan as they entered Isra's living room area.

"Well, the last soul, a witch, perished here. It was a strange circumstance. However, I know very little pertaining to it," Isra explained softly.

"I hope her passing wasn't too tragic. Sadly, a lot of our kind cannot survive the current climate. They either get to a place where they are accepted or a case of the love and light folk getting involved quickly develops. That is usually when things turn sour. I am afraid I try not to get myself associated with witchy business. It puts us on very shaky ground when one of our own vanishes from civilisation," he told her coldly.

This subject wasn't appeasing to him. He didn't seem distraught over it either; just numb, as if it was not interesting enough to beguile his attention.

"It seems it was rather mysterious. Nobody truly knows this woman's heritage, nor how she got vanquished. It is a little odd, one must admit, but I don't imagine I will ever find myself in the same fate," Isra mused carefully, pondering the notion that somebody rooted in darkness would attract much attention if they were to just vanish off the face of the earth.

"It would be challenging at best to dispose of an awakened soul such as yourself. You've unlocked the gateway to your shadow side. You've wholeheartedly embraced it unlike many who shy from that side of themselves. The love and light realms would struggle to try to disarm you without using a great deal of magic and sufficient force, which, if you ask me, goes against their fancy pants code of ethics," Alan enunciated in a displeasing tone.

Isra noted that perhaps Alan's transition to the darker side of life wasn't as smooth as he'd made it out to be. He seemed to harbour resentment towards it.

"Yes, I understand it would pose great difficulty for them, but I'm barely even aware of how I became what I am at this moment. I am not able to recall significant details. I just know I was meant to occupy Shambre Fell after suffering at the hands of Jonathan and Everilda, and here I am," Isra went on to explain.

Alan narrowed his eyes at her seriously, almost glaring at her for a second. "I've had dealings with Mr Reynaldi. He's a quiet soul. He's got the whole wisdom and etheric background thing going for him. However, he's also got one hell of a temper. He scolded me a lot when I was younger. The man has created this image that he's holier than thou but he too has a shadow side he'd rather nobody witness. He cannot handle the dark souls that have become too far gone. He just doesn't have the stomach for it. He flies off the handle the moment something doesn't go well. Trust me, I know," Alan explained with a wide-eyed glare.

Isra wondered how someone possessing a great deal of expertise in the darker side of life had ever managed to have dealings with a light-bringer.

Now, surely the worlds are disconnected. One doesn't interact with the other. They don't bode well together so it beats my understanding as to how Alan would know these things, Isra thought. "Forgive me for being ignorant, but how would someone as refined in this subject matter as you ever have dealings with a light-bringer? It doesn't seem right in my mind," Isra questioned, becoming slightly more bewildered in trying to make sense of it all.

"I was only ten at the time. I witnessed Samuel Reynaldi interrogating a young girl who was around fifteen. She would have been sixteen at the most, and Samuel was preaching at her like he usually does with all of us. However, she'd caught him on a particularly bad day, and he just lost it. I was wandering in his gardens but that man's flighty mood swings is not something I would wish on anybody, whether light or dark."

Alan made it clear to Isra that Samuel Reynaldi was indeed volatile but yet it seemed he was leaving some of the story out. Something indeed seemed amiss.

Astrid was still present to the conversation, having been perched on the exterior of the window ledge the entire time. He thought, *Yes, that does sound like Samuel for certain. It's funny, but I don't recall him mentioning Grimsbane or any other young warlock that fit Alan's age at the time. My memory is hazy but this seems rather odd.*

I can't help but wonder why Samuel would have animosity towards our young sorcerer unless, of course, Grimsbane caught him on a bad day.

He does have a right old temper and should take more effort to keep that under control. However, he's also in a highly regarded position.

He didn't choose this job, even if he'd wanted to. Being a light-bringer is not for the faint-hearted. It surely chose him, for there would have been no other alternative. Samuel is also not human, for he already ascended beyond the peaks of humanity so he would have inherited the role whether he deemed himself capable or not. I do find all of this wholly interesting but it is peculiar this chap had a rather unpleasant experience with Samuel. Then again, I do remember Samuel saying Grimsbane swooped in uninvited and tortured his beloved flower beds. Samuel can become very coarse if anybody messes with his darling garden.

Astrid chuckled away to himself. The notion of Samuel getting angry with a child was quite sentimentally amusing. *I can see him standing there with a pitchfork, attempting to shoo the youngins away as they wreaked havoc on his beautiful flowers. He's never had any forbearance whatsoever, but still, it is endearing.*

"He certainly sounds like a most disagreeable man," Isra concluded now that she'd heard more from Alan. Still, she didn't understand the big fuss between light versus dark.

"He is definitely so. I hate to be rude, but I must get on my way. Father will be expecting me. I'd rather not disappoint him. You understand, don't you?!"

Alan excused himself. He needed to head back to Immortal Yonder. He'd lost track of time since he'd been spending it at his leisure with Isra.

"Yes, of course. Please don't trouble yourself if it means you risk a reprimand. I never had a father to speak of but I surely know a good ear-bashing when I hear of one."

Isra reminisced on the many lectures from the male sex over her tenure. The bulk of them were wanna-be professors who deemed it necessary to harangue her for the slightest thing.

ALAN HAD ONLY JUST LEFT Shambre Fell but was fast approaching the vast land of Seclera, which would lead on to the veil that would take him to Immortal Yonder. He noted an eerie feeling as he crossed the boundaries. The skies suddenly became overcast with grey clouds materialising out of what had been a beautiful, bright blue sky.

Alan found this rather strange for a sunny afternoon that was soon to be striking four o'clock. He continued walking along despite the uneasy feeling surging inside his stomach, knowing he needed to persevere because he'd soon be home. He could discard this uncomfortable sensation and let it go.

I've got to shake this feeling. Immortal Yonder is just around the bend and whatever this creepy vibe is will bloody well sod off. These types of energies don't make themselves known where I come from, he conferred with himself as sirens screeched inside his ears.

The sounds hollered at him from an invisible source. He was getting closer to the infamous clearing when he noticed a woman standing in front of him. She had dirty blonde hair that looked like it hadn't been washed in months, but he recognised those sapphire blue eyes instantly.

Oh, come off it. What in the hell is going on here? Alan asked himself wildly, knowing exactly who was standing in his midst.

"So, you just thought you'd come over and associate with those who levelled up in the realm, eh?" Everilda probed Alan harshly.

She was standing in the way of his path so he'd be forced to face her, much to his disgust. She wasn't someone he wanted to bump into at any time soon.

"Everilda." Alan sighed impatiently. "I was just coming back from... " He trailed off, not wanting to admit he'd been visiting Isra. Quite frankly, it was none of Everilda's business where he went or who he saw. They had ended their dire union three years ago. "No. It's none of your concern. Now if you don't mind, I'll be going."

Alan attempted to move past her, but she refused to budge. She was practically right in front of his face and more than eager to have a standoff with him, much to his dislike as he hated confrontation. But it was crystal clear from the seething rage in her eyes that Everilda desired nothing less.

"Ah, yes. You consolidate with witches now. Oh, no; wait, you've always done that! How bloody marvellous that you chose *her*!" Everilda snapped. She folded her arms across her chest in a cross stance. Her feet tapped on the ground impatiently as her temper grew in intensity.

"For goodness sake, Everilda! I am a warlock. I am supposed to have romantic attachments with witches. Do you honestly expect me to shack up with a fucking pixie? Where on Earth is your head at, girl? We broke up. All right? Three damn years ago," Alan cursed at her.

His frustration was becoming apparent, and he eagerly scanned the area around him. The veil to Immortal Yonder was only a stone's throw away. Everilda had no magic to speak of so if he just dashed off pronto, she would not be able to catch up to him.

That whole mortality thing must be a real drag, Alan thought to himself with a sneer, imagining Everilda waving her arms in the air when she wasn't able to continue this little slanging match, one that she had started nonetheless.

"Very amusing, *not*! You've decided to court Isra of all wretched souls. I would have at least thought you might have some integrity within yourself," she mocked callously.

Alan was not able to tolerate any further remarks from her. Bumping into your former lover and being accosted by them was one thing, but being insulted for no apparent reason was not acceptable.

"Everilda, I don't know what the hell possessed you to think that this was a wise choice to engage with me in this manner, but my life and anyone who just so happens to be involved in it has nothing to do with you. If you must know why I am so deeply invested in this charming soul, well, she's undergone a remarkable transformation to darkness. She's been through damnation and back. I've been down in that dank hole and, quite frankly, just knowing her story summons up feelings that I haven't felt for a long time! Your grievance with the girl is none of my business," Alan said, overruling her.

I don't know what her problem is, but by golly, it sure as hell won't be mine. She's going to have to learn one way or the other to have respect for her fellow man. She constantly engaged me in this despicable argumentative crap when we were together and I didn't approve of it back then. So what; we were teenagers, but I'll be damned if I am going to allow it now, Alan thought righteously, having not been aware of why Everilda escalated matters in the first instance.

It was shocking to learn that Everilda was almost mute, barely saying a word the entire time Alan bluntly laid the law down to her. Nonetheless, her ability to strike up conflict out of nowhere was not fading away any time soon.

"What do you mean by my 'grievance' with the girl?" Everilda finally piped up.

"I'm sick of these nonsensical shenanigans with you. Evidently, you've been keeping an eye on my whereabouts. I cannot fathom why since we are history, but you stated very clearly you knew I was courting Isra. There has to be some kind of quarrel between you two or you wouldn't have retched up her name as if it had left a sour taste in your mouth," Alan provoked, reminding her that she was the same old person who discarded him all those years ago.

"I only mentioned it because since leaving the realm as I knew it, Isra has gone through quite the transgression. I mean, I heard she told the good and kindly folk at Wingdom's Academy where to go after she turned the tide, ascending to the foreboding forcefulness she acquired," Everilda commented while twitching from side to side. Her eyes shifted from the left and then back to the right. Something was irking her but she couldn't handle the feeling and she was spiralling from the inside out.

"Yes. She did. Whereas you, not only were you banished from their good graces but they rendered you mortal and powerless. Isra is the exact opposite. It's no wonder you're envious. Ha! You really have fallen from the heavens. The difference is Isra has immense potential. She wields incredible power that not even she truly comprehends, but it doesn't matter. That's not the point of this discussion. The real issue is you cannot bear to see me with another."

Alan humiliated Everilda further when he insisted that there was nothing between them but hatred.

"I didn't wish ill on you, Everilda, but if you keep up this charade, I'll be forced to detail to Isra exactly why you and I parted. As I understand it, she doesn't take kindly to betrayal. She won't be best pleased to know me and you were once lovers. So do me the kindest honour and stay the hell away from us both," Alan chided in a fierce tone.

He was equally just as angry as her now but perhaps even more so as something had stirred inside him. Alan's relationship with Everilda had never been plain sailing but now the harsh reminder brutally smacked him in the face.

"I shall stay away but I'm warning you, Isra is nothing but trouble," Everilda remarked, and then she slunk away behind the pine trees, disappearing as soon as she reached the woodland clearing.

"And evidently, so are you, Alan Grimsbane," Astrid remarked with high suspicion.

He'd witnessed the entire showdown between Alan and Everilda from his position perched on the end of a branch of a neighbouring elder tree.

"So Alan and Everilda, eh? Who would have thought it! Well, I must return to Shambre Fell. Isra must know about this. She may not be inclined to believe me but I am going to do my utmost in warning her," Astrid muttered thoughtfully as he swooped off into the skies.

9

Alan was still reeling from his encounter with Everilda after he'd slipped through the barrier back into Immortal Yonder. Thankfully, this was a safe place where only those witches who had darkness within them could tread. To Everilda, it was off-limits.

Sadly, Alan was befuddled. He leaned back against the black velvet armchair positioned adjacent to his bed. It was almost drawing on midnight but Alan glanced over at the black velvet canopy hanging elegantly over his deep violet bedding with contrasting onyx black pillows and sighed.

How I hated every moment. I never wanted to think of this. But seeing her today, seeing the pure rage and hatred in her eyes, brought it all back... that fateful day where I wanted to end my existence.

It was devastating for him to think that everything had come to pass over three years ago, but it was rushing back to him with a vengeance.

"I'll never truly understand why she was that way. We were young. It was to be expected there would be some juvenile qualities, but my goodness, where did everything go wrong?" Alan asked himself out loud.

Of course, it was fruitless because the reason why everything occurred the way it did was creeping in from the darkest depths of his mind.

~

<u>~Three Years Ago~</u>

"EVERILDA, it's a pleasure to meet you again. May I thank whoever had the good graces to send you over here?" Alan praised as Everilda strode over to him at the elaborate School for Young Souls Proficient in Magical Arts annual ball.

"And mine, too," Everilda responded with a cheeky half-smile.

She was ecstatic. She'd finally been able to put on the shimmery pink velvet gown she had holed up in her closet for weeks. Dancing with Alan was simply the icing on the cake for the charming socialite witch.

It was the big noise of the year whereby all the students, both female and male, were allowed to come together as one united front before being separated again for the next school year. Females and males at the establishment were deliberately kept apart but Alan and Everilda managed to break the rules on several occasions.

Alan had just come of age at fifteen, but Everilda was a few months older at the tender age of sixteen. Both had become acquainted by mutuals. Alan was the son of a high-ranking warlock, Nathaniel Grimsbane. Everilda was the daughter of an equally powerful miscreant in the dark realms, Damien Daughtry. However, Everilda's mother, Damaris, was mortal but the Daughtry name brought Everilda to fantastical places beyond any amount of questioning her Christian family could do, much to their distaste. None of them was able to tolerate their wayward young witch relative.

But we must give Everilda some credit. Her mother, Damaris, of whom was a Christian and God-fearing noblewoman, was an atrocious spectacle of a mother if you were to ever lay eyes on one.

Damaris resented Everilda, never wanting any part of marriage to Damien Daughtry. Damien's mother, Maria, forcefully persuaded her son to marry Damaris since they were betrothed when Damaris was a toddler.

Later, Damien was introduced to fourteen-year-old Damaris, who was seven years younger than him at the age of twenty-one. Damaris hoped that the marriage would bring her happiness. However, it was short-lived when Damien left her one year after Everilda was born. His rich interests in dark materials were too prominent inside himself and he couldn't ignore them any longer. Their marriage had at least given Damaris a child, which now was a powerful pawn for her to use whenever she pleased.

Poor Everilda was shipped off to every magical social event in the land, whether she agreed or not, and at one of these many events, she was introduced to Alan by one of her peers. They courted secretly for several months. Alan was vastly becoming more experienced at witchcraft and had mastered the art of invisibility, much to Everilda's delight as he'd shared the gift with her. And so, the two star-crossed lovers were able to sneak off into the night any time they desired.

Tonight, at the ball, would be the first time in many moons that Alan and Everilda could be seen together in public view without scrutiny. The good and kindly folks at the Magical Arts School didn't care if their students fraternised with the opposite sex at the end of term. It was the least of their predicaments.

Lady Vama Coheart was the main professor in charge. She'd caught sight of Alan and Everilda canoodling and simply turned her head, pretending she didn't see anything. The last thing a magical schoolteacher needed at the end of term was to drag one of her students into a cramped office piled high with end-of-year papers and behaviour reports and then have to write another report, as their behaviour would be seen as an incident of curiosity. And so, she turned a blind eye instead. Lady Vama had been a consort of Everilda's father, Damien Daughtry, long ago, and had great respect towards any Daughtry that set foot in her midst.

"Ha! Did you just see what Lady Vama did?" Alan mouthed comically into Everilda's ear.

Everilda seemed disinterested and replied plainly, "No, but I am bored stiff as it is. I don't want to play 'let's be jolly nice to my elders.'"

"But she looked right at us, glanced at you dancing with me, and then looked away. She knows we are an item. She has to know," Alan retorted with confidence.

"She's crawled up my father's behind. If any matter concerns me, she won't step a foot out of line, for the scolding she'd get would be susceptible to all manner of mortification and suffering," Everilda marvelled with high-pitched enthusiasm. "It's always been said that although my father abandoned me, he's never been one to allow me to be disrespected. I'll carry the weight because of the name Daughtry, even if the untimely day comes where I cascade from the heavens unto the downtrodden realms of peasantry."

"Hmm. It's not your father that concerns me but rather that I am dictated too often that I must be married to a woman of a hundred-per cent witch blood. My father will not accept a half-breed like you." Alan laughed with a sinister chuckle. "I feel they would reprimand us both. I am certain they'd be against us rather than for us because of your mortal lineage."

Alan clung onto Everilda's tiny waist in a fit of hopelessness, sighing impatiently. He wanted to get out of the crowded ballroom. The atmosphere of the mass of students clustered together in one location was overwhelming. Alan had come to be close to Everilda but it was no secret he too was forced to attend these high society galas.

"Anyway, you're bored? No wonder. Have you seen where we are? No, come on. Let us leave this banal devastation of communism to wilt whilst we have ourselves some convivial frolics," Alan suggested with a wink.

It was barely ten o'clock in the evening, so Everilda didn't hesitate for a moment. She grinned wickedly and said, "Oh, I'm there. You can bet your life on that. Just whisk me away!"

Alan welcomed her request, approving of her vast zealousness to go off gallivanting in the night with him. "Your wish is my command, oh, fair maiden!"

He reached down, placing both of his strong arms around Everilda's waist. When he had them securely wrapped around her abdomen, he lifted her into the air, carrying her in his arms, and dashing away before anyone could stop him.

Moments later, they were back in Immortal Yonder. Alan was caressing Everilda. She was lying on his black velvet bedspread, wearing the same soft pink velvet gown. The exhilaration was present on her face. She stared at Alan seductively while she lay in between his legs.

"You know, this is so amazing. I never want to relinquish this as long as I live."

Alan tenderly ran his fingers through Everilda's hair. "I don't either, but this is risky business, Everilda. I'm fifteen years old. I am set to become a high-ranking warlock, just like my father. You are a half-breed. Nobody will ever approve of us," he said gravely.

Everilda's eyes narrowed meekly and she uttered, "Are you saying you want to disassociate yourself from me? Because if you do, feel free to have at it. Go ahead, but I must appeal to you; if I am just some fleeting absurdity in your life, at least have the aptitude to inform me."

"I don't want to take my eyes off you. Not for a single second. I cannot bear to tear us apart. This love we share, it's real. I know it. So do you. But there are certain qualities in a female you'll be expected to have... you know, full-blooded witch. No exceptions. My father expects someone on the dark path, and you're barely starting your career in witchery," Alan elaborated, hoping she'd understand exactly what was required of her.

"So I guess that means I've got to become dark. I can't deliver on the full-blooded element but I can darken my soul to impress your family," Everilda implored, as though Alan would be pleased.

"It's not an easy road, Everilda. It means you'll take a part of yourself and some part of you will die. It won't be something you can simply just walk away from. Some folk just aren't built for it," Alan articulated with a somewhat worried stare, continuing to caress Everilda's forehead.

~ Three Months Later~

Everilda rapped on Alan's door impatiently. The loud tapping noise violently disturbed him from a moment of quiet solitude, but alas, Everilda was not one to muster the art of restraint.

"Yes, I am coming!" Alan hollered in response to Everilda's frustrated clanging upon his front door. She could have just walked in but instead proceeded to bombard him with heinous knocking.

"Finally! I was wondering when you'd get to letting me in," Everilda returned, nearly snapping at him.

She had a vengeful look in her eyes. Her jealousy was becoming more prominent by the day. Alan could barely have a moment's peace without her crashing in, suspecting he was entertaining a young maiden in his monastery.

"Yes, well, I was basking in the silence. So come in, why don't you? I'll make some tea," Alan answered, although a sardonic tone emitted from his lips.

I can't deal with her foolishness. How on Earth is she still behaving this way after all we have gone through together? Does she not trust me enough to maintain faithfulness in our relationship? Ordering me around, demanding I see only her; girl, have you seen any other women around me? No. Goodness gracious, Alan thought. His frustration was becoming more apparent by the second.

"Thank you, but I am not sure tea exactly appeals to me right now," Everilda snapped in response.

Her tone was so sharp it could have been the edge of a blade. She was rigid and coarse. Her mouth emitted pure acidity that was enough to burn off any positivity in sight.

"Well, if tea is not to your liking, then what would please you? I have to say, Everilda, I am not enjoying your company at this present time," Alan remarked boisterously.

"I am infuriated with you, Alan Grimsbane. I've ruined my entire existence, lost a dozen friends by entering this, er, dark path. And why? I did it for *you*. To please *you*. Thinking that in some strange nonsensical way, it would strengthen things between us, but you are just numb. You don't pay me any mind. Heck, half of the time, I don't know who the bloody hell I am!" Everilda shrieked. Her sapphire blue eyes had become bright red as she voiced her fury.

"Everilda…" Alan sighed with disdain. "I did say to you before you adopted this that it is not for everyone. It is not my fault if you cannot handle what you weaved yourself into."

"I only did what I believed would be adequate. I'm not well versed with this dark methodology. I truly sucked the life out of someone near and dear to me, quite literally, when I drained the very little life force they had left in them. Did I care? Do I feel remorse for what I've done? That I took a life knowing I had the power to do so? No," Everilda uttered solemnly, dropping her hands to her waist.

Alan narrowed his eyes at the woman he loved for a second and asked her calmly, "What did you do, Everilda?"

Everilda straightened herself out, taking a deep inhale of a breath as she uttered coldly, "I took one look at my mother today and I just couldn't stand it any longer. The insults. The disappointments I bring. Oh, how she relishes telling me just how much I've failed her as a daughter! So, I walked right up to her, closed my eyes, and drained the sheer ferocity out of her. She lives to tell the tale but she's barely anything more than a vegetable now." Everilda proceeded to sit on Alan's black velvet bedspread as she formulated, "I guess this means I've gone too far. I cannot take it back. I can't undo it. I've tried every spell I know."

Alan arched his back uncomfortably in his black velvet armchair, sighing incessantly. He just couldn't get his head around what Everilda had admitted so freely. He tried to remain impartial and chided in a dispirited voice, "I did try to warn you. There's a consequence here. If you can't handle this now, then just get out. This pathway is not suited for all souls."

Everilda didn't concur with Alan's line of reasoning. She shouted, "I would remove myself from this hellish vocation, but alas, I chose it.

I'm also in love with you," she beseeched him, causing Alan's face to fall almost to the floor. The shock of Everilda's admission did little to console him but he tried to maintain his composure.

"Truthfully, I don't feel as if you love anything in this world, never mind me. Perhaps we weren't meant to be combined into one soul. You resent me. You throw your ghastly hatred upon me when someone or something irks you. I am your wholesome whipping boy. Well, no more!" Alan commanded. "I am going to have to spend some serious time thinking about whether I want to remain in this... *situation* we have going on here. I used to deem it to be love but now I am very much convinced it may well be something else. Something wretched. Toxic, even!" Alan explained but he barely showed any emotion as the words descended out of his mouth.

"If that is how you feel, perhaps I should go," Everilda answered in a low voice. "I am not good enough to appease you at either end."

Alan sighed, once again frustrated. He exclaimed, "You just don't get it. I have cared for you all this time and this breaks me more than anything I've had to do in my entire life. I've tried accommodating all your jealousy, even making allowances for you, all in the hopes you'd move past it. But alas, you have not. I don't think I can create life with someone so self-deprecating as you. I'm sorry, but I need some time to think things through."

He seemed mournful, as if it pained him to depths beyond his comprehension. There was nothing worse than seeing someone you love go down the pathway to desolation, knowing you had somehow orchestrated it by being part of that darkness.

"Let me save you the trouble. You're right. I've messed up. I've done some real unmentionable things and I can't hide from them," Everilda admitted earnestly. "But I can't help but think you are looking for a way out. So let me ask you one last time, does someone else dominate your heart?"

She probed him with an angry stare. The redness in her eyes was still very much apparent but she calmed down significantly compared to what she had been earlier.

"There is nobody but you," Alan answered firmly.

"I wish I could stay..." Everilda began.

She twitched her hands all over the place. Her fingers tapped nervously on the black and purple velvet bedspread as she fumbled around awkwardly, not knowing where this next move would take her. The aggression in her was increasing once again, and now she was beginning to look very balanced.

"Alan, I don't think I can continue this either. It's been fun. I know I'm not truly what you are and, in some way, it saddens me. But I know in the long run, I'll be better off for knowing you. I wish I could end this better, but I guess it's best to just keep moving forward, that way any sourness can be promptly quashed before it decides to invigorate itself into hysteria," Everilda announced with an icy glance upwards at Alan.

"Well, I don't know what to say. You got what you wanted but you didn't for one moment bother to consider that I might have had some feelings towards you. You have dragged me through hell and back with the dirty looks, the rampant jealousy, and now because you can't handle me being troubled over *your* actions, you decide to just part ways? Have you no compassion at all? I've put my entire mind, heart, and soul into this. I'm besotted with you, for fuck's sake, Everilda. What more do you need to be convinced of that?" Alan pleaded as a tear so badly wanted to drop from his eye. But he dared not let it. It was a sign of weakness to cry.

Father always stated if you show emotion, you are a weak, worthless man. Foolish and unworthy. You must always stand by the code, unfeeling and rigid. Never show how you feel for a damn moment or the cost could be devastating. It's my reputation, too. I risked it all for her and now she chooses to cut me loose. What am I? Some toy for her to tangle with and then put in a box now that she's done? Well, there is nothing I can say that will make her change her mind. Good heavens only knows just how far she's gone to consolidate our union. But one step can sometimes be a step too far. I don't think she nor I can come back from this, Alan rambled away to himself in thought.

He wasn't entirely sure on how he should approach Everilda, but he'd have to be nonchalant with her, even if it hurt him at his very core. The stiff upper lip had a lot going for it and had been used for centuries. Men always held it under high regard. This wasn't a time to abandon an age-old tradition.

"There isn't anything for us to discuss. I will miss you until the sun ceases to shine, Alan Grimsbane."

She walked over to him and planted a kiss on his cheek before she solemnly faced the wall, knowing she'd have to leave.

"You never loved me. You only loved what loving me could do for you. I pity you," Alan hissed.

Everilda felt the pain of his words billowing up her spine. The soreness travelled up to her chest and she felt it surge around the muscles of her heart. It quelled her ability to speak. Helplessly standing by the door, Alan gave her his final parting words.

"You've made your choice. I am not to blame for your inane fuck-up. You can swan off now and find some other poor soul that hopefully will not devote his time to you only to be left hanging. Now get the hell out of here before my father lays eyes on you!"

Alan felt the anger inside his veins, and it went deep. He scrunched his fist into a tight ball as he watched her stand there before swiftly opening the door and walking out.

AND THERE IT WAS, the first time that womaniser Alan Grimsbane had ever been used by a woman. He had truly devoted himself to Everilda. He believed they were love's young dream, but it was not meant to be. The memory cut him up inside and he struggled to force himself out of the depressive stupor he was in as he rested his head against his faithful black armchair.

He couldn't understand why Everilda was so furious with him now. Three years had passed between them, so much time in which there was the opportunity for her to heal her wounded self that had caused her to become so violently jealous that Alan could do little else but suppress his true feelings for her. She was the reason the union came to a dramatic halt. She didn't possess the longevity needed to make a commitment work. She lacked the finesse, and after causing that harm to her poor mother... Well, anyone would feel sorry for poor Damaris Daughtry after that.

"I guess we'll never know, but her impervious feelings are the least of my concerns now. We make our paths in this vast existence. I am becoming strongly close with another whom I find intriguing for the first time in three years. I will leave Everilda to her misery, for she deserves no less," Alan mustered coherently, stifling a yawn.

The night was dragging on. He should have at least tried to get some sleep unless he wanted questions from Isra on why he was so worn out in the morning. The whole Everilda debacle had hopefully been put to bed.

I do hope she doesn't manage to get to Isra and tell her all sorts of rancid tales because the spiteful wench yet again cannot attain what she desires, Alan thought just as he found himself gently drifting into slumber.

10

Astrid was on his way to tell Isra all about Alan's former dalliance with Everilda. He believed Isra had a right to know, even if she didn't believe what he was saying to be true. Astrid started off just as the sun began to creep out from behind the soft white fluffy clouds, so he was making good time to get to Shambre Fell just as the bright orange and golden yellow hues were appearing in his line of vision.

It's quiet this morning; not what I imagined, but I hope I will be warmly received. At least we might have a natter before we get into the serious stuff that will either make or break this budding friendship, Astrid thought to himself as he prepared to land.

Shambre Fell's tower was visible as he edged himself downward, figuring that he'd be polite and land on the living room window ledge instead of his favourite spot, Isra's bedroom window.

"Ah. Not bad, Astrid. I dare say, old boy, you'll be getting better at this as time goes on. Now, where to placate myself, hmm?" he pondered. He was situated on the end of the window ledge, having a perfect view of Isra's living room. "Perhaps she is still asleep? Maybe I should wait a little while before I rock up in there and scare her half to death. It would be easier if she remembered who the hell I am, but we'll take baby steps for now until a proper connection is formed."

Astrid gently edged himself as close to the window that was left ajar as he could get. No less than a second after he positioned himself by the window that he heard footsteps descending from the spindling staircase.

"Ah, she's finally awake," Astrid remarked cautiously, as he didn't want to startle Isra.

That's the last thing that would encourage promising conversation. He didn't want to appear as if he was stalking the poor girl. Could you imagine the rumours that would come out if he was seen often emerging at this outlandish chateau, trying to curry the favour of a witch? Ooooh, unthinkable!

Isra walked in solemnly, clutching the handle of a warm mug of orange tea in her hand. Astrid sensed it was orange because of the strong aroma, reminding him of plump juicy oranges one finds in the heat of summer when they grew wildly without care. The citrus fragrance wafted to his nostrils as he eagerly anticipated the moment Isra caught sight of him watching her. Astrid decided to be bold in this situation, so he cawed loudly. He couldn't help the fact that the sound came out much more voluminous than he hoped.

"Oh, I... I didn't see you there!" Isra stammered.

Her mesmerising, glowing lime-green eyes met Astrid's yellow eyes awkwardly as she familiarised herself with the jet-black raven she'd already encountered. She noted Astrid's feathers were glossy; she envisioned they'd be soft to the touch. His beak was also black, but then she noted his fine legs and claws that one presumed might indicate he could sink those sharp talons into anything that came up against him.

"Yes, I do apologise. Nice tea?" he asked in an attempt to construct a conversation, although Astrid was anxious he'd mess things up and say something wrong.

"It's warm orange," Isra mouthed calmly.

She seated herself on a luxurious red chair with gold gilding located at the back of the room, which meant she was almost parallel to where Astrid was sitting on the window ledge.

"Oh, how scrumptious. I had some tasty earthworms this morning." Astrid noted Isra's sudden grimace as she resisted the urge to spit out her orange tea violently. "But they are probably not to your taste," he added quickly in the hope that this would salvage things.

"No. I'm afraid I am not very partial to worms, but I do enjoy things that come out of the earth," Isra commented with a cautious stare at the raven.

"I should explain. I don't mean to intrude upon your fantastical mansion but I do feel we should take it slow, especially after that nasty confrontation with your former friend the other afternoon. Oh, now what is her name? I'm atrocious with names. Faces? I'm fine with those, but names I'm a bloody abomination!"

Astrid appeared flustered, although he knew exactly what he was going to say. He just needed to act as though he had managed to forget it so that Isra would involve herself in the discussion.

Yes, I know it sounds silly. I have to prod her a little bit. If she thinks I'm just some old raven that doesn't know what he's attempting to say, she might interrupt me, thinking I am a gibbering idiot, thus smoothing the pathway that will enable us to speak more, Astrid gushed to himself.

He couldn't quite grasp onto the notion that this little brain wave of his was rather genius. He had to admit he felt a bit odd, pretending to be some blithering imbecile but he also felt it was needed since he had to win Isra's trust.

"Everilda?" Isra finished. "Yes, she and I were friends. Once." She stopped to take another warm gulp of tea. "However, circumstances change, and needs must," Isra voiced abruptly. The subject matter concerning Everilda was quite a sore one.

"Yes. That's it. I called upon your good nature to not quarrel with her because I believe your energies are better off elsewhere," Astrid appealed to her in a low voice. "You've been to hell and back, Isra. You've done some marvellous things. You've had your heart broken. All right, that was not one of your best moments, but you've accomplished so much more since then. I just want to be around to guide you forward, sort of like a familiar in the non-traditional sense?" he proposed in a somewhat formal voice, although he was trying to maintain a friendly atmosphere between them.

"Oh, it's not really a quarrel as such. She just keeps showing up at the most unpredictable times, and it irks me. She's always got to be present somewhere in my life. My goodness, you'd think all of this would be done by now!" Isra concurred with a tiny hint of animosity in her voice.

"It's never, ever done," Astrid remarked. "If she's as aggressive as she sounds and you keep taking the bait, it will not be finalized for centuries. You'll live on knowing you've surpassed her in terms of living but you'll never have conquered her, for she will die in her mortal body."

"How very morbid!" Isra countered with a grin as she asked inquisitively, "So what do I call you then? You've been hanging around me for a while. You could at least give me your name."

Astrid looked a little taken aback, but it didn't deter him as he replied, "Certainly. I am Astrid. I am known for helping witches find their feet as they tread upon their new path to glory and refinement."

He enunciated carefully, knowing his tale wasn't strictly true. He'd only ever assisted one witch, and it wasn't his professional vocation.

"That is a pretty name indeed. I like it. I am Isra, but you already know that since you had the gall to speak it. Tell me, what else do you know of me? I am wildly curious. Some would say it is my ultimate weakness but I believe it to be quite the asset," Isra pressed, nearly grilling him in some respect but he wasn't in the least bit intimidated by her.

"Actually, do you mind if I come in?" Astrid politely requested. "It's just the sun is too harsh on my feathers right now. I'd rather not be a sweltering mess. It's not pleasant if my feathers stick together."

"Of course you may," Isra invited him cordially.

Astrid gently strode forward, lifting his wings, and he flew into the living room. He marched forward until he was at Isra's feet, looking up at her from her throne before proceeding to hop onto the arm of her chair.

"Ah, thank you so much. It's very much appreciated and I hope that it's not too intrusive for you?" he inquired.

"Not at all. So come, tell me, what delicious secrets you know, hmm? I am intrigued," Isra began, softly licking her lips. "If I'm as wretched as they say, there has to be a story to tell. I feel like I am in the mood for enlightenment. Of course, not that love and light kind," she added coolly.

Astrid cleared his throat nervously. Just being around Isra again, sitting next to her on this exquisite throne, made his heart flutter. It was like he'd met her for the very first time all over again.

"I've known of you for quite some time. In fact, I feel like I have known you forever. I believe we were meant to be friends. The kind of friendship where you just look them in the eye and know you are exactly where you belong. You are home. I've seen your triumphs. I've witnessed you being defeated, and I've been present in your moments of solace. I know every last grim detail about you and yet I am still here! It doesn't matter what you do. I will not falter. I've been by your side throughout your climatic move to darkness. You've accomplished so much in such a short space of time. I am very blessed to know you, Isra," Astrid told her proudly.

"I am honoured to have someone by my side such as you," Isra retorted before she paused, realising there was a lot about Astrid and his materialising that she did not understand. "But wait... how come I hardly know anything about you? I mean, I've only known you existed since the day before yesterday. If you have been here all this time, why don't I recall it? You know, the strangest things are happening in my midst. Alan brought up a ton of stuff about me that I had no comprehension of, and now you do something very similar. Don't you think that's odd?" Isra asked.

She was baffled at the notion that two charming souls with the same tale could come into her life at the same time.

I seem to have this recollection with Alan. He was detailing me as this magnificent sorceress that had defeated the light or at least had done until they intervened and yet it's a similar story with this Astrid fellow. He too suggests I enacted magical feats that would make anyone proud to know me or maybe even fear me but yet I have no knowledge of it. How can this be? I don't understand.

Isra pondered quietly in her thoughts, although she was deeply intrigued by Astrid's appearance and what else he would say to her.

"I don't find it strange at all. I understand that all beings whether dark or light have their own mystical occurrences. Your journey is one of darkness. This Alan chap, well, he's sure to know that. As to why you don't have any knowledge of it, perhaps that is something we should leave for a much deeper conversation. Oh, don't misunderstand me; I am willing to tell you all I know but I feel other events must take precedence before we can push forward," Astrid relayed to her with a forewarning glance that he quickly switched to a warm smile, for offending Isra was the last thing he wanted to do.

"I understand. Well, I do admit, this has been indeed revealing but I feel the need to depart. My legs could do with stretching. I was leaning towards the idea of a brisk stroll in the woods," Isra motioned solemnly.

All of the enthusiasm she'd had before had drained from her face. She was very aware of her surroundings. However, a wariness was emerging from her. It was clear there was something about all of this she did not like at all.

Astrid nodded in agreement. "I feel that would perhaps be a good move in this case. Some fresh air will clear your noggin."

He stepped back a little, knowing this meant he was soon going to have to fly away back to his quaint elder tree; however, he was surprised when Isra softly asked him a question he never once imagined he'd be asked.

"Would you like to accompany me? I'd rather not be alone in these heinous times. It would be very much appreciated if you could spare the time."

She sounded apologetic, almost as if what she was asking might be too much for Astrid to do.

"I would be honoured!" Astrid piped up happily. "I was pursuing some earthworms but they can wait, for some things are simply best not avoided," he uttered in a tone that reminded Isra of someone she'd known once before that had this bizarre language. Yes, it often sounded like he was talking in riddles. Perhaps he had swallowed a book of poetry once, but yet again her memory was hazy on the details.

Isra's brain suddenly let loose one of her long-forgotten mirages. *I do remember this marvellous man. He was tall, well-mannered. He had a deep voice that reminded me of Magnus Wingdom but he was younger, maybe in his late forties. I don't think it matters but he began lecturing me one fine day over my dragon summoning. He introduced himself to me as a friend to the light but oh, goodness, how come I know that? I am not supposed to!*

"Excellent, let me grab my cloak and we'll be on our way," Isra announced coolly, feeling that despite the fact it was a sunny July day, there might be a slight chill in the air.

SAMUEL SAT up in his armchair. Alan Grimsbane looked mighty fidgety in his seat. He wasn't entirely sure as to why he'd been summoned to the eccentric realm of Spirisity, but he'd known of it from his prior dealings with Samuel Reynaldi. Alan had fond memories of poking around in Samuel's elaborate garden, making merry havoc in his flower beds as he tottered around with young feminines in tow, being the tearaway he was.

I don't know why I am here. Has Father sent me for a severe reprimand? Have I displeased him in some way? Oh, perish the thought. I have never come up close and personal with Mr Reynaldi like this. I fear I am in great trouble, Alan conferred with himself, feeling the unease deep within his bones.

His shoulders were incredibly tense, and he couldn't get comfortable in his chair that was adjacent to Samuel's desk so there would be no hiding how he felt by Samuel's interrogating ways.

"May I ask why I have been sent to you, Mr Reynaldi?" Alan piped up with a questionable tone.

Samuel chuckled, flashing Alan his trademark formal smile. "Of course, you may, and less of the 'Mr Reynaldi,' please. The 'on high' will think I am a stuffy so-and-so, and while I am indeed getting on in years, I am not senile yet. Now, old boy, what do we have here, hmm?"

Samuel paused, which left plenty of time for Alan to squirm anxiously in his seat. His fists clenched at either side of him as he tried to conceal how desperately nerve-stricken he was.

"Now don't panic. I am not going to turn you into a horned toad. Besides, your magic far outweighs mine. Ah, yes. That was it. You've become acquainted with our lovely Isra! She's a spitfire, truly and notably, and she's somewhat unhinged, right? But that's how things are. We don't count our failings here, nor do we fault others for theirs. Anyhow, I am very invested in your—how do I say it?—your *courtship* of the girl. I'd like to encourage it," Samuel announced in a friendly manner, leaving Alan dumbstruck, for he expected to be in for a wholly displeasing ear-bashing.

"Wait, I am not in trouble?" Alan probed with a worried stare.

"Not at all. Why would you be?" Samuel came back at him. "How about we have a proper man-to-man conversation, shall we? Please don't mistake my involvement as interference. I am very curious about your impending courtship with Isra, and I'd like to facilitate moving to the next step, if you know what I mean?"

Samuel took a sip from his mug of steaming coffee, eyeing Alan with bemusement.

"I am not entirely sure. I was thinking I was going to get a right bollocking for letting slip that you had—well, you know—stopped her from conducting the world's hellish end, discarding her memories of the torrid event," Alan admitted somewhat nervously.

"Ah, poppycock. Don't worry yourself. It's a perfectly normal thing to say to somebody. However, I would prefer if you kept those details under wraps in the future. It's very important to the world and to Isra that she never discover the truth of those shenanigans. It would be most embarrassing for 'on high' no less, never mind me. But enough of my predicaments. No, Alan; I will not be scolding you. In fact, I'd rather congratulate you. Here you are, a fine fellow at the prime age of eighteen. You are destined to be a powerful warlock one day. What better way to showcase that than by having one of the realm's most formidable sorceresses by your side? Think about it. You don't need to decide right away!" Samuel invited eagerly.

"But I must warn you of the tragic endings that have befallen your father and his friend, Damien Daughtry. They were both caught up in not being romanced, so they fell prey to stupendous circumstances that almost knocked them both off their pedestals," Samuel urged Alan in a cautious tone.

I don't know how the fuck Daughtry gets away with it. I know he assisted Astrid but nobody has heard from him for many months. I am intrigued to learn what has become of him, but then again, it's quieter without his unique brand of chaos. I know he made a big mistake by shacking up with that demoness. I have high hopes for young Grimsbane, I really do. Samuel waffled on in thought. He realised Alan was staring at him; he'd gone into a trance.

"Yes, my father often mentions Damien Daughtry," Alan replied as he reached over to grasp onto the handle of his hot mug of coffee.

He took a brisk sip and caught sight of Samuel's majestic bookcase that sat behind them at the back of his elaborate office. He also noticed a luminous lime-green glowing orb that was sparking with ferocious green energy.

Now that cannot be what I believe it is. Surely Samuel Reynaldi wouldn't keep the one piece of evidence of her transition, right in his freaking office? I mean, how imbecilic can one person be? It's unfathomable, Alan ruminated sceptically. He couldn't help but glare at the powerful object gleaming from its position on top of the shelf.

"Did he mention Daughtry's fall from grace? Being banished from the most promised establishment in the realm wasn't pleasant. Your father almost had the very same fate but his reputation was in tatters for decades. It's never good to play around with forces we don't understand," Samuel went on to explain.

Alan seemed to be tentatively holding onto every word he said.

"No. Father always glossed over that one. He just said that Damien ascended to higher ranks and that was all there was to it. I've never seen my father's career as being one I should aspire to," he confessed meekly.

"Hmm. Good. So, how do you feel about my proposition?" Samuel inquired with a wide-eyed glance.

The light bringer was smiling for the first time in almost a year. He was very keen to ensure Alan went along with his swiftly hashed-together idea. It was interesting that Alan was new to knowing Isra, so who knows how he would react? He was a young, buff man, focused on ambition and power. He may not want to include any old mediocre thing like love into the mix, especially at the age of eighteen when a young man wants to be in his prime, wooing the ladies and not caring about feeble things like commitment.

"I am a little unclear as to what is expected of me?" Alan asked cautiously. His nerves were very much doing all the talking since he didn't quite understand Samuel's meaning.

"Well, you'll be shacking up with Isra, keeping her in suitable check within the dark forces, and in return, you'll get a fantastic wife out of the deal. Well, in a few years, anyway," Samuel chortled, trying his best to detail the situation so that it was plainer.

"Ah. It's just a fleeting courtship right now. I don't really want anything serious just yet," Alan admitted with a worried glance at the light-bringer in the fear that anything he said now could surely land him into all manner of hot water. Samuel was a highly respected and most powerful man. Not to mention he was prone to going batshit crazy when the slightest thing didn't go his way.

"Well, nobody is expecting marriage at this point, dear boy. Just keep her out of trouble. You see, her outlandish behaviour is what got her in the midst of the light in the first instance. I wouldn't have had to magically disarm her in the metaphysical sense if she'd just left the dark side well alone. But alas, we cannot change the past now, can we, hmm?" Samuel elaborated as he took a large gulp of coffee before retorting in Alan's direction, "Just give it some thought. You never know; you may find yourself warming up to the notion. You wouldn't have to change anything about your relationship with Isra right now, but I do want her out of harm's way."

Alan narrowed his eyes at Samuel in a sceptical manner. It was as though Alan could sense Samuel was indeed telling an enormous lie to cover some prevaricating that had already been conducted. Samuel's role in Isra's destruction was a significant one but trying to convince anyone else that he had done what he deemed to be right was tricky since Samuel's story had many holes in it.

"You mean you want Isra to be distracted?" Alan assumed bravely, much to Samuel's displeasure.

He didn't like the accusation. However, he kept a cool head and quietly swallowed before addressing Alan.

"Whatever gave you that notion? Oh, no. Not at all. I just want her out of harm's way. You see, the reason Isra got herself into trouble is she got mixed up with someone, a servant of mine who couldn't handle their dark streak of rebellion. Naturally, I did all I could to stop it when I saw this attraction become an infatuation. Well, I tried my hardest to act methodically. You see, they meshed perfectly and that ensured it was even more challenging to stop them both. They were going to unleash Armageddon onto the world. Both of them had this ulterior uprising within that made their insubordination seem plausible, but I see things from a very high perspective. I knew Isra was ultimately going to travel down this path and she needed somebody to encourage her. Well, he was her partner in crime, so to speak," Samuel informed Alan before he motioned with a furrowed brow, "I just feel it would be better if she was placed under duress that doesn't involve me wiping her memory this time!"

Samuel turned fondly to his grandfather clock. "Well, look at the time. It's just around two. My goodness, how the time has flown."

Alan nodded in agreement. "It has."

He was awfully perplexed as to what the next steps were since Samuel was acting like the grouchy father-in-law and yet he had no relation to Alan... or Isra, for that matter. Still, Alan pursued the idea at heart.

Whatever I do now, I am under his watchful eye. If I fuck up for any reason at all and it means I am not going to be with Isra, he'll surely have my guts for garters. Damned if I do and damned if I don't. But on the plus side, Father will approve because Isra is a full-blooded witch so there's that to add into the bargain.

Marrying Isra would be seen as a triumph in the eyes of his father, Nathaniel Grimsbane. However, it was unlikely Alan wanted things to go that far. Deep down, he was still very uncomfortable about the entire affair.

"I must be getting on. I have things to do. Dark souls to dismantle, bringing them down to their knees. It was very enjoyable conversing with you, Alan. Please note, you are welcome to come into Spirisity anytime. Just don't play buggery with my flower beds, eh?" Samuel joked with a wink as Alan rose from his seat, relieved at knowing that their meeting was finally over.

"It was interesting, I must say, and thank you for the enlightening chat. I am sure to bear it in mind."

Alan excused himself and pushed that royal blue plush velvet curtain before lifting his hand in the air. He closed his eyes as he clicked his index finger together with his thumb, vamoosing the hell out of there.

11

Isra walked slowly with Astrid flying overhead in her direction. He didn't want to be intrusive and rest upon her shoulder, although the urgency was very much there. He wanted it to be a free-flowing aspect whereby Isra felt safe enough for him to be present in her energy sphere.

They had been adventuring for around twenty minutes and Isra was beginning to tire. She turned to Astrid as she spied the fateful open space of Seclera, knowing she needed a rest.

"Oh, let us sit here! It will be good to take the weight off for a moment or two," she suggested.

Astrid's golden eyes narrowed at her with concern and he asked carefully, "Should you honestly be here?"

The question provoked unwarranted intrusion; Isra hadn't considered she should avoid Seclera just because of a scuffle with Everilda, of which she had come out on top when she agreed not to pursue it any further. But as far as Isra was concerned, she had every right to be here whereas Everilda was trespassing on mystical ground.

She's not a witch anymore, so what is she doing in our terrain anyway? Seclera is home to Wingdom's Academy, which is exclusively for witches. Sure, I am not one of their students any longer, but I still have a right to inhabit their beautiful lands in any event. It does ponder the inquiry as to where she's taking up residency now since she's nearly always found around these parts, Isra casually mused, considering the notion that Astrid might be a tad overprotective. In any case, she would humour him, for he had good intentions.

Isra laughed in response to Astrid's pressing query and said, "I suppose, in some sense, I shouldn't, but then again, I never listen to reason."

"I wouldn't presume that to be amusing, Isra. Everilda had a significant climatic event in her life whereby she tumbled from majesty into a sheer abhorrence of everything she ever knew. This is what happens when tainted souls mess with things that are of no concern to them. Nobody likes a meddler."

Astrid drawled on, although Isra wasn't paying him much mind. She seated herself on the grassy bank, looking out onto the beautiful cobalt-blue ocean.

"If you say so, love," Isra acknowledged softly.

"All right," Astrid started, launching down beside her, "let's have a real chat, shall we? You're so much better than this. You don't need to keep revisiting this phase in your life. Trust me. Let it go. Everilda's luck won't change now anyway. It doesn't matter what you do but stop feeding into her bullshit. That's what she wants."

Astrid finished curtly. He was trying to be firm yet friendly but it didn't come across in that manner.

Isra looked at him with a sideways glance. "I see you wish for me to stop with it all but I must inform you that my ruckus with Everilda isn't one I planned to elongate for such a time. I never thought I'd see her again," Isra muttered with a long, drawn-out sigh.

"And that will be a blessing in disguise. You can't continue rocking up here and fighting with her. She's doomed whether you do or do not. She's going to pay the price for a vast amount of time. There's no getting out of the way of that fierce beast karma when she's about to best you," Astrid affirmed in a low voice.

He sounded incredibly wise. There was something about him

that had Isra's attention. Something in him was a rarity in itself. It was very seldom that she interacted with others.

He does have his good points. I do feel he's extremely worldly. I also wonder if that might be the problem. He's too close to this to properly understand where I am at with it all. I don't provoke Evie, however, she does irk me so. Maybe his reasoning for saying steer clear is astute but we won't know entirely until something occurs whereby he is proved right...

Isra came to the sincere conclusion in her thoughts and absentmindedly stared out onto the Seclera blue seas before turning to Astrid formally. "All right, then. Let's make our way back. Time is getting away with us!"

Astrid didn't need telling twice. He outstretched his wings, launching himself into the air, steadily hovering above Isra as they moved onto pastures new. The mass of Seclera led onto the infamous clearing that was just a stone's throw away from Shambre Fell. Astrid knew it well; however, Isra was somewhat of a novice about this location. She'd only been down it once or twice.

"This was enjoyable for me. I had a nice day!" Astrid remarked to her comfortably as they both kept a balanced pace moving through the woodland terrain.

"As did I," Isra responded coyly, pushing on.

She wanted to get home soon, for her stomach was rumbling. The gurgling sound startled her but she assumed if she moved fast, the pain would lessen and her hunger would be satisfied quickly, but Isra turned the corner around the scorched orange and brown clearing only to see something standing in the middle of it.

Isra couldn't make out what it was at this stage, but it was clear it was some*body*—a figure prominently standing out against the darkened colouring. Whoever it was, they had a white gown on, for two long white sleeves could be spotted as well as a long flowing skirt, but nothing else was visible.

Astrid stayed close to Isra, sensing something wasn't quite right, but Isra continued going on because she didn't care for needless distractions. She was going home.

"Hang back," Astrid instructed with a forewarning glare. "Just, please, stay close."

He tried to intercept, hoping she'd take heed of him this time, for even Astrid didn't like the atmosphere that was coming off this individual in waves. It was eerie. Something didn't feel right here at all.

"I've got it," Isra answered solemnly. She didn't mean to sound indifferent but she also sensed the icky feeling and was trying to keep her wits about her. "Even though it's not easy," Isra added as she slowly got closer to the white figure awaiting her presence.

She gawked at Astrid awkwardly. He didn't appear happy that Isra was going on ahead but since the figure was in the middle of the pathway, there was little either of them could do to avoid the upcoming situation.

"Oh, shit!" Astrid exclaimed.

This made Isra's ears prick up, for she was now seeing something familiar in the individual. Two blue orbs stared out at her from the space where they sat upon a modest beige stature. Isra couldn't figure out for the life of her why this seemed so customary until she saw redness emerging from behind the two shimmery sapphire orbs.

Oh, my, Astrid realised. This notion was dawning on him fast. *I say to avoid it at all costs and here it appears right in front of her. Damn. I cannot create this stuff into a fantastical conjuring even if I tried. It's just too surreal.*

The red lingering from behind those eyes is the energy of vile anger. Aggression can only be found in a person that is not at peace with themselves, thus unable to control their reactions when their dastardly life comes to haunt them in various forms. Hence the expression, 'Every dog has its day.' She's had hers. That is definitely beyond any source of possible lingering doubt. Nothing remains when one has not only lost their soul but all credibility of it having once been good.

Isra stopped. Her mouth hung wide open in shock at what was right in front of her. *Oh, my goodness. He tells me to do my absolute utmost to take myself out of the equation with her and yet here she is!* Isra thought as she prepared for a hellish verbal storm.

"Oh, well, here I am walking through the quiet and quaint marshes, and look what we have here!" she announced coolly. "I would say this was a pleasant occasion but then again, I have never one to prevaricate. I'll leave that tragic act to the lowly ones. The peasants. The downtrodden. More importantly, dear girl, I shall leave it to *you*."

She finished sharply, not taking a breath. She knew that there would be one heck of retaliation ahead.

"Isra," Everilda voiced sardonically. "It's always self-gratifying for me to bump into you while on these lonely walks. I was hoping I would see you on this fine afternoon because, my goodness, do we have a lot to discuss!"

Everilda snarled. She appeared to be very much angered. She had an icy exterior about her, signifying to a certain extent that she was past caring.

"We have nothing to discuss," Isra said, trying to stop her foe abruptly.

She folded her arms against her chest with impatience while making it clear in her short tone of voice she had no interest in whatever nonsense Everilda was babbling on about.

"I am sorry you feel that way, but I heard you have become rather close to Alan Grimsbane," Everilda uttered before confessing, "However, I must warn you that he seemed absolutely charming when I was once his beau also."

"How on earth do you know who I am courting? Can you not stay out of my bloody life? Are you predestined to throw chaos upon every dynamic I happen to form with another kindred soul?" Isra probed fiercely.

She'd had enough of Everilda doing this, since she had done the same with Jonathan, and although that was never going to be the romance of the century, it had its good points.

Everilda chuckled mercilessly. "Calm yourself down, dear. I am sure Alan has you wrapped around his little finger. He probably told you a tragic tale whereby a dalliance took a dastardly turn and not for the better because the person involved chose darkness against his prior warnings. Does that ring a bell for you?" Everilda sardonically provoked.

Isra scoffed nonchalantly. "I believe he did mention something of that calibre, but I cannot believe for the life of me it could have been you. No way would he have chosen someone as wretched, some so undeniably banal."

I'm past caring over her tomfoolery. Why, she just wants to stir the pot. It's any old excuse because I am a fully-fledged witch and she is a wee mortal. We all know it's simply sour grapes. Ha, so her latest attempt at winding me up is trying to implicate herself as Alan's former lover. Oh, my goodness, the poor dear just reeks of desperation, Isra cajoled wickedly in thought. She didn't believe a single syllable Everilda said.

"It was me. Once upon a time. Alan and I were very much besotted with one another but his obligations became too much for me to bear. His father was a rather stubborn fool and deemed his son should marry into an eccentric witch family but I'm half-mortal so that's technically not feasible," Everilda elaborated, and then realised she'd told a half-truth.

She wasn't half-mortal, as she was the blood daughter of Rhiannon, but she was created in the image of her father, Damien, and her human mother, Damaris. Both knew Everilda's true heritage for years and never said anything. But Everilda swiftly decided that was none of Isra's business.

"I've heard him say something similar but it still doesn't hold any credence that you were once in his good graces. If you ask me, it sounds as though you want to create discord between me and Alan. That, I cannot tolerate," Isra stated firmly.

Everilda realised she'd have to go deeper with her story. *I have to make it more convincing. Isra thinks I am mollycoddling the truth. Hell, I wish I was. Oh, Grimsbane has done a number on her, that is for sure. Damn him. He's playing her for a right old fool. Well, the girl is in for a harsh awakening because he never sticks to one woman for long.*

It's not that she wanted to end Alan and Isra's relationship but more so to let Isra know what she was letting herself in for. Everilda had no strange urges or desires towards him anymore and hadn't for many a time but she felt that at least Isra should know.

"I-I don't want him, if that's what you are so concerned about..." Everilda stumbled upon her words. It was a sore note because long ago this man that she now had so much hatred for had been her everything, her very reason for existing and being in this hellish cosmos.

"All right, let's hear it then. Get on with it," Isra ordered, still having her arms crossed against her chest. Her stubborn impending nature meant she could barely tolerate any childish palaver for more than a few minutes before needing a reprieve.

"Fine," Everilda snapped. "He and I became acquainted because we went to various social gatherings as witches. I had these thrust upon me from a very early age because my mother saw fit to have me showcased on some glorious stage. I hated every moment of it but Alan made it more bearable. He conversed with me at the glittering galas and dismal evenings I had no choice but to attend. We became good friends and within a few months, we became so much closer. I was sixteen at the time and he was only fifteen. His father would never have accepted our courting of one another so we conducted our business behind closed doors. You see, his father expected Alan to be with only a full-blooded witch of excellent prowess that would glorify their family name."

Everilda went on to explain, recalling the dire dilemma that became the biggest obstacle in their relationship.

"They don't want witches with damaged souls reigning supreme in their family line, for it soils their not so graceful reputation. That is what it comes down to at the end of the day. It's not about who is the most perfect divine counterpart to their imperious offspring but who is fanciful enough to create a pleasing impression for the families. So I decided one day I would indeed walk down the very lonely and wholesome dark path. He wasn't best pleased with my efforts and warned me it wasn't suited for all souls, no matter what their heritage."

Isra looked taken aback and remembered the very same faithful words Alan had used. "This path is not suited for all persons." All right, so Everilda made a slight adjustment and used "souls' instead of the latter but some part of Isra questioned whether Everilda wasn't lying for the first time.

"I don't mean to intrude, but did you honestly think because he's taken an interest in you that you are the only one he's delighting himself with? Because if so, be prepared to tumble into oblivion when your poor wretched heart learns the truth!" Everilda chided in a snide tone although she was trying to be cheery.

Isra huffed. She once again maintained her arms across her chest, a stance she had not grown tired. Everilda went on rambling on about things designed to bring about her instant gratification but she was about to get the brunt of Isra's ferocity.

"Everilda. Whether you were actually with Alan or not doesn't mean a damn thing to anybody. He's courting *me*. We are enchanting one another with our magic and mysticism. He has extensive knowledge of the realms. And maybe you fit in with him once but now you are powerless. You have nothing to offer anyone because you have lost that privilege. If you know what is good for you, you will stay away from me and in turn keep yourself away from Alan. It sounds as though he doesn't want you," Isra said coldly as she flashed Everilda an icy rivet.

"You choose to believe what you want, but I was once his and he was mine. It's just the natural way of things," Everilda countered. Her eyes flared with a searing red glow again.

"And that very same methodology is exactly the premise that landed you in the position you are now. Mortal. Human. Destined to exist in this desolation you call living." Isra taunted Everilda with a wicked grin. "But, I mean, if you must continue to linger in this haunted resonance, you could at least clean yourself once in a while. The stench of peasant is overwhelming." Isra turned her nose up in the air, giving a look of dismay towards Everilda.

"I see we are not going to agree on this. I can't promise I will stay away from either of you but I'll do my utmost to ensure I don't encounter either of you when this all becomes carnage," Everilda announced calmly, although she was pretty riled by the way Isra dismissed her claims.

"Whatever. It's the same old shit with you every time. You pretend you are the victim meanwhile you weave yourself in places you do not belong. Have you learned the lesson yet? One surely wonders because you've crashed down from supremacist unto extreme loserdom. Anyhow, it is none of my concern. I must be going. My friend here, Astrid, has a preexisting engagement with some juicy earthworms, and I'd hate to disappoint him by dragging him down into our chaotic shit while his stomach is rumbling."

Isra excused herself plainly while using Astrid as a getaway clause. Of course, Astrid didn't care. He wanted to fly away from here as much as she did but little did Isra know his mind was elsewhere.

Oooh, the moment has come. I don't know if this romance between Isra and Alan is going to last after this. It has become severely endangered now that Isra knows. And she won't admit it but boy, is she pissed. It's only a matter of time until the inevitable is her reality once again, Astrid callously thought as he looked down onto Isra, hoping that they'd be on their way.

"How fanciful," Everilda responded bluntly. "Well, I shall not keep you any longer but be warned, Alan is not a keeper. He's the last man you should get yourself entangled with."

She carefully turned away, heading towards the borders of Seclera, which was an odd thing for her to do since she lived in Rainfur.

"Goodbye, Everilda," Isra replied before proceeding to head straight to Shambre Fell with Astrid in tow.

The raven was preoccupied with Isra's welfare. *I want to say that I hope this will have a happy ending. I truly want to estimate that will be the case but history has a habit of repeating itself. She'll be heartbroken when he does the dirty on her and I'll be there to pick up the pieces once again,* Astrid murmured as he muddled through his anxiety because what he sorely feared would be coming up much sooner than anticipated.

12

Astrid tried his best to sit, although being a raven, it was difficult at best. Still, he thought it would be polite to at least humour Isra's kindhearted nature. Since her foray with Everilda, she wasn't as furious as he had expected her to be.

Perhaps she's just masking it. Everyone is different. She's secretly infuriated or she's burying it at the bottom of her soul. Isra must have some emotional response towards what Everilda said or she wouldn't be rummaging around, trying to accommodate some helpful raven who is concealing the fact he's her lover in disguise. Oh, how I wish Samuel hadn't managed to lower me to this harbinger form. I could have come to her by now and completely repaired everything he enacted. But wait! I still can, Astrid considered.

Suddenly, the idea dawned on him that perhaps he could support Isra in a much more reliable way.

"Well, you do seem quiet. I was expecting you to be abuzz, full of wonderful wisdom and cheery humour but instead, here you are brooding," Isra piped up.

She had settled down to a steaming mug of apple and cinnamon tea. The apple would soothe her soul whereas the sweetened spiciness of the warm, brown cinnamon would take the edge off of her extremely heated afternoon.

"I haven't heard a single thing from Alan since all of this commenced. I do hope he is well," Isra muttered as she took a sip of the hot tea through pursed lips, although her eyes were all over Astrid.

"I am sure the warlock is fine. But I must admit, I do have something on my mind. You are right about that," Astrid confirmed. "It seems that even those with whom we share diabolical pasts have the sheer habit of unleashing the very worst in us all. I wonder if sometimes I am doing enough to resolve the issues of those nearest and dearest to me," Astrid said in a melancholic tone of voice.

"And how is that then?" Isra pressed with curiosity. Her piercing, bright lime-green eyes were still very much focused on him but she had reduced the rigidness.

Astrid looked at her with a forewarning glance. "It is easy to neglect that which we believe will take care of itself. The reality is the latter. That it will, in fact, not subside, yet we choose to delude ourselves with the notion we've done enough. It was just a passing thought. That's all." He ended the line of questioning from Isra, afraid she'd discover his meaning. *Alan has not been in touch. To me, it is a dire sign of what lies ahead. She's not even remotely prepared for what is coming.*

Astrid gravely realised he needed to act swiftly if he was going to be able to sweep in at an unexpected moment.

"I may have to depart sooner than I anticipated. I have some business to take care of," Astrid exonerated himself meekly. "I will be back by this evening though, should you need any company? I do understand that Everilda's revelation may be troublesome to you, even if you do not care to admit it," Astrid added thoughtfully, knowing he'd need to do some investigating of his own because the time was drawing near when he'd be needed in Isra's life once more.

SAMUEL SHOOK Nathaniel Grimsbane's hand and introduced himself calmly. "Thank you, Nathaniel, for agreeing to see me. I do appreciate it in these murky times. Anyhow, you're probably wondering why I am here."

Nathaniel Grimsbane, who was overshadowed by the light-bringer, barely noticed Samuel. At just around five feet ten inches tall, he didn't resemble his son, Alan, except for the resounding bright blue eyes the shade of azure. Nathaniel had brown-black hair combed back and wore slim framed spectacles in the shade of gold to complement his large eyes. Nathaniel was confined to the back of his dining room, which also made for an excellent gentleman's smoking room. The large oval-shaped mahogany table nearly took up all of the space.

This meeting wasn't met with pleasure but Nathaniel decided to comply since the light-bringer suggested—or more accurately, threatened—it would be in his best interests to be obedient rather than cause an unnecessary ruckus. The last thing anybody needed was an all-out war between the light and the existing warring witch families of which Nathaniel was part.

"Mr Reynaldi, I don't wholly comprehend why you've summoned yourself over in our lands but I hope you aren't trying to be taxing in some way," Nathaniel remarked with a sardonic low growl. "It would infuriate me no end if I discovered you were trying to butter me up in order to benefit your cause."

"Nathaniel, that is not why I am here. No; I'm rather concerned about your boy, Alan. He's come of age and taken an interest in a witch I am very much aware of. In fact, she's been under my radar long before she transitioned over to your side," Samuel articulated with fervour. "And I was hoping you and I could come to some sort of arrangement since you are the boy's father."

It sounded as though Samuel was attempting to smooth things over with Grimsbane before cleverly engineering it so that Isra was kept distracted but he was not going to go into that with Nathaniel. Samuel had decided that Grimsbane didn't need to know.

"Our side?" Nathaniel questioned implicitly.

"The dark realms. Your fortress of undeniable rebellion against everything I fight for," Samuel retorted bluntly.

"Oh, *that*. Well, we don't rebel. We live to please only ourselves. Nobody gets hurt. Not a soul has anything adverse eventuate on their person unless they happen to be skirmishing for the opposing side. What calamity has Alan got himself involved in now?" Nathaniel chided with a fierce sigh.

He was vehemently abrasive towards Samuel and all he stood for. That was the trouble between light and dark. They could never co-exist with one another. One entity was always combative with the other.

"That's a fine attitude to have until all hell breaks loose!" Samuel admonished with anguish. He was angered by Nathaniel's uncaring mannerisms.

"I've seen more dark souls tumble to despondency than I care to count, and it's always the innocent bystanders that suffer most from it. I don't care how it irks you but your boy isn't in any trouble. He's taken up with a witch. Isra. She's from a highly respected warlock, although I am not at liberty to discuss who at this juncture, but she does meet all of your strict requirements as a woman for your son."

"Interesting how you want this to occur but yet you keep certain details under wraps. Isn't that always the way?" Nathaniel groaned with scepticism. He raised an eyebrow cautiously at Samuel as if he couldn't quite believe that Samuel travelled all the way to Immortal Yonder just to ask his permission to consolidate a potential union between his son and a witch. "And why would you ask me, anyway? I don't really care much for what the boy does behind closed doors. As long as he doesn't drop his ambition, that's all that matters to me."

"I feel his *ambitious* nature would be somewhat problematic if he doesn't have a good woman by his side. Isra is a sorceress of high esteemed prowess. She will encourage him if nothing else. She is nineteen and although her journey to darkness has been eventful, she is a good fit; marriage would ground her immensely," Samuel elaborated, hoping his reasoning was made clear although he was hesitant in giving away Isra's true heritage, which caused Nathaniel Grimsbane to roll his eyes in disbelief.

"Such a hater towards the darkness, eh? Oh, boy; is the darkness going to swallow you whole Reynaldi? You avoid it so relentlessly anyone would think you need to let loose some of that impenetrable tension. Give yourself a decent release," Nathaniel retorted, not caring that Samuel was offended at such a remark.

Samuel turned his nose up, looking disgusted. He recited questionably, "I am quite fine where I am, thank you very much. Aren't you worried about the ramifications, old son?" he countered with a wink.

I am in no need of your pity. I do not deem myself to be somebody that will dwell upon the negative. I don't hate the darkness. However, since fighting it as Lord and Chief Light-bringer of Spirisity, I know the damage it brings upon anyone stupendous enough to welcome it unto themselves, Samuel ranted away in thought.

Nathaniel was trying to goad him into a verbal tirade of obscurity. "I could say the same to you," he argued in response to Samuel's comment.

The two old men were bang at it now, both insulting the other without a care. They were missing the mark as Samuel had come here to discuss the impending matrimony and not to trade derogatory remarks with the groom's father.

"Whatever. You'll be dragged down to hell one of these days. I am wholly sure of it," Samuel jibed ruthlessly without due care. "Damnation is almost certain to find you. I'm surprised you aren't worried about it finally coming to bite you on your oafish backside!"

Nathaniel scoffed. "Hahahahaha, so narrow-minded!"

He fumbled under his table and fiddled before he pulled out a cigarette, reaching to the lit candle adjacent to him. He merely looked at Samuel as he turned to light up, watching as the glowing orange embers flash back as grey smoke billowed out from its end.

Samuel went on to enunciate his meaning. "I am not narrow-minded. I am simply stating your pathway in darkness is bound to result in repercussions. Sooner or later. I've seen it time and time again. And they all think they're holier than thou. Oh, karma won't get me. I mean, honestly, do you think the universe is stupid? That it doesn't prey witness to all you do? Trust me, old chap, damnation is coming for you. I don't mean to be intrusive or rude; I am just concerned."

Goodness, what is wrong with this buffoon? I come here as a humble man wanting to conduct business surrounding his son and my Isra. Well, she's not strictly mine in the paternal sense but I am her guardian; that's another long and boring story we'll not pay mind to. He's so freaking ignorant to the cause. Is he happy for his child to be the same as him? There is so much better in the world than to be a failed warlock desperate for attention by putting his son centre stage to gain clout, Samuel thought to himself, dumbstruck at what was staring Nathaniel in the face. *Sheer arrogance.*

"Aren't we all?" Nathaniel joked, taking a long drag on his cigarette and leaving Samuel absentmindedly trying to wave the smoke away. "So, you say the girl is a perfect match. Why don't we just let those two kids engage in this fraternising for themselves? If they are devoted enough to one another, all of that wholesome love stuff will soon emerge not long after. I'm not a sole believer in forcing anything."

"Except discharging all manner of carnage," Samuel returned candidly.

"Well, there is that," Nathaniel admitted nonchalantly.

He truly didn't care. There wasn't one shred of guilt to be found within him. He was blameless.

"I would have hoped this alliance would have gained your approval. Alas, it has fallen on deaf ears. With that notion in mind, I'll be going," Samuel muttered, getting up from his seat before he waved his hand above him angrily, dissipating into thin air before Nathaniel could hurl another insult his way.

Isra still hadn't heard anything from Alan and she was beginning to despair, feeling as though something was gravely wrong. Her newly made raven companion had gone and deserted her to attend to some business, or at least, that was how he had worded it, but Isra wasn't entirely sure as to his meaning. She didn't presume ravens did much else other than soar through cloudless skies and gobble up earthworms but perhaps she was mistaken in this case.

Maybe he is a messenger. I don't really know. Ravens and crows herald great mystical symbolism but that is all I am aware of. If I was gallivanting in search of Alan, perhaps I could find the answers I seek. It is very unorthodox that he's said nothing to me ever since Everilda tried to imply she and him were once lovers. And they might have been, but the thing is, that's the past. It's not where we are in the present moment. Oh, how Evie loves to hold onto things she should have let go of goodness knows when, Isra blundered along in her thoughts. She was alone yet again, and not hearing from Alan was causing her discomfort.

Isra made haste in leaving Shambre Fell, knowing she would have to trod down to Immortal Yonder much to her pleasure. Only witches could dwell there, meaning there would be no chance of bumping into Everilda since she was mortal now, which thankfully, reassured Isra. She was vastly enraged with Everilda's childish, nonsensical crap.

"Alan must be sitting at home in his quiet solace. There won't be any preexisting circumstance that would have kept him from communicating with me, although in these times, we never know for certain," Isra mumbled as she edged on closer to the clearing where the border of Seclera subtly turned into Immortal Yonder. The invisible veil kept it a closely guarded secret from those who didn't need to know of its whereabouts.

Isra reached the entrance to Immortal Yonder, taking heed as she stepped right through. It was such a miraculous sight to behold. The glorious orange melted in between the golden and fuchsia just as it was before. This beautiful light show that dominated the cobalt-blue skies was ever so serene set against the eventide. Isra found herself distracted by the lavish colours that made the stormy sky look almost plain but there was no sign of Alan's brilliant white farmhouse, which Isra found rather odd. It was always here. It was his domicile.

"That's strange. Where is his home?" Isra asked pressingly.

She began walking clockwise around the brilliant deep blue lake, the very same way she'd normally get herself over to the farmhouse since the large body of water surrounded the vast area of Immortal Yonder.

"Oh, no! Are you lost, dear girl? My, now that is most unfortunate," a low voice chortled out to her.

Isra couldn't see anyone behind or to the side of her so she looked straight ahead only to find herself face to face with a man with jet-black, slicked-back hair. Whilst a pair of silver half-moon framed spectacles sat upon the bridge of his nose, they only complimented his sky-blue eyes. He had a forlorn expression plastered onto his face as though Isra shouldn't be here. He was dressed head to toe in a tailored black suit with a long black coat jacket to match his smart trousers and crisp white shirt. All that would be required would be a black top hat and Isra would have assumed that he was some kind of magician.

And if she'd have known better, she'd have swiftly realised that this was none other than Samuel Reynaldi. However, she'd lost her memories long ago so could not place him. Her ability to recall these things had sadly been lost to her, much to her befuddlement and Samuel's revelry, for he knew exactly who she was.

Ah, it is our young enchantress. I did wonder when I'd lay eyes upon her again. Well, she's looking very well, I must say. Although I am a little sore on why she's in this bewildering wasteland. Alas, it must pertain to that Alan chap. He seems to have skedaddled far out of sight much to her annoyance, I'm sure. She's searching for him for some reason, Samuel gushed to himself. He had never expected to bump into dear sweet Isra so soon.

"I am not lost, no. I was looking for a friend of mine but his domain seems to have vanished into thin air. An odd occurrence, I am sure," Isra proclaimed with a slight groan. She had expected to find Alan, not some wandering stranger that had managed to land in her midst.

"Oh, well... I don't see any buildings here, do you?" Samuel called out to her with a grin. "I was just leaving. I had a rather unfortunate incident to deal with. I'll tell you what; how about you tell me who it is you are seeking, and I shall see if I can assist, hmm?"

He beguiled her with his intriguing offer although Isra had no idea who he was. How could he help her? It was baffling, but she couldn't help but sense some familiarity there underneath all that charm and sophistication.

I know him from somewhere. I just cannot think where. I am sure I've witnessed this man show up many times in my dreams. I recognise that suit coat and those silver spectacles. That formal yet somewhat brash attitude has many young souls perilously running from their chosen calling for fear of displeasing him. Certainly, he lacks finesse but I can almost definitely agree that there is something about him that is so customary to me. He always appears as an irritated guardian that is practically foaming at the mouth, knowing I'm about to wreak havoc again. In my dream space, I give him quite the escapade, Isra thought, feeling as if she were in a hazy daydream but the details weren't completely crystal clear.

"I don't. You're right, but how can you help me?" Isra asked with a forewarning glance. Her piercing lime-green eyes gleamed back at Samuel auspiciously. She had no trust in him at all.

"Ha, I can see you are sceptical. All right, how about I let you into a little secret, hmm? The house is *there*. It's just not *here*, if you pardon the expression. It's viewable only by those who are locked into that infinite consciousness," Samuel detailed, becoming very serious for a moment.

"I can get you in there, but you must promise you won't tell anyone about our meeting. If they were to feast their eyes upon the fact that the high esteemed light-bringer of Spirisity let a young, relentless witch into their domain who was determined to find out why her young man had been ignoring her, well, my head would be on the chopping board," he admitted carelessly.

Yes, giving Isra access to the unthinkable realm of Immortal

Yonder when it had been cloaked off was dangerous indeed, even to her. Isra was a remarkable force to be reckoned with on the sunniest, brightest day of them all.

"All right, so please, may I ask why you can smuggle me in there when you are stating that it is closed off?" Isra pressed further. "Aren't light-bringers supposed to be good and pure like the soft white snow? Although I've never had the pleasure of meeting one, I've heard things from my friend." Yet again, she threw another question in the direction of Samuel Reynaldi.

"The very same companion who is reigning in his ignorance towards you. Yes, I thought as much," Samuel retorted. "We light beings are pure but since you are a soul very much drawn to the dark ways, you'd never be able to comprehend that. Nevertheless, whether someone is light or dark, they have a marvellous knowledge of the realms. Where one door is slammed shut, we can burst the other wide open," Samuel stated honestly.

"I see." Isra nodded in agreement. She still appeared extremely bewildered as to how all of this could commence when this man was light and, as he had already said, she was dark as sin. Isra implored him to answer her. "He is a challenging one. But I must beseech you to tell me, how do you know it is hidden? Surely being surrounded by the light, you cannot see anything but sweet, white fluffy clouds and punchy pink unicorns while you all prance around like fairies with something stuck up your rear ends?"

"Hahaha, prancing around like fairies. I'll have you know that we do not. However, you wanted to know how I could tell that the house was hidden. Well, my dear girl, after exchanging sour dialogue with Nathaniel Grimsbane for just over an hour, I sensed disapproval over my coming here but more so an impish atmosphere like someone didn't want to be found. It doesn't take a genius to figure out that this house isn't viable to the naked eye. But I did feel the energies lingering from the dark magnitude saturating the house instantly as I made my way out of there, quick as lightning," Samuel confessed stoically.

He had a rather perplexing glance about him. It seemed he might be unsure at what he had experienced but that it was a vibe he had that the Grimsbanes were trying to desperately conceal something.

"All right. I do soberly apologise for my callous remarks," Isra rebuked herself in a formal tone.

"No matter. Now, let's just get you in there, shall we?" Samuel suggested.

Time was getting away, and he had the sinking feeling that all would not be well when Isra entered that fortress.

"Of course. I thank you for this also, if it hasn't already been made clear."

Samuel raised both of his hands at where the farmhouse traditionally stood and to Isra's amazement, bright silver sparks imploded from Samuel's palms, surging to the open space. They became more prominent. The effect of it all made Isra feel slightly dizzy. She couldn't handle the ferocity of the energy being unleashed by someone that called themselves a light-bringer, no less. It was unimaginable that his amazing skills had gone from seeing gleaming silver energy manifest from his fingers to then seeing the brilliant white house materialising in Isra's line of vision within seconds.

Samuel still held his hands firmly against the farmhouse as he instructed Isra, "Go. I cannot hold this for much longer."

He was standing in front of the magnificent energy portal as shiny silver lightning bolts flashed back onto his hands with sheer veracity whilst Samuel used all of his life force to wield it open for her.

Isra wasted no time in hurrying herself along to the doorway of the farmhouse before she turned to Samuel one last time, about to say something further to him, but then it mysteriously vanished from her mind.

"Good luck. I'll be seeing you, girl!" Samuel called out in an echo, just as Isra set foot into the open portal Samuel created. Still hearing his words, she found herself standing in Alan's bedroom.

13

What have I done to deserve this? Father is berating me. Mr Reynaldi is bargaining with me that I absolutely must consider courting Isra or else there could be infallible consequences arising. I mean, where is the sacred divinity? The freedom to do as one pleases? It's all just falling by the wayside and nobody else can see it but me.

Alan jolted out of his reverie, sitting bolt upright as he saw Isra materialise in front of him. "What the hell are you doing here, Isra?" he exclaimed in a petrified voice.

He was shocked to see her appear in front of him like that. It was a severe knock to his system so much that he could feel the bourbon he'd been drinking surging back up through his oesophagus as he tried to maintain his sense of calm… Whatever that was.

"Oh, I am sorry. Did I startle you?" Isra asked in a melancholic tone. "I was concerned. I hadn't heard from you in a while and after a troublesome afternoon, I wanted to ensure all was well."

"Trust me," Alan stammered. "All is not well at all. I almost jumped up to death. Not that I'm not displeased to see you, but my goodness, you scared me half to death!"

"I am sorry. I became concerned because I hadn't heard from you.

I certainly didn't mean to intrude upon your 'lonely' time," Isra advised with a furrowed brow.

He could now see that she was deeply worried over his welfare and therefore it was unlikely she was going to enter into a slanging match with him.

"I needed a break, is all. I have Mr Reynaldi on at me. My former lover is also goading me into an all-out war. Father isn't best pleased with my efforts," Alan enunciated, plainly demonstrating his frustration, but Isra quickly caught on to hearing him say his former love, which made her twitch nervously, shifting uncomfortably from where she was standing in the middle of Alan's bedroom. The irony was Isra was beginning to believe that perhaps Everilda was telling the truth, although the former witch rarely ever did keep herself honest. Everilda was well known for creating the sob story and then making whoever was dumb enough to fall for it jump to her defence when they learned just how much of a victim she was.

"Former lover?" Isra asked, trying to be as casual as possible, for she didn't want to rock the boat too hard.

Let us not fall prey to one's indifference. Just because they seem similar on the outset doesn't mean they are. I suspect it's Everilda. He won't admit it's her but I can't shake the feeling that he's been wholly dishonest with me this entire tenure. And hey, it's not like I pursued him; I just so happened to land into his mystical land of self-loathing and unhealthy infatuations. He was the one who harangued me into becoming something more. I am not to blame if he didn't want anything more than a fleeting flirtation where we'd connected due to circumstance.

Isra questioned the idea that maybe Alan was in fact toying with her but honestly, she had nothing to prove otherwise. Just his word that something was awry, which wasn't incredibly helpful at this juncture.

"Yes, the one who fell prey to darkness. She's been harassing me of late. I cannot fathom why, but she's taken it upon herself to be my shadow all of a sudden. It's very peculiar, not to mention unnerving," Alan explained coldly.

He was barely giving Isra any eye contact for fear that she'd be cross with him. A witch with a temper was never something that came highly recommended in these parts.

"Oh," Isra said, stopping there and not saying anything else. "Mr Reynaldi is the light-bringer, is that not true? Why would he place pressure on you? Surely you are the opposite of everything he deems worthy and just to be in his midst?" Isra quizzed with not one but three questions simultaneously.

"He is but he also has business with me. It's somewhat difficult to explain but I'm on very thin ice with the man as it stands. He could throw me into the lion's den in a nanosecond just for going against what we agreed," Alan went to explain, making sure he wasn't giving away too many details, for he couldn't let it slip out that Isra was the business Samuel Reynaldi had bargained with him over.

"Oh, I see now. That sounds challenging at best," Isra concurred. "Perhaps you just need to take yourself out of the equation with this former lover. Maybe her reappearance in your life is more harrowing to you than you first deemed to be true," Isra recited back to Alan as she pressed her index finger to her lips as though receiving some kind of intuitive notion that only she knew.

"Yes. Maybe. Anyway, it is very hard for me right now. I cannot be what people want me to be. I'm not going to overexert myself. They are going to be angered with me either way," Alan continued, tripping over his words as he realised he'd made the biggest faux pa right in front of Isra.

"Does that little conundrum also include me? To be what people want you to be?" she questioned with a solemn glance.

"It does. Yes," Alan admitted in an icy tone. "I am sorry. I know you burst in here to hopefully clinch onto some new age answers or whatever, but I think we should simmer down a little bit until things calm down."

He made his connotation known as he was almost saying the words, "I think we should stop courting," but yet at the same time he hadn't.

"Does that mean that you don't want us to court any longer?" Isra probed, folding her arms across her chest in disbelief as to where this discussion was now taking the pair of them.

"For the time being. My ex is far too perilous. She will stop at nothing. She knows about you, me; the whole shebang. Quite frankly, Isra, my mind is getting tired. I'm running away with myself, questioning how this has all unfolded. I was unceremoniously dumped by this woman three years ago and here she turns up like a bad penny," Alan blurted out, not giving Isra an inch of leeway.

She would have grilled him over this no matter what he'd confessed so really, he was just digging himself an even greater hole, one that he should probably slink right into and hide from both vexed females. There's nothing worse than rampant hormones running riot in a woman who has not yet mastered her emotions. A charming feminine, sweet on her outer exterior who could easily fly into a rage without warning, without prior invitation and he couldn't do jack shit about it because he'd got himself into this mess.

"Well, I guess that is one way of telling me what I needed to know. But why don't we get the elephant out of the room here, eh?" Isra nudged Alan. "It's beginning to grate on me," Isra hissed nonchalantly.

"And what might that be?" Alan came back to her.

He was on edge now. His body language was rigid and there was a very compact space between him and Isra so he couldn't exactly high tail it and avoid her intrusive energy although he really wanted to.

"I know your former beau and my ex-best friend is none other than Everilda Daughtry. It's all right. I don't blame you for it truthfully. She's a spineless git, focused on her own gains, always has been, but I'd rather we'd be honest with each other instead of dancing around this," Isra pronounced carefully, her eyes narrowing upon Alan as if she was checking for signs he was lying again.

His eyes zoomed upwards and then back down onto the floor. He sat upon his bed as he had been the whole time but he kept on nervously turning his eyes away from Isra, which to her only confirmed she was indeed right.

I know it. He knows it. Let's just get it all out in the open and perhaps some resolution can be found. I get the feeling he doesn't truly want to abscond from me. It might just be the fear of it all. But I want to at least give him the chance to redeem himself. If he messes up after this, then it's all for the taking, Isra thought to herself.

She might have been better off in isolation after all. She'd seemingly come across yet another selfish man who only thought of his own needs. Even someone that had helped encourage her upon the dark wasn't much better than Jonathan, the mortal who had been the catalyst for Isra's journey to darkness in the first instance.

"All right, it is Everilda." Alan straightened himself as best as he could muster after his confession. "She's been following me about the last couple of days. It's why I demanded that Father protect Immortal Yonder in a cloaking enchantment. Please don't mistake my intentions, Isra. It wasn't that I wanted to keep you out, but that I needed to keep myself in," Alan blurted out in a cautionary tone.

He was anxious. There was no denying that but he was trying to maintain the harmonious equilibrium between himself and Isra by painting Everilda as the villain.

"But you still choose to end our courtship after such a brief time?"

Isra motioned to him in a low voice. Her eyes were slowly welling up with tears. The sheer betrayal hit her in the face once again. The same feelings she'd experienced with Jonathan and Everilda were coming back to her as if it was yesterday.

"I am afraid so. I can't make myself love another when I am so unloving. I just cannot bring myself to do it. I do like you, Isra, and I hope in some way that we can still be connected but we don't work as a united front. I hope you understand it from my perspective and not jump to unaligned conclusions," Alan made it clear to her.

"I hope you find the time to sound off to Everilda and let her know she has won," Isra retorted sardonically.

There was just the tiniest bit of sadism in her tone. She was wholly angry with Alan but also upset as was expected due to his untimely manner of which he had chosen to end things with her.

"I won't be doing that," Alan resounded solemnly. "Everilda is the least of my or your problems. I would still like to assist you with that memory spell should you wish to receive my help?" he asked in a low voice.

"I am not sure I want to recall anything that has happened now. So you and I are no longer lovers... All right, I shall see myself out. I am sorry if I disturbed you in any way," Isra countered as she turned to leave Alan's bedroom, which instantly reminded him of the very same way that Everilda had stood right before he'd told her to get the hell out of his home.

"We can't be. I'm sorry. I'll tell Mr Reynaldi that it's a no from me," Alan admitted, which left Isra reeling.

Her head spun around in an anti-clockwise fashion as she affixed her gaze onto him questionably, wondering what exactly he meant. To her, it seemed perhaps Samuel Reynaldi had tried to encourage Alan to court her, which suggested another idea to Isra.

I wonder if any of it was real. Was I in some kind of a daze? Had I been knocked into a stupor, not knowing where the hell I was and somehow finding myself in his very enigmatic presence? Could it be that this entire thing was orchestrated on my behalf to distract me? Isra considered the questions, for now her suspicions were on high alert.

"Wait, how is Mr Reynaldi involved? He was the one who..."

Isra's voice trailed off momentarily as she began piecing some key details together.

He was the one who greeted me here at the entrance and was more than willing to admit me into this realm, knowing I couldn't get in without him. But how on Earth did I end up being used as a prize for a young warlock? What does he gain out of a union between a witch and a sorcerer who likely may never have met if it wasn't for his help? It doesn't make any sense! Isra surmised as she pondered the idea that maybe Mr Reynaldi wasn't all that he seemed to be. Her mind revolt was disrupted when Alan interrupted her train of thought.

"He was the one who what? Let you in?? How?! He's part of the love and light brigade," Alan pumped, becoming even more confused by the second. He couldn't fathom for the life of him why a light-bringer would get himself so involved in matters that were none of his concern.

Why would he be there? Did she meet him coincidentally? Perhaps he had a word with Father? But then again why would he of all people converse with Isra, knowing what she is? There has to be an agenda of sorts here. He wouldn't just help her out of the kindness of his heart. No, that's not how it works. There has to be some end game he's not disclosing but I cannot figure out what. Isra is none the wiser. She's just as perplexed but it does beg the question because even she is bemused as to why it was him and not somebody from our lands. Alan mulled it over in his thoughts, slowly formulating together all of the parts of the story. Some of them made sense, while others were nonsensical at best.

"Does it really matter?" Isra pressed but was becoming withdrawn as she seldom had any interest now that there would be no resolution to the relationship between them.

"It does to me," Alan argued. "I know that light-bringer; he is as slippery as jellied eels. Just one false move and he can bring down your entire operation in a flash if he deems it right to do so. It's not like anyone in Immortal Yonder has ever gone against the light either. Many are born and bred into the darkness. Some have never even set foot in their so-called lightworker lands. Neither do they care to. It's just so..."

Alan was trying to find the right word to describe it, pausing for a second as he aimed for an accurate understanding of his meaning.

"Pointless?!" Isra interrupted.

She had always found the light to be a little far beyond the parameter. Something so meaningless that it had barely any purpose. Why being good and doing kind gestures for unloving souls only to have them ripped from underneath you, chucked right back at your face, just didn't make any sense.

The souls residing in the dark are the true queens and kings. The awakened ones. The ones who have experienced true sorrow and never want anyone to go through that wretched pain they have thus become accustomed to. It is not good enough to simply wish away that desolation. One must make the required changes in themselves in order to benefit their existence to the highest level of being. Yes, I understand him more than I dare admit, but the little shit is removing himself from my midst so I cannot garner much sympathy for his plight.

Isra relinquished her sense of empathy as she mulled over the current predicament she found herself in intensely.

"Irrelevant," Alan concluded. "Nobody here cares enough for the do-gooders of life. It's so ridiculous that it may as well be almost petty. Everyone in the darkness has already known so much hatred in their long or short lives that the art of kindness comes naturally to them. It's just our ways, but we are so easily misinterpreted for being devil worshipers or begging a divine being to answer our every whim. If only that was the truth," he finished quietly.

"Well, I don't know what he wants with me or why he's got himself involved but then again, I am past caring. I seem to find myself in this situation time and time again. I get close to a man and then kaboom! He goes AWOL or blames some external source for our separation and I get burned. I am becoming increasingly tired of all this." Isra stifled a yawn.

If he carries on blabbering, I am sure to find myself falling into a slumber. He's not even that intriguing anymore. I don't know what changed. He used to be so confident, so brass and bold. Now he's just a shell. I have no use for a man that has allowed himself to be struck down into a feeble imagining of something he used to be, Isra wondered to herself, taking care to notice the time on the antique golden cuckoo clock situated at the back of Alan's bedroom affixed to the wall above his bed. It showed the large hand striking at twelve and the smaller one hovering on seven.

It was seven o'clock in the evening! She'd been running around chasing this man for almost three hours and what a sheer waste of her resources and energy that had been. Oh, well. There was no time to cry over spilt milk. There were more important things for her to focus on, such as asking the relevant and impending questions as to why certain folks were getting their noses invested in her business all of a sudden?

It doesn't bear great witness that a light-bringer would focus his attention on such a wicked foe like myself. If I am deemed to be such a troublemaker, surely he would have not wasted his energy on me and would have moved on by now. It doesn't give a lot of credence when you look at the philosophy of the love and light brigade. They are supposed to be loving and do some good deeds, so again, it provokes the question, why is he interested in helping me? I just can't fathom it. I don't understand the inner workings of some of these people and the sordid worlds they are so callously entwined in, Isra pondered with a fierce glare in Alan's direction. He was yet another person she was now sure didn't have her best interests at heart, a self-serving man with only one desire, and it didn't take much thinking to decipher what that was.

It would probably be a smart move for her to head back to Shambre Fell soon. If nothing else, perhaps she could comfort her weary soul with a warm cup of tea. She wasn't sure what flavour would be appealing. What does one indulge oneself in when they're discarded like yesterday's trash? Would you appreciate the sweet sentiment of ripe strawberry mixed with pungent elder flower? Perhaps something more calming like vanilla teamed with chamomile would be more welcoming.

"Well, I'll be going. I have things to attend to. It was nice knowing you, Alan." Isra smiled as she turned to face him one final time.

"Wait," Alan implored. "I know I've been a fool. I should have realised you and I were just an infatuation and nothing more than my reckless lust. It's a habit of mine. I'm not capable of love, truly. I am very sorry. I think it would be best if we never laid eyes on each other again."

Isra looked dumbstruck. Her face was numb and she said nothing in return.

"Aren't you going to say anything?" Alan called after Isra. He was shocked that this young woman he had grown to know wasn't reacting to his admission at all.

No, because you'd love that wouldn't you, eh? Another carcass to add to your shrine of broken hearts. While I may weep for you, I'll never give you the satisfaction of knowing that, Isra thought coldly as she felt her chest tightening inside her tiny body. The pain surging from her heart was almost burning into her. She'd have to get out of here soon or else it might become uncontrollable. This suffering pain she had thought she'd been able to discard so effortlessly long ago had returned with a vengeance.

Isra turned away from Alan solemnly as she emitted, "Suffice to say, I think there is nothing more for us to discuss."

And with that, she walked out of his bedroom, not caring that Nathaniel Grimsbane had seen her, for she descended so fiercely down those stairs that her feet felt searing pain once finally reached the bottom. Isra wasted no time in swiftly making her getaway, tearing out of the farmhouse entrance before anyone could stop her.

Isra ran like a shot around the blue lake, not even taking in the glorious sunset that normally held so much majesty. She yearned to get to the veil of Immortal Yonder, which she did much to the bemusement of the onlooker, Nathaniel Grimsbane, who twitched his nose, tutting in disapproval as he caught sight of the flighty light-haired maiden dashing away.

When Isra pushed past the barrier without a care, tears billowing down her face, she didn't notice the black tail feathers of Astrid as he lingered from the nearby elder tree apologetically.

Astrid felt awkward as hell; he had foreseen this, after all. It had only been a matter of time for him. He'd already grasped what Alan was like, even if he portrayed a kind soul image to Isra. Astrid had Alan figured out although Isra deemed him to be worthy of her time.

He watched closely as Isra flung herself onto the grass. Her head was in her hands and she cried uncontrollably while her entire body shook. Her skin was like electricity. The energy she'd taken so long to release left her but she was inconsolable.

"I'm sorry," Astrid whispered meekly, peeking down at her from his perch where he'd been sitting.

The feeling was so uncomfortable he was left unable to truly express what he'd wanted, for now Isra was in pieces once again. Of course, there was the hope she'd build herself back up but Astrid wasn't entirely sure on how he should approach this now Alan had done the dirty on her. It was bad enough for a mortal ripping her heart in two but now it was a warlock who had committed the sinful deed, leaving Astrid much more perturbed than he had been previously. This would prove to be an entirely different situation.

"How the hell...?" she gasped.

Isra lost her words. Her face showed little emotion except for the straying tears that still resided on her cheeks. She didn't know what else to say, for she was exasperated at him being there, having expected this to be a quiet moment of solitude where she could sit and attempt to be at peace with her thoughts. Not that she was going to be, her state of mind was somewhere between unleashing chaos unto the world and reigning hellfire without due care.

"Don't worry. I'll leave you alone if my being here troubles you. I just heard the commotion and wanted to check if you were all right before I departed?" Astrid voiced cautiously.

He felt tears welling up inside him. It was overwhelming. Astrid was lucky that his feathers were black because they would not show up easily on his onyx plumage but he was determined to hold them in because he had to be the strong one now. He was going to have to lead this connection out of obscurity because his beloved saw herself as damned.

"You don't irk me. Not like the rest of them. It's just I can't believe how gullible I am. Is something like love so unattainable for someone like me that the relentless universe will show it to me being crushed every single blooming time? Am I that hopeless?" Isra asked although she was banking on an answer that showed she was worthy since she felt so desolate. All of the colour had drained out of her. Her normally bright, glowing, piercing green eyes had become somewhat murky, which was odd for a delightful evening at dusk.

"You're not hopeless," Astrid started.

He wasn't clear on how he should amplify his meaning that Isra was deserving of love without triggering her into further bleakness. That was the last thing that he wanted to do. It was a delicate matter that had now been placated into his midst. It was going to be challenging seeing how Astrid would handle the dissolution of Isra's brief affinity with Alan without causing her further heartache.

"Listen, you've been through this before. You did all right then.

Maybe the idea of destroying the mortal realm wasn't that well thought out but it gave you that fire. It's the strident zeal inside you that keeps you from dying. Hold onto that. It will be all right in the end. You may not view it that way right now but I promise you, all will be well," Astrid instructed, rolling the words off his tongue as if they were butter.

"It isn't enough just to want love. You need the zest. The burning passion that sets your soul alight. I know with every fibre in my being that you will find it, even if it doesn't happen tonight," he finished, not stopping until he made his point explicitly clear.

"I guess you could have some resonance there, but I am so unsure of what to do now. I stood up to Everilda. I told her so vehemently that she was wrong, and here she has managed to beat me once again," Isra muttered soberly, under her breath so that her voice was barely audible.

"Go home. Get some rest. I might come in and check on you in a little while. I cancelled my little trip. It can wait. You are far more important to me," Astrid commanded in a low voice.

He was soft yet formal with her. This was no time for his true rebellious self. He needed to ensure she was all right before he showed her just who he was. The brass and bold anarchist she had fallen in love with would be able to hold himself at bay for now.

"I suppose sleep could do wonders," Isra mumbled, slowly lifting herself off of the grass and proceeding to head home.

Astrid remarked solemnly, "Well, I'm sticking around. Screw Samuel and his banishment. She needs me. To hell with his legislation."

14

Astrid made it back to Shambre Fell just as the clock struck midnight. He wanted to get there sooner but he had been formulating a plan of attack. Since Isra was heartbroken once more, he needed to tread carefully. The last thing he wanted to do was cause further issues for her. Even if he did feel like saying some things that may result in offence being taken, he was going to do this with finesse. Astrid would be Isra's friend, first and foremost. Her confidant. The one person she would be able to trust above everyone else.

He proceeded to launch himself downward as he spied the spindling tower of Shambre Fell and aimed for Isra's living room window so he could push past the window that was always left ajar. He probably would have given preference to the one in her bedroom but he didn't want to be intrusive, so the main window would have to suffice.

"Well, let's hope she hasn't decided to hit the hay early," Astrid chortled to himself confidently, veering over to the window which had been left slightly ajar like he had predicted it would be.

Just a tiny golden candlelight lit up the area between the window and Isra's red couch, which was usually her place of solitude during the long nights. Astrid pushed past the tiny gap, taking care not to get his feathers stuck in between the window's edge as he squeezed himself through. Much to his surprise, Isra eyeballed him from her position on the couch. Her lime-green glowing eyes were ablaze as she stared at him intensely with much interest.

"Normally, I'd get testy if someone walked into my home uninvited, but I don't seem to feel that vibe with you. Isn't that strange? I'd offer you some tea but I'm afraid I'm short on ground-up earthworms," Isra suggested with a chuckle.

Astrid noticed she had a large tome in between her hands. Her right hand rested against the open page whilst the other dropped by her side. She wore a long black and purple silk lace contrast nightdress with beautiful black embroidered detail on the chest and straps. She had a long-sleeved nightgown to match in deep violet. Astrid had to admit, he was still very much attracted to her, even in his raven form.

"I'm not feeling partial to earthworm tea right now. I imagine it would be delicious. However, one shall abstain from such pleasures. Anyhow, I'm not here for refreshment. I merely came over to check in on you. I know it is somewhat rude of me, dropping in at this hour, but it looks like you are up and well," Astrid stated plainly.

"Yes. I don't exactly feel the call of sleep right now," Isra rambled apologetically. She closed the book abruptly before placing it on the table.

"I would imagine that sleep is the very last thing on your mind," Astrid motioned in a sympathetic tone. "It's not easy being tossed out like the cookies you ate for dessert by somebody you grew to love. Not to mention thus believing they truly loved you. It's brutal. It's soul-destroying, and it kills you from the inside. The painful feeling of not knowing just what it was you did wrong will eat you up. But Isra, you did nothing at all," Astrid summarised pointedly. "Still, the night is young and you, young lady, look like you could use a midnight jolt, so how about it, eh?"

This wasn't exactly an amicable break-up. He didn't even have the balls to come to her to inform her of what was occurring. He locked himself in his elaborate fortress by means of a magical invisibility shield that kept anyone out who didn't have the in-depth awareness of his realm. That, to me, speaks volumes. If he cared enough, he'd have been running here on his hind legs, begging her to give him five seconds of her attention. Alas, this was not to be. Then he threw salt into the wound by suggesting all they had between them was nothing but lust. Yes, of course, those grapes are going to be sour. Do we expect them to be plump and bursting full of flavour? I think not, Astrid thought as he waited for Isra to answer his impending question.

"I must admit, gallivanting around does sound delightful," Isra implored with a low voice. She had some enthusiasm towards the idea, which was better than none at all. "However, I am still reeling over that Samuel Reynaldi man's involvement in all this. I don't quite fathom why he'd be so hell-bent on taking an interest in my romantic conquests of all things when I am indeed dark."

Isra voiced her opinion elegantly, but some perturbing vibes were emitting from her as she said it.

"Samuel Reynaldi?" Astrid asked, looking extremely worried. His face was awash with melancholic concern. He looked right into Isra's shiny lime-green enchanting eyes with wonder.

"Yes. The light-bringer of the realm nearby. I can't quite recall the name of it. Oh, now I am going to seem like a fool." Isra blustered awkwardly, wracking her brains for the bewildering answer.

Astrid beat her to it before she could delve further. "Spirisity. Yes. I know it. More to the point, what does he want with you?"

He had to remember to be careful of how hard he was on Isra. This wasn't supposed to be an interrogation but he needed to know why Samuel was suddenly weaving himself into Isra's sphere when he was supposed to be far away from her.

"Do you know this is the most peculiar thing for which I have absolutely no idea! He appeared out of nowhere. He gave me entry past a formidable force-field of which even I was deemed unworthy to pass," Isra mustered carefully, mulling over the situation intently.

"That is very concerning to me. I understand Samuel more than most. He's not as light as he claims to be but I feel like I am in a position to spill the beans on the most dire predicament I find myself in at this time," Astrid confessed, although he was being deliberately vague. He didn't know if testing the waters was wise in this situation or whether he should just come right out with it. And to hell with the repercussions.

What have I got to lose? She's trusted me thus far. She's allowed this unorthodox raven to come and counsel her when she hardly knows me at all. Isra is far from aware of what went down and yet she's still given me that leeway to come in and relay what I've been able to. The fact of the matter is Samuel is playing a very dangerous game by wiping her memories in the callous, shallow way that he did, and I feel Isra should at least have some idea of who she's really been dealing with.

Astrid perused this idea cautiously in his thoughts. He was courageous, and for a moment, he didn't care that Isra might misconstrue what he was saying because it damn well had to be said.

"Why would you be worried?" Isra asked.

She narrowed her eyes in a scrutinising way as if she didn't exactly believe that things were as they seemed. The normal piercing green glare dimmed slightly but it was still prominent even though Isra's living room was saturated by soft candle flame illuminating the entire room.

"I could tell you a tale where a most powerful witch found herself on the darker side and then she was magically castrated into a neverwhere of unknowing," Astrid recited candidly. The words rolled pleasantly off his tongue as he elaborated his meaning. "She was drawn to the darkness after being betrayed once too often and thus her true identity was born. Up she rose to the tips of obscurity only to find herself with an enemy in her wake, an unsuspecting foe that set out to obliterate her. However, the witch's biggest asset was a man who saw her true potential. He encouraged her, allowing her to grow all the more preeminent. He loved her endlessly. He would have done anything for her no matter what the consequence but alas, he was quashed, too. The light-bringer reigned supreme but he was the worst of them all," Astrid disclosed with a sigh.

"I am afraid I don't understand." Isra pressed in his direction, "Who is the witch that found herself in the dark?"

"The witch is... you," Astrid confessed meekly.

Isra clasped a hand over her mouth, unable to comprehend what he'd just said. *Wait, didn't Alan say something to a similar effect? They both know something I have no conscious awareness of. I do sometimes dream of this Samuel Reynaldi fellow and I swear it is indeed him but none of it makes any logical sense. I am trying to pull myself back to the moment where Alan said it. He dropped that bewildering one-liner that paved the way to me becoming curious about my lineage. 'Ah, so you were the one the light folk placated in that monastery.' He even said it himself. I was placated by the light beings. But why doesn't anybody in these parts elaborate on their meaning?* Isra wondered as the memory flew away from her.

She returned her attention to Astrid. "And how do you happen to know this?"

Isra probed him with somewhat of a sceptical glare. She had to give him credit, for she couldn't see one single facet of him that would have reason to lie. He was very open in his body language. His feathers were effortlessly unfazed. His shiny golden yellow eyes were staring right into her mesmerising bright green ones without judgement. He was also as cool as ice.

"I was there," Astrid uttered softly. "I know of your deliverance because I was right by your side the entire time. One minute, I was handing you this magnificent green spectacle imbued with your velocity. The next, you had been eviscerated. I saw it all." He recalled gravely, "The light make themselves out to be the most eccentrically gifted of beings; however, they are very dangerous if you get on the opposite side of them. Believe me, for I surely do know."

"I see. And may I beseech you as to why I have no recollection of any of this?" Isra asked.

She had a bemused look upon her face. It was as though the truth was incredibly frightening but yet the notion of it not being known to her was far more impervious. Astrid would have to detail to her just how relevant it was him telling this because he knew better than anyone else why Isra couldn't remember a single thing surrounding that gloriously sunny day.

"Of course," Astrid admonished sullenly. His eyes grew increasingly prominent. His voice deepened as a serious tone emitted from his beak, "You were swiftly warned to stop all you were doing. You quite rightly refused to go along with Samuel's pathetic demands and thus he placed his right hand upon your forehead. Within moments, you became dizzy, losing your ability to stand still, and then he softly whispered into your ear, 'I told you I'd disarm you,' strategically sweeping away your precious memories in the blink of an eye."

"Interesting," Isra muttered finally. She exhaled deeply. Some of the pieces of why she couldn't remember emerged but only one question remained. "How can I retrieve those memories?" she asked with fervour.

"Good question. The only person that will know the answer to that is Samuel. I would say I'd escort you there to ensure all will be well, but I am banished. I am also not supposed to be anywhere near you, but I'm a rebel." Astrid winked at her cheekily.

"And where do I find this Samuel?" Isra probed further.

Of course, it went without saying he was more than cooperative in being forthcoming with all the seedy information she craved.

"You'll find him in Spirisity. That's his patch. It's in between the border of Seclera and Wingdom's Academy. The light realm. It's locked to only those that dwell in the light but you're mighty fine at breaking and entering into places you are strictly forbidden from being in. You'll have no problems getting inside there, I am sure," Astrid told her candidly.

"I guess one might pack themselves off for an excursion after all. Please excuse me. I need to put on something a little more sensible for a night's stroll," Isra commented before she pegged it upstairs.

Seconds later, she came back down, and Astrid seemed bemused as to how she'd managed to slip into a black lace dress with long black lace sleeves with delicate black roses embroidered on the sleeves and the chest.

"That was mighty fast! Well, I'd say there's much to do but there isn't. I will take you some of the way but wait for you by Seclera," Astrid instructed in a serious tone. He knew he'd have to detail again why he could not come with her. Isra didn't completely understand the implications of Samuel's banishment yet but she soon would.

"You really can't come in with me then?" Isra asked, just as Astrid predicted she would.

Her mind was extremely curious. Isra loved asking questions. One could even go as far as to suggest she rather enjoyed it. She was incredibly suspicious but also marvellously adept at detecting the slightest hint of tomfoolery. Her desire for delving deep into the way life worked only gave her more precedence, as there's nothing more the enemy hates than you knowing far more than they'd like you to.

"Alas, I cannot." Astrid sighed. "He banished me from the lands and also from you. I don't take most of what he said lightly but I'm also a strong believer in not getting caught. It will be better for us this way!" Astrid concurred, realising he'd just made a major faux pas.

"Us?" Isra narrowed her piercing lime-green eyes.

Again, she didn't fully comprehend Astrid's role, other than he was here assisting her for now while she undertook this next dynamic phase in her life. As far as she was concerned, he was just a raven companion.

Damn it. I wasn't ready to detail to her the subject of 'us.' Eurgh, let's not worry about it now. You've already dropped enough hints, Astrid. Next time, try not to let loose so easily these snippets from the tongue, eh? he scolded himself, quickly taking haste to correct his mistake.

"Ah, don't worry yourself, trouble. Just get on over to the land of pleasantries. Samuel won't be best pleased with being disturbed at this hour. But it's you. I think that will provide you with enough leeway to guarantee a lack of resistance? After all, you are a witch. Him? Well, he's a light-bringer and a stuffy one at that. You'll be fine, kiddo," Astrid answered coyly.

"While you're off gallivanting to the realm of supreme illumination, I'll be off checking out some things for myself. Don't worry. All will be well," he reminded her.

Isra promptly took her leave. She strode down the steps of the spindling grey stone staircase with Astrid in tow. They disappeared beyond the front door of Shambre Fell into what would soon be considered oblivion.

Isra was going into the lion's den. Would Samuel welcome her? Or would he be so vastly engrossed in his narrow-minded vendetta that he will have lost sight in keeping up his dynamic pretence with her? Ultimately, Isra was about to give Samuel Reynaldi one heck of a rude awakening, one that he was not expecting.

15

How does one hack into the greatest fortress known to all humankind, the landmark realm, Spirisity—home to none other than Mr Samuel Reynaldi? Ha! He thinks he is so scrupulous that no one other than who he deems worthy can slink their way inside. Well, my dear heart, I have a plan that may just scupper any forthcoming agendas you have...

Isra wrestled with the notion that Samuel had conducted a most elaborate feat upon her personage as she fumbled around awkwardly with Spirisity's barrier. The guardian gateway that stood at a crossroads between Wingdom's Academy and Seclera was not visible to the naked eye; however, Isra was drawn towards dark forces so she sensed it from a mile off.

It was the gleaming green flash of serenity that gave it away. The sparkling lime-green energy called to Isra beautifully as it stood so pristine in its archway form. Of course, one would expect that a barrier designed to keep someone like Isra out wouldn't appear to be so magnificent in nature. In any event, Samuel was known for his lavish displays of finery so how could you deem it to be anything else?

Isra perused the contents of her pocket as she aimlessly stood before the glowing artifice that began searing soaring flames towards her. This wasn't exactly a deterrent but sure enough, after she lifted her hand out of her dress pocket, she pulled out a tiny jar of mugwort, followed by a swift pinch of cinnamon. Isra swiftly hurled it at the protective gateway, patiently awaiting a response as to whether she had been successful at breaking the enchantment.

Much to her surprise, the shimmery green gleaming flames parted so that there was a tiny crevice, which Isra was able to step through. She ambled through the archway only to find herself staring up at a majestic grey castle surrounded by green vegetation with delicate little violets and yellow crocuses dotted everywhere.

"So, this must be the famous Spirisity. Well, it's not much to write home about but I suppose light-bringers have to oversell," Isra conferred with herself as she marched over to the steps leading up to the front door.

I mean, she really could have just materialised herself over there, but since it was past midnight, not a soul would notice her coming. However, Isra wasn't going to be stupendous. She was uninvited in this place. The last thing she needed was attention drawn to herself by popping up out of nowhere and let's face it, she wanted to give Samuel a fright.

She quickly muddled through the iconic hallway, taking in a vast amount of unappreciated art in the sacred paintings hanging idly in the hallway, evidently much neglected, as the dust on them was just over an inch thick. Still, Isra pressed on until she came to the plush royal blue velvet curtain.

Now, she didn't know where she'd find Samuel but something in her intuition told her that this was remarkably profound as blue is a spiritual colour. Samuel was bound to have it showcased somewhere around here, so Isra presumed this would be the entrance to his office. Now that she thought of it, Astrid hadn't given her much detail on what Samuel's place looked like but she imagined it would be a fortress of sorts. She wasn't far wrong from that estimation.

WELL, old son, I'd say you've got it made. It's just past midnight and all these loose ends are now securely finalised. Good job, sir, for you have done yourself proud and oooh, look! Caffeine. Hmm, tranquil moments of pleasantry! Samuel murmured as he proceeded to satisfy himself with his favourite beverage.

He'd made it himself this evening. James was off somewhere, and since Astrid had been banished, Samuel no longer had a right-hand man. James was good, don't get it twisted, but he was no Astrid, that was for sure.

Samuel sat idly at his desk as he hastily took a large gulp of black steaming coffee. It was just after midnight so he thought it was the ideal time to finalise some paperwork. Being a light-bringer wasn't all prancing about on clouds, you know? Samuel was responsible for signing contracts, ensuring all details were in place whereby strongholds were placated on those who strayed from the light. He also made a sincere effort to communicate constantly with "on high" on the regular to avoid mishaps occurring.

Samuel assumed he'd now be able to relax for the rest of the night, taking delight in sitting outside on the grey steps that led to his eccentric home located in the ethereal land of Spirisity, a beautiful idyllic location where his very tall castle stood on a grassy carpet covered in sweet violets and yellow crocuses. He thought he'd be able to chug back a potent Irish whiskey while watching the stars circle around the bright glowing full moon.

"Well, Samuel, old boy, you've done it this time! Another dark soul kindly taken over by the generous folk at 'on high.' If I said so myself, I think my work is indeed done!" Samuel muttered cheerily to himself, not taking his eyes away from the mass of papers laid on his desk.

"I'm not so sure your work is done. Actually, I'd say you're in for quite the intriguing evening!" a young feminine voice called out in a melodramatic tone.

Samuel stopped, looking upwards as he gazed at her from his silver moon-framed spectacles. He couldn't believe it. *Oh, my. It cannot be, can it? No!* Samuel exasperated in thought, wondering if he was indeed dreaming.

The young female was dressed from head to toe in black. She had a very slender frame that was only enhanced by the lace dress embedded with black lace roses. The sleeves were frilled on the outside so her delicate hands were put on display. A pair of unmistakable lime-green glowing eyes stared intensely at Samuel. He then noticed her golden-white shimmery hair that perfectly hung down to her bottom.

Oh, dear... it was her. She'd finally found him after all this time. It was unthinkable. He'd only spoken with her the other afternoon, but here she was!

"Yes, I can see that may well be the way of it. I have to say, I didn't expect to see you so soon, Isra!" Samuel gasped. He sounded concerned. He nervously twiddled his right index finger and thumb and tried to maintain eye contact with the lady standing before him.

"I see you managed to find the place then? Interesting, as I never had you down as the breaking and entering into the realms type. But then again, Isra, we never really know with you, do we?" Samuel pressed eagerly as he awaited his young female guest to open her mouth and say those immortal words he'd been dreading for the longest time.

"It wasn't hard," Isra excused herself. "You love and light folk don't exactly cloak yourselves from the likes of me. I played around with a few spell charms. Added a little mugwort here. A pinch of cinnamon there. I broke open your cloud of invisibility and here I am. But that's no consequence as to why I'm really, here is it?" she asked Samuel boldly.

She knew there was something he had concealed from her so in her mind he'd better start unravelling the web of lies sharpish.

I barely remember this man, but yet I am told how I ought to know him. How on Earth is one meant to recall something they don't feel truly happened? But the way he calmly composes himself while also looking like he might throw his head into his hands tells me he knows far more than he cares to admit. Astrid is indeed right but if only I could retrieve that knowledge for myself.

Isra blundered anxiously as she waited for Samuel to give her a response other than him nervously pandering over the situation.

"Aha. I see. You've been working on your magics. Very impressive, young firecracker, but perhaps we should get right to it, eh? Now I don't have much but I can certainly rustle up some coffee for you," Samuel suggested. He'd changed his nervous tone to one that was significantly softer in nature. "Although, I could forage in the pantry if you'd like something to eat. Here, take a seat!" he added hastily, trying in vain to keep up the level of formality. He was doing his absolute best to be accommodating although Isra wouldn't be able to discharge her magic in Spirisity. Only Samuel had the ability to do that.

"I'm not thrilled by the delights of caffeine. It's a little bitter for my liking. Like many of the human souls I've come to know. Or warlocks, as it happens of late," Isra countered. She sounded irritated and somewhat frustrated.

Isra looked taken aback as she seated herself on the black leather armchair positioned parallel to Samuel's wooden desk. It was clear she felt uncomfortable around Samuel but yet this was this alluring vibe he gave off. It was almost endearing but also strangely familiar.

"Oh, no. That is most unfortunate, but perhaps I can indeed sweeten it up for you? I'll add in the tiniest bit of sweet salted caramel and you'll never have known it was bitter. Honestly, you should try it. It's a game-changer!" Samuel offered kindly, lifting himself off his red velvet armchair, proceeding to head into the kitchenette.

"Well, maybe I could be persuaded to try something new but I seldom do. It's a rarity for me to step out of my comfort zone, you see? I find the people I encounter so wretchedly vile but they have a sweet exterior like butter wouldn't melt. I always seem to get burned by the ghastly illusion," Isra vented casually.

Samuel momentarily excused himself for a second, saying, "I'll be back in a minute or so. I'm just going to conjure this delectable caramel coffee for you. I promise it will make you feel better, if only for a short while."

Isra merely nodded as Samuel stepped out. She found her eyes wandering around Samuel's office. In front of his eloquent wooden desk, Isra caught sight of his charming red velvet armchair, perfectly positioned next to the window, which, of course, was always left ajar. The colouring of the walls was an antique ochre but more yellow than beige. Just at the entrance to Samuel's office was the very distinctive plush royal blue curtain.

However, the thing Isra found most entrancing of all was a tall mahogany bookcase that sat against the back wall. It was just around five feet in height and had six separate shelving dividers on which an array of dusty old books sat and also some very intriguing odd-looking objects. On the top shelf, was a majestic lime-green glowing sphere carefully placed on it.

Now, Isra really couldn't shake off the fascination she had with it but it was bemusing indeed. How she was so attracted to this mystifying entity, she had no knowledge of. Little did Isra know she and it had met before. Samuel took a liking to the rather mystical artifice and although it was dark in nature, it could only do harm in the hands of its creator so he'd stupidly left it sitting on his bookcase after he'd confiscated it from Isra. Notably, she had no memory of this since he'd snatched it away, too!

Isra was still staring at the glowing entity when Samuel walked into the office, carrying two mugs of caramel coffee. Naturally, he was a little remiss as he realised what had kept her attention for such a time but again, he wasn't overly concerned since he'd wiped her memories.

"Ah, I see you've been distracted. Here you are. Tasty sweet yet salted caramel coffee to awaken your senses. Now perhaps I should level with you," Samuel started although yet again, he appeared nervous.

He handed Isra a bitterly hot mug of the caffeinated beverage. He then placed his mug on his desk before settling back down in his extremely comfortable red armchair. Samuel arched his back against the warm, soft velvet fabric, leaning back in the chair so he could directly face Isra.

"I imagine you should since you have me down as some vile queen of the night!" Isra interjected.

Samuel gazed at Isra awkwardly, paying close attention to those bewildering lime-green piercing eyes glaring back at him although she seemed relatively calm at this juncture.

"Aha, so you do know then?" Samuel probed tentatively.

"I know you were tracking me for the longest tenure until something occurred whereby I was deemed harmless in your eyes. I'm afraid I'm a little lost on the details but I was told you assisted me in a very difficult time. However, I cannot remember it at all so I was hoping you could fill in the blanks," Isra implored modestly.

She maintained her composure as she still didn't have any recollection of what had happened but she wasn't going to outwardly strike up conflict with Samuel. It seemed more reasonable to be diplomatic with him; after all, Astrid had only been too kind in revealing the sodden truth that she was the witch he'd famously disarmed, a miraculous feat to embark on for a light-bringer.

"Yes, I am indeed responsible for certain events occurring in your life. However, it was done with your best intentions at heart. You wouldn't remember me due to the trauma of it all, but not to worry. That was then, and here we are now. Must I say that you've blossomed so maturely," Samuel expressed casually but was still took due care, for he wasn't sure exactly what Isra knew.

"I see," Isra mouthed. She breathed in the warm velvety aroma of caramel emitting from the steaming hot mug she clasped in her hands. She took a small sip reluctantly through pursed lips. "Hmm, it's not that bad. It appears I was wrong," Isra said apologetically. Coffee had never been top of her palate. She always imagined it to be bitterly foul rather than a delicacy.

"I stated it could be made to dazzle you. Still, I presume you didn't come here to solely sample the finery I have to offer. I imagine you have a lot of questions for me," Samuel mouthed openly.

He took great diligence in taking a large gulp of his caffeinated beverage but made sure he had his eye on Isra the entire time. He wasn't clear on exactly what she knew regarding the whole debacle that went down between her and Astrid versus him on that shimmery sunlit beach.

If she's come here for revenge, it's sure to be fruitless but I doubt that's the reason. She's far too calm for that. Something would have commenced by now. She knows something, but what it is I have yet to learn. I wonder if our rebellious foe, Astrid, has indeed spilt the beans, Samuel wondered to himself as he didn't yet want to show any signs he was suspicious of Isra.

"I don't have any questions. I barely know anything, just that you played a huge part in it all. I heard tall tales but I seldom believe anything that comes out of the mouths of mortals these days. Light and dark waging war against one another sounds a little cliché, don't you think?" Isra probed in earnest.

"Well, yes, it does, but you know as well as I do that peasants are prone to prevaricating about the minutest things. Sorry, I should explain. I call them peasants because of their sheer lack of recognising how wretchedly stupid they are. They rather irk me! I mean, quite honestly, I don't think too many souls would complain if a bunch of mundane peasants were suddenly gobbled up by dragons. I'd call it the universe paying them back but hey, I guess I should refrain from such thoughts, being the light bringer, Lord and Chief," Samuel mumbled carelessly. *Shit, one really must take into consideration the words coming out of one's mouth. But I truly don't take kindly to peasants. Horrible. Vile individuals. Oh, well,* Samuel guffawed to himself in a comical manner.

"A dragon apocalypse! Oh, how wonderful!" Isra's lime-green glowing eyes lit up instantly at the thought of it.

Yes, she's no stranger to unleashing beasts onto the world. In fact, I do recall the time our dear little witch summoned a rather vicious draconian beast. I believe the bugger's name was Franco or something similar. Anyhow, he bloody scampered by the time I came to lay down the law, Samuel thought.

It was ironic that Isra had the opinion that a massacre involving dragons descending onto the land would indeed be presumed joyful.

"Of course, you'd think such a thing is rapturous. How silly of me!" Samuel cajoled in high-pitched laughter as he attempted to correct his naughty misgiving.

"Well, I'd do a damn sight more than let a few dragons loose. As it stands, a warlock made the decision to end his courtship with me, so I've been toying with the idea of how to repay him," Isra remarked sharply, acrimonious venom distinctly prominent in her voice.

Oh, golly. She's already delving back into that darkness without a care. Evidently, it's not just the mortal men that are the catalyst because when she goes bad, oh boy, does it get critical! And notably fast, too! Perhaps our young miscreant would indeed benefit from no interactions from any males for a significant time period. She was undoubtedly fine with Astrid although there was that whole chaos with them both unleashing Armageddon but the majority of men just don't gel with her. At least not for the long haul, anyhow, Samuel mused to himself sardonically. He'd seen this scenario play out once before with Isra.

"Well, I suppose you could indeed give him a taste of his own medicine but would it honestly make you feel any better about yourself? You could make merry with him and still feel abhorrent inside. Does a typical revenge scenario even uphold its expectations anymore? I seriously doubt that it's not all that it's made out to be. You see, even a light-bringer like myself understands the lengths a person can go to when they are tested beyond comprehension. Your whole life can fall apart in a flash, even when you are a most heinous sorceress. Oh, believe me, it's true. There's no escape for any of us. None of us is getting out of this reality without some despicable, cruel trick played on us, courtesy of the good old universe. Are you certain you have no questions for me, girl? I am happy to answer any way that I can."

Samuel made it clear that he was going to be transparent in any way possible although it went without saying there was a strong probability he'd make some swift edits here and there.

"I am unsure of my place in the world as it stands right now. I am already questioning so much. I have been conquered by an unlikely foe that has masqueraded under the guise of a friend; however, I cannot fathom certain details, as my memory seems hazy. So, you see, while I'd like to grill you on these fantastical notions, my brain just will not have it!" Isra exclaimed nonchalantly. She was doing a marvellous job so far of not letting Samuel get the better of her.

Let him think he is indeed superior to us all. I am not going to disclose that Astrid has been completely cooperative in revealing his underhanded shady dealings. No, time will let him know in due course. I am not going to assist it in any way. If nothing else, this little trip has been insightful because I know my enemy is doing his utmost to be as close as possible to me, Isra professed to herself with wit. She believed she had an upper hand over Samuel.

"Hmm. A warlock rebuffed you, eh? Well, that is novel. I don't mean to be presumptuous, but aren't you one of the most formidable sorceresses this land has ever known?" Samuel questioned with a grin. "Suffice to say, girl, I don't think this little blip is going to matter in the long run. You may not see it now but it will soon become clear. Warlock or not, you don't need a male companion in your life," Samuel affirmed to her with enthusiasm.

"Well, he said we were nothing more than an infatuation. A desire for him to peak beyond his limits while he evaded his buffoon of a father," Isra concurred sardonically although Samuel could detect the slightest hint of sadness in her voice among all the seething resentment.

"Believe him. But note what I say. You don't need a man. You've got this entire thing figured out. You'll see. Things will become clear in time. It's not always clear cut at first, but everything happens for a reason."

Samuel winked and then turned his focus to his salted caramel coffee sitting idly on his desk. He and Isra sat in silence for the remainder of the somewhat awkward impromptu meeting but Samuel underestimated Isra since she left Spirisity with a whole new lease on life and motivation to boot, for now, she knew her greatest foe was someone who claimed to be on the side of good.

"There she is," Astrid called out to himself.

His voice filled with joy as soon as he caught sight of the shimmery white head bobbing up and down as Isra walked at a brisk pace towards Seclara. She had just come from the well-placed crossroads that led to Samuel's infamous ethereal realm, Spirisity. It was ironic that it was so well connected to two places very near and dear to Isra. Astrid couldn't help but feel that was deliberate, although Samuel's establishment had been there for aeons, even before Isra was crawling.

Astrid wasted no time in cornering Isra immediately. He launched himself into the air, coursing right above her head. He waited for her to acknowledge him.

"Goodness!" Isra squealed, reeling from Astrid's sudden appearance.

"So come on. How did it go?" Astrid nudged as he hovered in mid-air above Isra while awaiting her answer.

He was antsy. Unbeknownst to Isra, he'd made a decision that could potentially change everything, but Astrid needed to hear the words from Isra first.

"It was interesting. He comes across as very charismatic. I do feel, however, I've just had a meeting with my enemy," Isra confirmed to an aghast Astrid, who now knew he had to do what he planned.

"I am afraid that will be the case for the foreseeable future. However, Samuel won't come to you as a foe. He'll be compassionate, kind, and appear to have a dozen principles wrapped up in formality but he'll be there waiting for you to trip up now," Astrid said gravely. "Get on home. I don't want you near Seclara with Everilda lurking around. The last thing you need is another squabble with her bringing too much light onto you. I have to take care of my errand but I'll be back before dawn."

He gave her a warm smile. "Hey, don't worry, kiddo. You've already surpassed my expectations. You've gone past the hurdle. Now, we have to get moving, setting things up for the world stage! Well, in a manner of speaking," Astrid corrected himself as he prepared to fly off once again. "I'll be back soon. Get some sleep; it's almost two o'clock in the morning."

She hardly sleeps a wink since this Alan idiot played his wicked game with her. Not that she slept much beforehand being nocturnal and all but one needs sleep at some point. Unless, of course, they're immortal. Oh, wait! Astrid stopped his reverie as he realised just how true it was.

"I find myself seldom caring whether I get rest or not," Isra mumbled unapologetically back at him.

"You'll need it when I return. Things are going to change." He hinted the notion to her although it was vague and Isra had no comprehension of what Astrid meant.

"Sounds elusive," Isra remarked as she stifled a yawn. *Hmm, maybe he is right. A few hours of slumber might be highly recommended, although I don't care for it at all.*

Isra shrugged off her tiredness as the thought remained heavy on her mind. Finally feeling satisfied that Isra was going to head back, Astrid surged into the midnight-blue skies. It was time for him to call on an old friend.

16

Journeying to Sprawnbell at this hour was ill-advised but Astrid had little care for that as he perused the darkened skies, keeping his eyes peeled for the monstrosity that was the Daughtry mansion. Last he'd heard, Rhiannon and Damien were slowly bonding with Everilda, although there were hiccups in the proceedings between Everilda and Damien. Needless to say, since Astrid had lost Isra to Samuel's regime, he seldom cared to know the gritty details but Damien Daughtry would be the key in Astrid getting back to Isra. Without him, Astrid would be screwed unless he managed to seek out another way of getting right back to Isra.

Astrid finally laid his eyes upon the eccentric black mansion that stood out amongst all the darkness, which was peculiar for a demon dimension. Even in these places, you'd normally see some kind of illumination. Whether it be a candle burning on a window ledge or a light dimly lit in one of the back rooms, there was always something alight to remind the joyous folk here of what they'd been fighting all their lives—the freedom to be themselves.

Peering into the adjacent window that he was sure was Damien's dimly lit office, Astrid prepared to swoop downward, and much to his delight, the window was left ajar. *Perfect. I shouldn't have any mishaps with this,* he said to himself as he walked right into the dimly lit room on his claws.

The room itself was chilled to the bone. Someone had carelessly left the window open aeons ago, not caring that the tiny office was practically an icebox. Astrid stopped to look around. Parchment papers lay untouched on Damien's usually immaculately tidy desk.

"Something is wrong here. Damien would never show this much tardiness. He'd be in here, sweeping all of this up or at least keeping it in one spot. This office hasn't been inhabited in months," Astrid summarised gravely.

His worst fears were coming to the surface that maybe Isra wasn't the only one Samuel took care of.

Samuel might have latched onto Damien but he's a warlock. A mighty one at that. It would surely be impossible but Samuel is no stranger to manipulation, just as we have all learned in recent times, but I cannot fathom why Damien would have just abandoned the ship like this! Astrid conferred with himself for a moment.

He considered the idea that Samuel may have done a lot more than just take care of Isra. If he'd been stupendous enough to try to take on a most wretched warlock, there was no telling what would commence. It was time to seek answers. Astrid needed Damien to not only transform his bird form into something more aesthetically pleasing, but Astrid also cared greatly about the situation at hand. If he was right in his assumption that Samuel was targeting all sorts of dark beings, it seriously didn't bode well for future occupants that happened to take a fancy to the forbidden arts.

A light whooshed and Astrid found himself face to face with an aggrieved onlooker in the form of Rhiannon, who looked deeply baffled to see him. "Can I help you, Astrid?" she asked plainly.

Rhiannon didn't seem privy to anything even remotely friendly. Her face was careworn. Her eyes almost dropped underneath heavy bags showing inquisitive dark eyes whose lids were usually firm and upright. She seemed distressed and most importantly on edge, which was extremely peculiar for a demoness of Rhiannon's stature.

"Actually, you can. I was hunting for Damien, but evidently, I have missed him," Astrid replied.

"Damien hasn't been here for many months. I don't have any idea in relation to his whereabouts. There is deep intensity surging around all of us right now. Even my daughter, Everilda, is antsy being in her form. Of course, she's mortal and that is beyond her control. But even she feels the change in the air. It's not good, Astrid," Rhiannon admonished with a sullen tone.

"No, it's not. That's why I am here. I have to sorely apologise for my absence but Samuel took the knowledge of Isra ever knowing me from her memory. He disarmed her in the process. I am back in her life now, but it has been a torturous process. She's just been discarded by a warlock who decided she was no longer useful to him so as you can imagine, I am anxious to get back to her," Astrid explained with a low brow.

"You want to reclaim your once glorious masculine identity?" Rhiannon asked curtly.

"Yes. If I can get up close and personal to her, then maybe I can stop her from going too far. She's already got the attention of the light. Their ears are well and truly heightened, ready for when she tumbles down. If she does anything now that they view as unsavoury, well, it will raise an all-scale red alert," Astrid commented as though he was outlining a plan, one he'd dreamed up not only in a bid to get close to Isra once again but to also stop her before she did something irrational.

"Her mind is focused only on pain. Is that right? Her heart screams revenge. The poor thing. She's spent so long wilting in the shadows that she hasn't mastered how to rise from the ashes. Emotions from someone so touched by the darkness of which we all have inside us but yet have been conditioned to reject it are haughty creatures at best," Rhiannon remarked as she stood by the door in a deep trance-like state before opening her eyes.

She stopped immediately upon seeing a clear vision that prompted her to be softer toned. She whispered, "Come. Downstairs. I feel there is more to this delicate little arrangement than you deem yourself worthy to know. Come," she commanded, leading him down a narrow passageway filled with old pictures of previous Daughtry descendants, including a peeling image of Damien in his peak at age seventeen.

Down the far end of the corridor, they came to an archway next to a steep staircase. Rhiannon grabbed onto the gilded gold bannister as she swept down the stairs, opening a dark stained wooden door. She turned to Astrid and gently invited him to come join her.

"In here. This is my private room where I do my most profound work, the stuff most don't know or wish to have known about me. But it's a part of me I cannot shrug off, so here we are," she admitted.

Astrid was in awe. He had never been in here in all of his years working for Damien Daughtry and his beloved demoness, Rhiannon. It was like a fortress of sorts. There was an old rusty portcullis hanging indiscreetly upon the back wall whilst thick dark violet drapery shrouded nearly every single wall in the room. However, the most entrancing part of it all was the round table, which was positioned by a quaint little wooden chair with a red velvet cushioned seat for comfort.

On the table was a clear, shiny crystal sphere that sat perfectly on a raised golden stand. The ball was enormous, almost taking up the entire space as it was around a hundred centimetres in diameter. Cobwebs decorated the entire room. Their soft, silvery tarnished webbing hung from nearly every facet of this darkened, gloomy artifice that Rhiannon called her working room. Astrid noted that as Rhiannon sat to gaze into the transparent crystal sphere that on the wall behind Rhiannon was an extremely well-stocked rack of miniature jars filled with all sorts of powders, crushed herbs, oils, and a fine array of ingredients you might find yourself needing in a witch's kitchen.

"Sit," Rhiannon ordered as she looked up briefly from her serene, translucent orb.

Astrid hopped up onto the table, perching himself on the opposite side of Rhiannon so he was parallel to her. Now he'd be able to see exactly whatever was going to manifest in this magnificent crystalline entity.

"Aha!" Rhiannon mumbled as she stared into the ball with interest. "I see it now. Oh, dear, there is a man involved. Isn't that nearly always the way?"

There was a pause as she closed her eyes. Both of her hands were placed delicately at either end of the ball. Rhiannon began concentrating meticulously and Astrid wondered just what it was that she was seeing.

"What?" Astrid inquired, since Rhiannon still had not come out of her silent pause. His curiosity was piqued more than ever.

Yes, there's a man in the picture, we know that, but who is he? Is it me or that Alan Grimsbane imbecile? I am betting it's not likely to be me although I do play a considerable part in her life. The way she described it is this man isn't there to shower her with love so clearly that's not me, Astrid retorted earnestly to himself as he awaited Rhiannon to answer him.

"Oh, he did love her? He regrets it. Why, I see her weeping over him. She hid her true feelings but this thing crashing down the way it has brought her to a dark place. She doesn't feel her heart anymore. It's there, but it's numb. A hardened rock that sits inside her chest. She's emotionless but he shows he has some kind of yearning for her," Rhiannon concluded as she finally opened her eyes, taking some focus away from the clear crystal sphere for a moment.

"It's a bit late for that," Astrid cut in abruptly.

He had no sympathy towards Alan, even if he did have time to mull over his stupidity. It wouldn't change what had happened to Isra and for that reason alone Astrid wasn't going to be forgiving.

"I agree. However, he seems to have spent some time rationalising over it and now feels remorse," Rhiannon murmured solemnly. "Your witch in question won't be receptive."

"Isn't that good, though? She won't tolerate any of his shit?" Astrid pressed the matter as he had wrongly presumed that Isra would reject Alan's reprieve as a way of her being assertive. But he was about to discover he was way off in his estimation.

She paused again and then uttered, "In fact, there may well be a confrontation of sorts as an admission of guilt is made on his part, but Isra will not suffer fools gladly. She won't accept his apology. The olive branch will be promptly castrated in a manner of speaking. He must be careful because if he says the wrong word to her, catastrophic circumstances will be afoot." Rhiannon felt tingles in her hands, indicating that the crystal had no more to say.

"Oh, my! This doesn't sound promising at all. Well, I need to get back to her. Perhaps I can talk her around. It may prove challenging, I know, but if this Alan chap wants to find himself in her midst, I feel it may just be a step too far, in the sense it will provoke Isra's elongated anger to the point of no return," Astrid surmised.

He was beginning to understand the imagery emerging. Alan would attempt to regain Isra's good graces after having given the situation some solid thought.

But then again, you were the idiot that annulled things in the first place. You were the one who insisted it wasn't working out the way you wanted. it was too much pressure for you to bear on your shoulders, having already been at loggerheads with Everilda. And while I do understand that what commenced was no fault of your own, you made things go belly-up when you said Isra was nothing but an infatuation. That's not the way to woo young females unto you, now is it? Telling them that it was a crush for you. A fleeting attraction and nothing more because your interest had wavered. I'm not surprised you barely see any interaction from the fairer sex.

Astrid cursed Alan sullenly in thought as he realised that if he took action now, he could potentially be waiting in the wings at the very same moment Alan would try to appease Isra.

"Well, that is all. The energy has withered away. I hope it is at least of some use to you. I'd hate to have delivered something and find it had no purpose," Rhiannon elaborated. She always felt even being dark that if she did one thing to help another then she was indeed on the right path.

"No. It was insightful," Astrid remarked. "But I am not close to getting back to Isra. I can't do much for her in my raven form and although she has accepted me in this manner, I know it is simply not enough. I need to be physically there by her side so I can provide the additional support she needs. Emotionally," Astrid went on to explain in great detail.

He'd spent a lot of time mulling this over. This wasn't some haphazard whim he'd dreamed up overnight. That was for sure.

"I understand. I think you and I both know what needs to happen. So, this plucky light-bringer managed to sink his teeth into Isra, stopping you both from being yourselves. I have a rather novel idea that might just put the kywash on his diabolical plans," Rhiannon mused, perusing the notion that more could be done than she had originally deemed possible.

"I am following. I think," Astrid replied.

He understood that when he was transformed into human form before he was still his immortal self underneath it all. He wasn't mortal like his appearance beguiled those unsuspecting souls to believe.

"You'll have the upper hand. We're going to make you invincible to anything Samuel Reynaldi attempts to bestow upon you, anything he tries to destroy. Basically, whatever he decides isn't what he wants you to do, he will sit back and attempt to make a meal of it, right? Well, now you'll be impenetrable to that chicanery of his. His magic comes from the light lands but it's not his to own. That's the tricky conundrum in all this. If he is expelled as a light-bringer, there is no power there to speak of. This is why we must take a much different approach to this. He's going to expect you to stay banished. To keep your distance from Isra. What we are going to do will ensure the exact opposite. Reverse magnetism," Rhiannon continued with a high-pitched voice. She was bursting with overexcited enthusiasm at what she was proposing they do to remedy Astrid's predicament.

"All right. I never would have thought anything like that was possible. How will you make it so that he cannot taint us like he did before?" Astrid questioned.

He wanted to make sure all would be well this time around. The last thing Astrid wanted was to be within close proximity of Isra once again only for Samuel to come up trumps at the last second, snatching all of it away with a wave of his hand.

The smug, methodical, grinning bastard would love that. He believes he is right but really all that regulating and controlling to meet his expectations of which people should be shows a lot of his shortcomings. He sees Isra as such a threat otherwise he never would have done what we had, Astrid concluded as he thought carefully about how Samuel bested him.

He had cleverly turned the situation upon Isra and Astrid being the wrongdoers. They were committing atrocities in his realm, under his holy name. Oh, he couldn't have that. It was such a risk to an already bruised ego. His desperate need to undermine anyone who displayed a shoddy amount of power that rivalled his own was extremely prominent for all to see. Astrid had been disbanded from Samuel for just over a year but he had begun to psychoanalyse him in ways that would make the light-bringer quiver because of how much of an expose it was.

"I will seal the magic with some of my own. There are no absolutes, you understand, but it will give you a greater chance than if we did nothing whatsoever. Let's begin. I need you to focus on the image of Isra for a moment. It will help strengthen the spell," Rhiannon instructed as she got to work.

Rhiannon took great care in visualising dark energy around Astrid's raven form; however, this materialised in his reality within seconds. Then bright green specks of light emerged, hitting Astrid with such force that he struggled to keep himself calm. Rhiannon closed her eyes and was almost rambling something barely audible but Astrid managed to detect some of the words she used.

"Now it's time. Astrid will be strong and tall in his immortal shell. It doesn't matter what the light says because now all will be in favour. The darkness of his connection with Isra is going to be her almighty savour."

And the second Rhiannon said the word "savour," Astrid didn't feel himself anymore. He was overcome with dizziness that quickly surged all over his body. The energy was so strong he didn't notice that his feathers had been ripped away from him, as had his wings, for he had grown over six feet tall.

Now his shape was beginning to emerge and a mass of clean-cut, silvery hair manifested on top of his well-endowed head to match his fine body that was symmetrical with the rest of him. Astrid's eyes were screwed shut; he couldn't take the dizzy sensation he was feeling but he took a breath and gently opened them only to find himself looking down at large hands donned in peach skin, covering a svelte torso peeking out from under a crisp white silk shirt.

Rhiannon took a blade to her right hand, letting some blood drip onto Astrid quickly as she knew the energy was taking over. A sizzling sound was heard as the red blood collided with the ferocious energy surrounding Astrid. He stood taken aback at his fine self. The mesmerising pillar box sparks emitted from around his toned body. The magic had been mystically sealed.

"Well, let's get a look at you. I think you're ready to grasp your beloved into your arms. I must say, you are some of my finest work," Rhiannon gushed, stopping to admire Astrid's newly endowed, muscular appearance. His usually golden sheen eyes were now a musty ochre colouring with that deep golden shade ablaze in the centre.

"Wow. I cannot believe it. It's just like from when you changed me before. Only now it feels so surreal. But it is real. If you pardon my bewilderment, I just feel so animated. It's wonderful!" Astrid exclaimed happily.

"Excellent! You are sure to go on ahead now. I don't want you to get there too late. The sooner you arrive at Shambre Fell, the better. Here, I'll give you a helping hand. We don't want any mishaps now," Rhiannon suggested.

She closed her eyes once again, envisioning bright green energy all around his elaborate form. Only now, he swiftly dissipated in a flash, completely gone from her sight as the energy took him exactly where he needed to be.

17

It was approaching sunrise. The warm, fiery sun was just about to poke its head out of a mass of white puffy clouds that showcased the brilliant blue morning skies. Shambre Fell's grey spindling tower stood out among all the blue and white. Tall as ever, it reached up to the top of the soft powder-blue heavens.

Astrid had been walking a good few miles after Rhiannon had magically deposited him over the outskirts of Seclara in his newly humanised appearance. He was still adjusting to the fact he was now made of flesh. He had no wings to speak of. His claws had been replaced by hands and feet and all of that black he'd had on his person before was simply changed to a very handsome mass of grey hair with silver specks that sat upon his head. And his forever fateful warm eyes with that golden gleam resided inside them. He did feel triumphant now that he had been transformed into a man once more because he'd have the opportunity to assist Isra the way he wanted.

Being a raven gave him limitations; claws could only accomplish so much whereas robust hands and fast, fetching legs gave him more of an advantage. He could chase after Isra now, ensuring all would be well without having the dreary hassle of squeezing himself through a tiny gap into her window. Now he'd have the impressive ability to walk in unannounced. And hopefully, it would be welcomed without making him feel as if he was imposing upon her energy. The last thing he wanted to do was irk Isra.

He finally arrived, and he felt it was a good time to take stock of everything before he plucked up the courage to go over and speak to her outright although he was intimidated by the prospect of it. Astrid did have an overwhelming amount of joy pertaining to his very expertly created body that he now inhabited.

"I haven't felt this good in aeons but it's been just a little over a year," Astrid mused as he took a moment to admire the wondrous sights just outside Shambre Fell looking on at the idyllic grounds.

The verdant, luscious green grass blades had grown considerably since the last time he was here. And the stunning blood-red and deep violet roses were blooming beautifully for a hot month in July. Of course, it was worth mentioning that the minute apple tree was also seeing rapid growth, which was interesting. Astrid took that as a sign that Isra was about to mature to full bloom.

For a nineteen-year-old, she had been through an immense amount of experiences that would cause most teenagers her age to shudder and in turn, voluntarily shun the world in favour of something bearable. But not Isra—she kept her momentum going despite all that was thrown at her. Sure, she was feeling pretty wretched over Alan discarding her like pungent-smelling excrement from the back of his shoe, but even Astrid knew she would get over that in due time.

She doesn't know it yet, but this is just a roadblock. Most importantly, this crisis of faith is needed because without the chaos one cannot restore the balance required to gain confidence in yourself to bring about the magic you truly possess within you. Isra won't see that just yet. She's drowning in the betrayal aspect. Possibly some part of her is just waiting for Alan to fuck up, admitting what a fool he's been, but what will that achieve? I'd say nothing. But only time will tell how she'll handle this.

Astrid broke the situation down in a nutshell in his mind, considering Rhiannon's vision that this strange, bewildering Alan chap just may make a reappearance in Isra's life.

It would be stupid of him to do so but then again, he's also young. A strapping lad adorned with a prideful attitude and an arrogance to boot. Full of himself. He deems every single facet of his personality as gold dust but that's just his overzealous ego.

Astrid suddenly caught a glimpse of a fair-haired maiden coming out of Shambre Fell's grand ornate wooden door and felt an insurmountable amount of glee and nervousness as it was confirmed that it was indeed Isra. You can't exactly miss those two glowing green eyes of hers that radiate enchantment and vulnerability. Astrid felt uncomfortable and stood awkwardly at his spot at the bottom of Shambre Fell. It wasn't something he was wholly confident about. He knew it was just a case of marching right up that brown ochre gravel pathway and introducing himself but he was wracked with guilt over having left her before.

Yes, it had not been his doing. If he'd had his way, he and Isra would have ridden off out of Nefaria Sands, dancing to their tune of darkness. But alas, Samuel had turned up in the nick of time to put all of Astrid's ambitions pertaining to Isra to a grand halt.

In any case, that was then, when Samuel managed to get his way. And this, Astrid standing here, finally able to physically intervene with Isra for the first time in a year, was now. He'd be a fool if he didn't snatch the chance with both hands. The last time Astrid checked, he was certainly not an idiot. A smart man he was with ambition, integrity, and immense power to boot. He would not let this chance get away from him.

Astrid slowly put one foot in front of the other, gently striding up the rough gravel pathway that would eventually lead him to the entrance of Isra's fine chateau of Shambre Fell but just as Astrid was almost halfway, he witnessed the most extraordinary sight.

No! it can't be. No. No. No. Astrid voiced in exasperation.

Alan Grimsbane ran past him, tearing through the grassy knoll at the speed of lightning before Astrid could even properly work out what the hell was happening.

"What in the blazes? He's gotta be blinking crazy just turning up here like that! Oh, my! Is this quite the catastrophe!" Astrid commented as he watched Alan bang on Isra's grand ornate wooden oak door erratically. "Oh, dear lord. No, he's going for it. Fucking hell! That boy is insane!"

Astrid dropped the sardonic commentary as Alan got no response for his rapturous knocking so he had proceeded to let himself in much to Astrid's bafflement as he looked on nervously.

"Oh, shit. Now things are going to get rough. Damn! What the hell is wrong with that man? But hey, Rhiannon was right on the money. Unfortunately for me, she was extremely astute in her knowledge. But by golly, if I ever wanted an excuse to get in there! Well, there's no time like the present, Astrid!" Astrid coached himself, bracing for the worst when he tumbled straight in after Alan Grimsbane, who had now collided up the narrow, unwinding staircase of Shambre Fell before Astrid could catch up to him. Now it was time for Astrid to make himself known.

"Alan? What in damnation are you doing here?" Astrid heard Isra shout.

Astrid couldn't see what was happening but by the sounds of it, Alan was a whimpering, befuddled mess that was seeking Isra's attention much to her disgust. Judging by how much Isra was yelling, she was not receptive to Alan's emotional outburst.

Astrid raced up the grey steps at record speed, stopping as he reached the living room door much to Isra's dismay as she sat upon her elaborate red velvet chair at the back of her living room, showing nothing but contempt at Alan, who was pleading with her for forgiveness. The poor soul was on his hands and knees, almost crying as he reached out to Isra in the hope she might hold some compassion within her heart, although this was likely falling on deaf ears.

Grimsbane pleaded his case. "Isra, I have been an almighty idiot. In fact, I'm more than that. I am a fool. I should never have said the things I did to you and for that, I am truly sorry. Please accept my humble apologies. Please, I beg of you. Do not leave me hanging, knowing that I could so easily have gained your trust and your friendship. I want so desperately to make it up to you. Just allow me the chance. Please," Alan begged.

He looked upward from where he was kneeling on the cold stone floor. But before Isra could address what Alan had said, her focus changed to that of the living room door creaking, for it startled her. Astrid pushed past the door bravely as Isra's piercing lime-green eyes fell upon him at once. However, she was furious.

She beseeched angrily, "And who the hell are you?" in his direction.

Her voice was cold and lacked empathy. Well, what do you expect for someone who had just had two men break into her home? Not one, but bloody *two* of the buggers. It was understandable that she was a little on edge.

"I do pardon myself. I heard the commotion and wanted to check that you were all right," Astrid excused himself.

He was careful, for Isra was extremely irritated at present and he didn't want to further anger her. He needed to get her to reason with him right now. And he wasn't exactly sure how he was going to accomplish that because she was looking like a raging fireball about to implode. It wouldn't be at all far-fetched to say that she needed to cool off for a little while.

"Who *are* you?" Isra asked once again.

Her tone was more formal now but just as icy. She was showing Astrid no mercy. There was no sign of a reprieve with her as the callousness in her voice was noted.

"I am Astrid. Please don't be alarmed by my appearance. I can assure you that it is indeed me. We have spoken very recently. I'm here to... well, I came to assist you," Astrid continued warmly.

"But the Astrid I came to know is a raven, so how do you expect me to believe you are who you claim to be?" Isra pressed, flashing him a sceptical glare.

Astrid knew he'd have to convince her and fast. The situation was getting very heated and it was only a matter of time before Isra would lose her patience completely, not caring that there would be consequences for her actions if she happened to lose her mind at this very moment.

"I am him. You have to believe me. All right, here's the deal. We talked about a story about a very powerful witch. I detailed a tragic tale in which the light had become her ultimate enemy and then cleverly snatched her memory so she'd never recall the sordid event. I then announced that the very same witch was you. Please do not misunderstand me, Isra. I am not here to cause malice. Neither do I intend for you to have discomfort. I am here because you bloody well need me. Look at this that is happening here. Only days ago, this pathetic man discarded you from his loins as though you were nothing to him. Trust me, I have risked ultimate banishment from the Lord, Chief and Light-bringer of Spirisity, Samuel Reynaldi, in order to get right back to you! Hell only knows what he will do when he discovers I am back in your vicinity," Astrid explained in great detail. "But I don't care for that. Call me irrational. A loose cannon about to spin his wheels into unfiltered chaos. I'm really not bothered. None of those fickle things means anything to me. But you do."

Astrid finished with a furrowed brow. He looked intently into her bright gleaming lime-green eyes, hoping that when their eyes met, she'd see the true him inside and have that inner knowing that he had finally returned.

"All right, let's say I believe you. Why would you come back now? You've appeared to me at the strangest times, and yet I cannot recall how I seem to know you. Don't you find that most peculiar?" Isra asked.

Her eyes narrowed as though she didn't quite deem what he said to be true but part of her was wholly invested in it.

"It's the right time. Now more than ever," Astrid replied. "I know you're hurting and that's why I am risking far greater repercussions to come back to you. It may sound silly, but in my dreams, you always remember!"

Isra lowered her gaze, softening her rigid stance for a moment as she uttered, "Your dreams must be truly remarkable entities then, as I daren't say I am able to recall this dalliance. I assume that is what it is. I doubt it could be anything else."

"Oh, it's a little more than that. We are the most excellent of friends but all will be revealed in time. Now this Alan fellow, I know he's riled you something chronic but let us be sensible. Whatever you decide to do to him will not fix the sacred carcass that is your heart. I know you more than you dare to admit. It won't repair the broken lineage inside you but I know the comforts of revenge can be satisfying. Even for just a time," Astrid mentioned, pausing halfway through as he quickly realised this situation could be far more dire than he'd originally foreseen it to be.

"And if that is so, why would it matter?" Isra pressed with wide-eyed suspicion. She yearned to know why it meant anything whether she chose to vanquish Alan or not.

Why would he care? It doesn't change anything in his reality. In his dignified realm, we are the best of friends and while I cannot see his entrancing vision for some reason or another I am inclined to believe that it is indeed possible. Just not so much in the cosmos we currently inhabit, Isra conferred with herself, pursuing the idea that perhaps Astrid knew far more than he was letting her know.

"It won't. Not in the long run, but every action has a karmic consequence. I know you don't have any care towards the rhyme and reasoning of the realms but I can assure you with my fullest understanding that just because you don't understand it, it doesn't mean it is not in existence," Astrid implored with bated breath.

This was the penultimate moment. Had he managed to talk Isra around? Or would he be the one cleaning up her abhorrent mess in a few moments? Only time would tell if she was taking any notice of his damn reasoning.

"So why care if I decide to disembowel this poor wretched soul?" Isra hissed with a subtle lick of her lips, venom practically dripping out of her mouth and effortlessly rolling off her tongue as though it was silk.

"May I please interrupt this iconic moment of lover's lane for a second to add that it's rather unconventional to talk about someone in such a harrowing way when they cannot add in their defence?" Alan entered in such a manner that he felt as though he was breaching boundaries by saying it as he had come here to rectify his situation with Isra. In any event, she wasn't exactly receptive to his offering of making amends.

"Shut up!" Astrid shouted in Alan's direction. He was sick and tired of hearing about Alan. *Oh, he's a warlock and such an intriguing being. Alan's so fucking wonderful. Blah, blah. Nobody cares, you undignified bottom feeder. Honestly, at least she's finally turned off of him now but ha! His pathetic begging is somewhat entertaining,* Astrid chorused in an amused tone, quietly keeping his thoughts to himself.

Isra's face lit up immediately upon hearing him say it so it was only right that she responded in kind. "Yes, shut up, you imbecile," she responded cruelly, not caring that Alan was in two minds whether it was worth him attempting to apologise further or whether it was best to follow Astrid's advice and keep his trap shut.

Well, she's not going to take me back. So, what the heck do I do now? Is there any purpose in making a run for it? She's got this eccentric stranger in tow that seems to know her but yet her memory fails to conjure up knowing him. I do need to be careful in any event because if it comes between me and him, I'll be in a whole boatload of trouble. I don't know who this man is but he clearly is more than what he proclaims to be. That in itself is dangerous. I have to think on my feet, or it could all go to hell. Now! Alan thought, deftly dreaded what was coming next.

"Well, as enterprising as this is, surely one cannot at least have a defence at hand? I can't be hung, drawn, and quartered without a chance to explain," Alan pressed the question to Isra earnestly.

He hoped that being diplomatic would save him. Oh, how wrong he was.

"Hmm. I haven't given it much thought!" Isra remarked. "Say, Astrid, what do you think?!" She expertly turned the question over to Astrid, much to his delight as she had been paying more attention to him than he had believed to be true.

"Oh, this has nothing to do with me, trouble! But I'd bet that it would be in your best interests to let him go. That's if it was me running the show, which, of course, it is not," Astrid answered in a sympathetic tone.

"Hmm, not terribly helpful there, dear. Oh, well." Isra shrugged as she was still considering Alan's plea.

"But if you please," Alan implored, "it is I who should be extending my heartfelt gratitude to you, for it was you who inspired me to tell dear old Everilda where to go when she began harassing me. As far as failed dalliances go, my courtship with her is surely up there among the worst of them," Alan confessed meekly, lowering his head down as he still knelt on the floor.

Isra's eyes narrowed at him angrily. Her normally bright lime-green eyes flashed a vengeful shade of pillar box red. She glared at him with such veracity that even Astrid took a step backwards, unable to decipher whether he should stick his neck out on this one or just give Isra the floor to do whatever she deemed right because let's face it, she was going to do it anyway.

"So it is true. How interesting! And now the only probing issue is how I'll deal with you, my dear? Hmm. Oh, the possibilities are endless."

Isra licked her top lip wickedly. Astrid looked on silently, not saying a word.

This is none of my business. It's totally up to Isra how she delegates this now. She may choose to castrate him and then again, she might not. It's not any of my concern. What I have reservations over is what happens after it, Astrid thought.

Standing aside was the best thing he could do while watching on to see how Isra reacted or responded, however the case may be. But Alan was certainly one for putting his foot in it and this was no exception.

He blurted out, "Everilda and I were young. It was high society times, where we did nothing but go to communist galas. And thus, we became close. Some would say we had become good friends, but it soon turned into more. I am sorry I did not detail this to you sooner, but needs must."

Needs must? That's just about gone and done it. He's made a step too far this time.

Oh, and there it was. That fateful little word. One tiny verbalisation propelled Isra to snarl at Alan in one piercing glance and within seconds, shimmery white lightning shot out of her right hand, scorching Alan right at the core of him. The violent sparks emitted at him in all directions.

He began screaming in a high-pitched voice, "No, no. Please Isra. I beg of you. Please don't do this."

It was to no avail. Isra's dominant hand was fiercely positioned from her spot where she sat so regally upon her golden clad throne. She didn't come to any resolve as she continued to hurl lightning bolts at Alan, who was clinging to the cold stone floor in agony. He had surpassed all forms of pleading and howled out in pain. The ferocity penetrated throughout his body to such intensity that it was a fruitless effort to call out to Isra's good nature, for it was non-existent.

"Well, that has put paid to that!" Isra cursed sullenly.

Her hand finally dropped. Alan didn't bother acknowledging Isra's culmination as he realised everything had stopped. The quietness was unnerving; you could almost hear a pin drop.

He gathered the courage to look upward only to find he was completely paralysed from head to foot. There was no fluid movement in him whatsoever apart from the ability to roll his eyes but he wasn't going to be brassy enough to attempt that, as it would surely anger Isra more. But he did notice the bright, shimmery silver sparks that formed around him, creating a metaphysical cage. Isra had callously holed him up in here and that was why he had no bodily movement. He wouldn't be able to shift himself out of here, even if he was able to.

Astrid looked down at Alan, seeing him in the confused and discombobulated state he was in and felt a mediocre amount of pity towards the warlock, but even then, Astrid knew Alan had brought it upon himself so he seldom cared much. Astrid turned to Isra, softly walking up to where she sat on her gallant throne.

He gently reached for Isra's hand, whispering to her in a delicate voice, "Come. Let's go for a stroll. There is something I want to show you."

Isra reluctantly allowed Astrid to take her by the hand, leading her away from her extravagant throne room. He quietly suggested his alternative in them disappearing for a while so she could regain her focus as he whispered in her ear once more, "Leave him be. He's not important. Besides, you've got him more than occupied for now. His time will come, but what I am about to show you will change everything you believe!"

"Where are we going?" Isra asked with curiosity. She didn't look behind her while Astrid swiftly removed her from the living room, proceeding to take her down the spiralling grey stone staircase before she could change her mind.

"To the very place it all began. Trust me, you won't want to miss this! Come on."

He urged her, knowing they needed to get going if they were going to get to Glamvein without anyone from the light lands getting a glimpse of what they were up to. Astrid clicked his index finger and thumb together, visualising the eccentric wasteland inside the pit of his mind as if it were yesterday whilst he transported himself and Isra there in a flash.

ASTRID MUTTERED APOLOGETICALLY, "Sorry for all the theatre, but if Samuel knew where we were going, there's a significant chance we'd be on his radar once again," as he gently held onto Isra's right hand. When they arrived at their destination, he said, "Well, here it is. It's strangely vague compared to the last time I was here."

Astrid paused, mulling over the situation where he'd been perched above the mountain crevice and Isra had been enchanted by the vast green energy locked inside the monstrosity of Glamvein's deserted mountain for years. He was awestruck as he had witnessed her soak up that vibrant ferocity, and her connection to it had made the entire entity abuzz with mystical energy.

"With you," he added. "Yes, that's right."

Isra stared at him dead on in his warm brown eyes with their honey-ochre coloured sheen that was somewhat dimmed by the majesty of what was before them.

"But that isn't why we're here. I want to enlighten you on what's going down. I could only do that by taking you here. I know it's all very mysterious. You're probably wondering what I get by handing you all of this on a plate. Well, let me tell you. I gain nothing, but you will have everything at your disposal after me telling you this," Astrid voiced soberly, turning his attention to the tiny crevice where Isra had, once upon a time, truly found herself on that cold, damp rainy night where everything came full circle.

"I was there. The very same night you became attuned to the dark side. I watched as you offered up your heart to the darkness and although you were heartbroken, I saw it. Something went through you. You became one with it. And then everything was different. I was still there in the morning when you awoke, awash with the fervour from the previous night. Sleep did little to calm your rapturous energies," Astrid explained carefully.

His warm brown eyes showed how serious he was as he fixed his glance on Isra carefully. "I was right there from the very beginning. I know you more than you know yourself." Astrid lowered his eyes at her and admitted, "I was sent to watch you. It was me that was by your side throughout your triumph and your defeat with that pathetic weasel, Jonathan. I was right by your side the entire time, and under strict orders from Samuel to do so."

Isra gravitated towards him with every word he spoke. If this had been anyone else admitting all of this to her, she'd have been wholly cross by now, but for some reason, she was indisputably lured in by Astrid. There was something so familiar to her and she caught a glimpse of it as she remained focused on his big, dark eyes with their shimmery golden-yellow gleam.

"I see; and so this means you knew me long before we actually met then?" Isra queried him plainly." She stared up at the mountain peak before her, sensing the familiarity that also resounded from the historic landmark before she paused momentarily, looking back at Astrid as she remarked, "Why do I get the feeling you aren't quite telling me all that you know?"

"That's because I am not. Nothing is ever what we set it out to be. I never planned to be with you in any capacity but I have been. Always," Astrid candidly told Isra with a forewarning look in his eye.

The fear that he was detailing to Isra the powerful story of how they came to be in each other's lives was overwhelming. It was just one truth. This big thing he needed to get off his chest and had been keeping from her for the longest time was just waiting to be released from his lips. To give him that sanctimonious sensation of peace knowing he'd maintained his integrity with Isra was priceless to Astrid. There was no going back after he told her the harsh, cold truth, and knowing Isra, she would see it as nothing else.

I could have done this a million different ways. I tried my utmost to conceal it from her but now things have drastically changed and not so much for the better. Without Alan, I may not be in this moment with her right now. Oh, well. Best get on with it, old son, there's no time to lose but everything is up for the taking. Astrid thought, as he knew if he was ballsy enough to strike up the nerve and say it to her now, there would be no return after this.

"I first heard of you because of Samuel Reynaldi. He asked me to keep watch on you for 'on high' had predicted you would turn to the tide. That's a fancy pants way of suggesting you would switch over to the dark side, by the way. I was there on the stone steps of Wingdom's Academy when you wept over Jonathan. I was there when you were courting him. I have been there throughout some of the most prominent moments of your life," Astrid admitted, swallowing a little as this was a big deal. Much more enormous than he'd originally anticipated.

"I appreciate you may not be too comfortable with the notion of me watching you in some of your less than favourable moments in life, but because of it, we are the great esteemed friends we are now. I know you cannot remember the times we have shared and believe me, if I had the ability to reconcile you with them, I would have done so in a heartbeat. Alas, Samuel cast the spell, so he is the only one that can remove it. Suffice to say, I've been trying to get to you for a very long time. He banished me, of course, after he'd taken your memories, but we were there, side by side, about to relish every second, when I presented you with your magics months after he stole them away from you!" Astrid announced proudly.

He felt awkward; Isra had yet to give him any kind of reaction. He was almost perturbed, wondering if she was going to be all right with him after this.

"I see. So I was the girl destined to go dark and no matter what I did, they had me down as some vile creature that needed putting down," Isra pointed out plainly. She wholeheartedly agreed with the light's reasoning.

"What do you mean?" Astrid asked. "Don't you see? It was all the light's doing. 'On high' is responsible for this and don't think for one second that Samuel wasn't grabbing a slice of the action for himself. I still don't understand it but you were the big fascination for him," Astrid explained curtly.

Samuel benefited from the very start. It was all about Isra. He was so transfixed on her going to the dark side that he wouldn't pay much attention to anything else. Can you imagine how many other souls turned to the dark side during that time that he blatantly ignored? Does he even comprehend just how besotted he was with the notion that Isra was the main theme in his life at that time. Well, still is, if you consider his latest behaviour, Astrid thought as he stared at Isra pointedly.

She wasn't exactly being receptive to his way of thinking. He was somewhat flustered. He expected that he'd have made some progress with her by now; however, she showed no signs of faltering. He assumed Isra would take on board what he'd said to her. Only for her to completely reject his idealisation. Isra was not even caring much for Astrid's incredibly vivid explanation as she said it candidly to his face.

"Darkness is all I am," Isra interrupted while he was still so deep in his head about it all.

Astrid cut Isra off abruptly. He vehemently disagreed with what she'd said. Some would say he was even infuriated with her suggesting that the love and light brigade were right about her.

"Oh, no. You are so much more than that. Trust me, I've been working in the service of the light for longer than I care to know. And I've never seen them get so flustered as they had with you. Samuel made me stake you out from the start and I never really understood why but something about you had him high tailing to the seven seas. Pardon me for making assumptions, but that isn't very love and light now, is it?"

Astrid knew Isra needed him to break it down. Because, by golly, she needed convincing. And if it meant Astrid spilling the beans, all the gory details, then that was exactly what he was going to do.

"Not to mention, you were such a formidable force, he wanted you out of the way sharpish. It was easier for him to confiscate your magic than it was for him to consider you a worthy opponent. Let's face it, our light-bringer isn't quite the hero he's made out to be. I've worked with him for aeons and I've seen more darkness in him than I've ever seen in anyone," Astrid retorted solemnly.

His eyes dropped back onto Isra as she threw him a bewildered glance as though she didn't quite believe him to be telling the truth but also wanted to probe him further. Her curiosity was taking her places she didn't dare to go.

"If that is so, then why did you agree to watch me?" Isra asked with a wide-eyed stare burning into him.

Those bright lime-green eyes of hers were alight with fascination. There was still so much about Astrid she was yet to discover. He was so enthralling and yet so mysteriously closed off. It frustrated her a great deal as sometimes she truly couldn't decipher what he was thinking. He was such a dark horse and his critical mannerisms irked her somewhat. She yearned to know what was going on in that brilliant mind of his.

Astrid straightened his stance, resisting the urge to fidget. He felt a little uncomfortable with the question. He paused as he tried to rid himself of the awkward sensation inside him. That energy pulsating inside his chest. That knowing that he'd lied to her after gaining entry into her life once again. That feeling of knowing he was finally coming clean but that Isra may not be best pleased with him after all of this.

"Truthfully, I don't know. You were the big noise for months. Samuel barely mentioned anything else. The light realms are supposed to convert those who turned to the dark side but he never mustered that approach with you. You hadn't even turned over to us yet. He went straight in for the kill. Sure, he scolded you a hell of a lot, tried to show you there was another way, but he didn't for one moment make a single attempt to bring you back to the light. It was all theatre. I never realised just how fixated he was until he seized the opportunity in taking your magic. All of a sudden, you were gone, holed up in that eccentric tower. I was banished, told to never come back and Samuel remained victorious," Astrid told her with a worried glance.

"I am afraid I do not recall such an event," Isra mouthed soberly.

"Well, you wouldn't," Astrid explained with a look of concern. "He not only snatched your magics but he also ensured you'd never remember him doing so. I had no idea until a few days ago that he'd kept hold of your dark ferocity but he'd made out to us all that he'd destroyed it which is obviously false. I know this now," Astrid confessed; he'd been spying on Samuel, too.

Isra gasped, pressing the question; for even she didn't fathom as to why he'd grab her dark magic for himself. "So if I am so dangerous to his precious realm, why hold onto my magic?"

That's quite unorthodox for a light-bringer. It makes you wonder what goes on inside a man's head to think that being all high and mighty makes it okay for you to just get a tiny taste of something dark and mysterious. He seems quite tempted by it all. But his love and light facade isn't one that will be easily broken down, Isra conferred with herself in her thoughts, mulling over the whys and wherefores, for now she was understanding more than she originally had intended to.

"That's just the question. You see, our famous light-bringer isn't as good as he proclaims. Deep down, he's just a terrified old man, scared of a young enchantress. However, he portrays that holier than thou attitude to the rest of the world," Astrid clarified.

"It seems he has some deeply rooted issues but a man with such a powerful position isn't the easiest of foes to take down," Isra presumed with accurate precision.

She'd grasped the concept! Samuel Reynaldi, light-bringer, was the enemy, whereas Astrid, a bemused and yet marvellously enchanting creature, was indeed her friend... although she hadn't put all the pieces together yet. He was so devoted to her though in telling her all of this that Isra was certain he was trustworthy. Nothing else really mattered although she was rather baffled he hadn't said something sooner but she guessed that in the greater scheme of things it wasn't important.

"That's why I don't want you making any moves that might get you noticed. By exacting revenge on Alan, you may well have the spotlight shone upon you once again and the last thing you need is Samuel breathing down your neck. You'll be famous for all the wrong reasons," Astrid appealed to her.

He hoped she'd drop this ridiculous notion of executing revenge upon Alan, knowing that her energies were best placed elsewhere. However, this was Isra he was talking about. It wasn't often she listened to reason. After all, she was rather superior in this way and didn't believe others' opinions were worth hearing.

"I see. So, you don't want me disembowelling him then? Shame. I was planning on having quite the frivolous afternoon," Isra remarked with a cheeky smile.

It was the first time she'd shown her more adventurous side to Astrid. She was almost being flirtatious but she still had that sharp edge to her that showed she meant business.

Astrid flashed her a dead stare. "No. That's not what I recommend. How about you go home after this? I have some business to attend to that unfortunately I couldn't take care of before. Let Alan go. He'll fester in his own impetuous emotions but he'll be so terrified he won't dream of coming back to you again," Astrid instructed her with a forewarning look.

I hope she releases him. The last thing she needs is Samuel getting wind of her extracurricular activities. Toying with lovestruck warlocks will not impress our fateful light-bringer. Neither will it bring Isra any peace. Well, she may find some satisfaction in her vengeful deed but not much else shall come from it, Astrid concluded in thought as he maintained his sense of whimsy, knowing he needed to get off soon now that Isra was in a fairly calm state of mind. He didn't want her doing anything that might direct attention to her from the very wrong sorts of beings. That was Astrid's biggest concern.

"All right. I'll go on my way and let the pathetic man go."

Isra agreed although she didn't seem happy about it. It seemed she was just going along with what Astrid had wanted. It's not like he was demanding anything from her but already Isra was investing a lot of trust in the mysterious man she'd previously known as just a raven.

"Good, and don't worry about getting back. I'll transport you over to Shambre Fell before you can think of it," Astrid announced in an assertive tone.

Oh, golly! How he wanted to ensure that Isra toddled straight over and did nothing but. He wasn't being controlling but he was extremely protective of the witch and wanted nothing but what was best for her. Whether Isra chose to see that or not was ultimately up to her.

"You're persistent. I'll give you that," Isra retorted coyly.

She wasn't used to having someone around that pretty much told her what to do but was incredibly casual about it at the same time. Astrid wasn't forcing her to do *nada* but something about him made her want to obey. It was fascinating for her to have such an influential person in her life because she rarely encountered anybody that even had a shred of intelligence. Most of the souls she managed to come across in her short but interesting tenure were the dim-witted, lost, and desolate wrecks of life you expected to find at the bottom of a pile.

Astrid was completely different. He was confident yet not conceited. He showed kindness but was also firm with her. He was resilient yet also remarkable with his immense knowledge on a variety of subjects especially since he knew so much about life and since he was predominantly a raven Isra couldn't help but find him even more enticing.

"Trust me when I say I've been called far worse. Now, let's not dawdle. I'm getting you back to Shambre Fell. I don't want you tempted to stray and go off path." He gave her a firm glance. He knew there was a part of her that desired to give Alan a taste of his own medicine but Astrid wanted to give Isra the benefit of the doubt.

She may as well just listen to me. I don't know for certain if she will follow through but at least I've calmed her down to the point she's not exhibiting violent tendencies so prominently. I'm sure she's still relishing the idea but is less enthused over it now. Astrid mused to himself as he pursued whether Isra was at ease over him practically insisting he send her home pronto. But then again, he wasn't going to give her any leeway.

"Ha, I could have walked, dear heart," Isra responded with a bewildered look although she had a tiny half-smile resounding upon her face, so she wasn't at all offended.

"Yes, but that's not going to suffice for me. Off you go now!" Astrid enforced, his tone becoming hoarse. He wasn't letting Isra slip out of his grasp now.

"All right, Mr Snappy. I was going to go off anyway!" Isra guffawed in his direction. Her tardiness was showing as she was becoming more brazen by the second, which, Astrid had to admit, made her far more attractive to him.

No chance. Not on your life, my girl! Astrid chortled as he softly concentrated on her elegant form. *Oh, if only I had a spare few moments to get my bare hands on you. You're lucky I've got to saunter off and find Damien. If not for my sanity and your salvation. Perish the thought I might be able to have myself a jolly old time exploring your inhibitions. Disappointing, but shit happens.*

Astrid surrendered his unsavoury ideals for he could always come back to them after everything had been taken care of to the highest order.

Those piercing green eyes of hers distracted him somewhat but he didn't let it get the better of him. Just imagining her standing there so perfectly while her golden-white hair sparkled in the sunlight was enough to have him dreaming up what might commence if he managed to find the time to be alone with her, but there was no time for illicit thoughts.

He enveloped Isra in soft, gold glimmering specks of light enough to tumble down onto her, showering her with the energy's amazing vitality until she was completely saturated in it, and then Astrid pictured the tower of Shambre Fell along with Isra's living room whereby Alan was now captured, trapped in her wicked midst. Next, he visualised Isra back inside the tower, positioned perfectly right by her red chair with gilded gold. After that, it was way too easy and before Astrid knew it, Isra had dissipated in a puff of glittering grey smoke.

"Ah, now that's more like it. I'll be along soon. Now you best be good, kiddo," Astrid remarked softly after Isra vanished from his sight.

18

Isra eagerly opened the door to her living area, not expecting to be greeted by anything less than a docile Alan, who would inadvertently be trying not to push the boundaries further.

"Ha, well, that was modestly entertaining, but now I find myself a little bored," she mused as she leaned against the oak door, pouting as her eyes met Alan's nonchalantly.

"Oh. I forgot you were here. Anyway, I trust you have had a most quiet afternoon? I was thinking I might run myself a hot bath. Take the edge off after a marvellous day!" Isra gushed, feeling immensely good about herself. She smiled at Alan comically. "You know, you could have left me alone. But you had to come back here, didn't you? Silly, really, but then again, you boys never truly learn your lessons, do you? Hmm."

She posed the question inquisitively, although she didn't care to acquire the answer.

"I should have believed them," Alan uttered in exasperation. "I knew you were an amazing woman, wise beyond your years, but I never pictured you to be ruthless."

He finished slowly and sat on the cold stone floor of his energetic cage. Of course, it wasn't a real one but it was impenetrable and he knew couldn't get out of it.

"Hmm. You'd do well not to insult me right now," Isra cautioned with a probing finger. "You know, I've tolerated a lot of crap from men like you. Men who think they are pushing past their lowly status. Nearly all of them have an overinflated ego. Well, my dear, you just surpassed them all. Aren't you a prince?"

Isra sneered sardonically but her tone of voice suggested she was joking, almost mocking him as she callously slunk over her elegant yet comfortable red couch. "It has been a very invigorating day, but I am not burned out yet. I still have a lot of energy in me, and if you don't play nice, you might be on the receiving end of that so quit it... boy."

Isra threw him a death stare as she laid back against the soft cushioned fabric of the couch, letting her cares pass her by. She sank into a lack of consciousness, allowing her eyelids to fall closed just as Alan made the fatal mistake of opening his mouth once again.

"I don't mean to be insolent, but you were so chaste, not to mention naïve. I mean, girl, I am not trying to belittle you, but you are so beneath all my other conquests! Yet here you sit, leaving me to rot. Is there nothing left in that rotten heart of yours?" Alan inquired sarcastically as he lay desolate, his brow dripping with sweat, awaiting his untimely fate.

"Naive, eh? Interesting how you weren't saying that when you were charming me with your divine cookies. But it doesn't matter. Your end is in sight," Isra retorted dryly.

"Hahahaha, do it! End my self-imposed misery. But hey, we both know you don't have the gusto. Deep down, you still feel something for me. I mean, underneath all that blasphemy of how much you hate everyone," Alan sniped in a condescending tone.

However, it was enough to incur Isra's wrath. She marched straight over to his cage and stood over him. Alan flinched nervously. He wasn't certain what Isra was about to do, but the glaring red flashing from her eyes indicated she was really pissed.

~

A STRID STOOD by the weeping woman statue that was the landmark of Wretchenheart. He hadn't been here for many moons but he knew it was the perfect place to find someone that had been declared missing in action... or more accurately, staying out of sight. Astrid turned, noting the skies had suddenly become almost black. The air was dense and thick as were the fluffy clouds that were emitting humidity all around the atmosphere.

If Astrid wasn't immortal, he'd probably struggle to take a breath, but that was the least of his problems. He needed to find Damien Daughtry sharpish because a lot was about to commence. Astrid figured that Damien could help fill in some of the blanks; he had a lot of questions buzzing around inside his head. Rhiannon had been less than forthcoming with answers and so Astrid had gone straight to the source.

The weather was less than favourable. Lightning surged across the land, singing everything in sight. Astrid wondered whether he'd be best to seek out Damien elsewhere. However, amid the chaos, a long black shirt jacket emerged from the bramble thicket.

"Astrid. I didn't expect to find you out here." Damien gasped awkwardly as he clutched a lit lantern in his right hand. His eyes looked tired, presumably from all the running. Still, he looked on wearily.

"Actually, I am here looking for you," Astrid voiced clearly. "It's been a long time, Damien. I had no idea if Samuel Reynaldi had vanquished you, too."

"No. He doesn't have that kind of power. Sorry to say but he's not as worldly as he claims to be. Anyway, why are you here? Not that I am not pleased to see you but I get the feeling you don't bring good tidings," Damien urged, taking careful eye of the storm playing out above his and Astrid's heads.

"Luckily, that shit can't touch me. Nevertheless, can't be too stealthy now," Damien mouthed quietly.

"No, we can't. Still, let's not stall here, Damien," Astrid commented.

He had an eyeful of the illumination show taking place overhead. Bright silvery sparks hit Wretchenheart in every direction but yet none of it went near Astrid and Damien. The benefits of immortality, eh?

"What's up, old chap?" Damien piped up. Damien had probably envisaged that Astrid had woman troubles again.

Astrid jumped straight to the chase, not even breathing as he made his opening statement. "Your daughters are at each other's throats again."

"I'm sorry, I beg your pardon? I have one daughter, and I know she's a nightmare, but may I remind you that she's also mortal now," Damien concluded with a low brow. He didn't appreciate being scolded about Everilda, for part of him blamed himself for the way the poor girl had turned out.

"No. You have two," Astrid blurted out. "Isra and Everilda."

Damien stopped, red-faced, as he connected the dots of what Astrid was saying to him. "No, not the same one you wanted to be with? But wait... How? Oh, my goodness. This cannot be true. It absolutely is impossible!" Damien blundered nervously and stood shaking. His legs trembled as the rain pattered him from head to foot.

"The very same one I wanted to be acquainted with. Yes. I found out by complete accident. It's a riveting conversation. I happened to be eavesdropping on Samuel Reynaldi, my former employer," Astrid confessed with a serious glance.

Damien dropped his nervousness immediately and retorted, "Yes, I know who that bloody buffoon is. He's the self-righteous git that was given way too much power, if you ask me. But may I ask how on Earth you're sure it's the same baby I handed to him?"

Astrid answered pointedly. "How many young witch babies are just simply handed into Samuel's care? Believe me, it's her. I didn't even know you had a child out of wedlock, nevermind Isra. I've been reeling over it but the damage is already done. I can't undo it. Neither can I change my feelings."

"No, you can't. I wouldn't ask you to. Nevertheless, yes, I did have a second child. I happened to be in a romantic connection with a young witch, Gwendolyn. She was afraid of her power but we had a very interesting dynamic. Anyway, the baby... Well, Isra was causing all manner of havoc and so Gwendolyn sought help. That help turned out to be Reynaldi, standing on airs, looking down his nose down at us," Damien admitted carelessly. "I didn't much like him then. I certainly do not like him now."

"Wait, Gwendolyn is a witch?" Astrid probed.

"Yes. Not a very good one in any event, but yes," Damien responded solemnly.

Damien paced on the soaking wet grass, trying to fathom what would be the best course of action. If he knew what to do, this situation might be handled a lot more methodically than he had done thus far.

"Which means..." Astrid stopped mid-sentence, trying to come to terms with this latest bombshell that had been hurled his way.

"Isra is a full-blooded witch. Yes," Damien finished abruptly.

Astrid straightened his stance, and his tone got way more gloomy as he looked Damien dead in the eyes and muttered, "Isra currently has a well-known warlock, you may know him, holed up in her tower. Alan Grimsbane," Astrid detailed, but the bewildered look upon Damien's face told Astrid all he needed to know.

This isn't pleasing news to him, is it? The Grimsbane name seems to strike fear in his heart, which is odd for his status, Astrid remarked candidly to himself.

"Oh, goodness. Tell me she hasn't taken up with him. He's notorious for serenading virgins! Wait, did you say she has Grimsbane in her tower? Are we talking against his will? His father will kick up a stink!" Damien muttered.

"Yes, they had a brief dalliance. And he's rocked up there today, wailing and apologising for his bailing. Only, Isra has taken matters into her own hands and he's currently locked away in a magical energy field cage right now." Astrid did not hold back on the details.

"Ah, not good. That won't go down well with the warring families.

Grimsbane is the son of Nathaniel. He's a wayward chap, been disowned by most of his relatives but he's untouchable. If Isra puts one foot wrong down... Well, it could end badly," Damien warned Astrid bluntly. "Not to mention, Isra is in serious danger, as he is well known for captivating unknowing virgins so he can fill his energy reserves and continue growing in power. And for a witch of Isra's calibre, as you have described, he'll drain her energy in a nanosecond," Damien informed Astrid with a grave expression.

"I hate to break it to you, but Isra is not a virgin," Astrid retorted dryly, although he still had a serious tone in his voice, for this was a very important conversation and now wasn't the time to kid around.

"Oh, gosh! How do you know that?" Damien inquired.

He looked Astrid right in the eyes. Astrid only responded by giving Damien a somewhat bemused glance. It was awkward; the men exchanged blundering looks with one another.

"Because I am the dastardly fellow that took her innocence," Astrid finally confessed solemnly.

"Oh. Astrid. You didn't?! Oh, my! That is not a conversation I want to have with the warring families!" Damien paused, feeling as though he'd overlooked the situation somewhat but maintained his optimism despite what he'd heard. "Well, it cannot be helped now, I guess. Still, it's not good news for Isra if she has him captured in her not so humble abode. Dare I ask how my other daughter is somehow incorporated in this mess?" Damien boldly asked.

"Everilda had an alliance with Grimsbane," Astrid mouthed so quietly it was barely loud enough for Damien to hear. "We are talking romantically here. Your wayward daughter decided to hound Grimsbane shortly after she discovered he was courting Isra. Naturally, Isra is out for blood. She won't care that the stakes have been lowered with Everilda being mortal now."

"No. I can only imagine. Fucking hell. Is there anything my stupendous daughter won't get herself entangled with? He's connected to one of the biggest high-ranking witch families. Boy, you think I'm high up in the food chain? The Grimsbanes have been around for centuries. Shit!" Damien exclaimed as he put a worried finger to his lips, signalling his deep concern.

"Is it that dire? I've been trying to persuade Isra to let Grimsbane go but she's on the warpath as one would expect when their heart has been toyed with," Astrid continued, looking equally as perplexed because of how the situation was unfolding.

"It is that bad, yes. So Isra has managed to get Grimsbane in her grasp and now she's planning on avenging what he did to her. Well, dare I ask why he suddenly decided to rock up there after deserting her? He's not right in the head, you know, but he's also bloody untouchable. A spoiled brat, if you ask me, but his grandmother is Zelena Grimsbane. Nathaniel's mother. So, if she was to get wind that her precious grandson's life is being threatened... Well let's not even go there," Damien articulated, dreading just how serious things were about to get.

"So, you're saying Isra is playing with fire by possibly intending to unleash her fury onto him?" Astrid pressed the worrisome question in Damien's direction.

"Yes, and far more than that. You better hope she drops this charade and soon, old son. Is that chap, Reynaldi, involved? I know you were concerned over his interference last time you and Isra tangoed together," Damien asked out of interest since his intrigue was expanding.

"No, he's not. He'd be doing all he could to take her down if that was the case," Astrid muttered, remembering how forceful Samuel had been with the last incident about Isra.

"Right you are. Not to mention, he's also in charge of the warring witch families. Isra is really in a lot of hot water if she pursues this, Astrid. You don't even want to know how serious this could get!" Damien warned with a cautionary glare.

"I cannot lift a finger. I wish I could, but I'm in exile. It's my untimely punishment for helping you snatch back Isra's magic from that dastardly man's office. However, Rhiannon, the sweet soul she is, let me know you were looking for me, so I decided to make an appearance. I can't stay for long, it's far too dangerous, but you've gotta stop Isra from undertaking this line of inquiry or we are all in deep trouble!" Damien cajoled before adding in, "With severe ramifications. Honestly, Astrid, it's not worth the hellfire we'll all roll against. Get her to stop what she's doing immediately. Don't wait any longer."

Astrid took heed but was also rather bemused to hear of Damien's plight. He knew there had been something keeping Damien out of the spotlight but never for one second did he suspect it would be something so consequential as being forced out of the land.

"What do you mean, you are in exile?" Astrid asked coldly.

He didn't mean to be harsh towards the man he'd known very well. It's just so much was becoming apparent now and he was unsure what to expect next. Since Samuel had so cruelly managed to do away with Isra knowing Astrid the way she once had, everything else was left hanging in the balance. Astrid needed to be reassured there would be no more ghastly surprises.

"It's not forced, if that's what you are concerned about. No, I heard there was a ruckus between you, Samuel, and Isra in Nefaria and I got myself out of harm's way. Not that he can do anything to me, you understand, but he's a power-hungry man, desperate to cling onto anything that keeps him in the supremacy he has become accustomed to. I refused to add myself to the equation," Damien candidly told Astrid, which caused Astrid to question how the hell Damien knew that afterwards when he hadn't told anyone what had gone down.

"Oh? And how did you manage to hear about what occurred in Nefaria?" Astrid probed earnestly. He seemed calmer now, like more his methodical self, which was a big difference compared to what he felt like only moments ago.

"News travels fast in our world. You'd best be on your way now, Astrid. I don't think it's wise for us to be seen together right now. I wish I could be more helpful and I know it's an absolute shit show for all concerned. I don't wish to sound cold. There's nothing I can do from my position here. I'm counting on you, Astrid. You'll be the one to save us all," Damien elaborated with a furrowed brow, the tension getting to him as he backed away, leaving Astrid reeling. It was all down to him.

"No pressure, huh?" Astrid remarked abruptly.

"Sorry, old boy. If she had her powers removed as they wanted years ago, we could have avoided this mess!" Damien scoffed angrily.

Yes, Isra was his daughter and a part of him knew he played a significant role in her ending up the way she had, but he felt as though the light-bringer had majorly cocked this up.

"What?" Astrid countered. "You've got to be kidding me! She was supposed to have her powers removed. Oh, come on, Damien. I am not going anywhere until you explain yourself!"

You could tell from the look in his eyes that he was practically boiling over with rage. At any moment, he could tip over the edge, but he was trying to maintain his composure. He needed to know now more than ever what the hell was going on.

"Isra was going to have her powers extracted when she was an infant but it's clear that never happened. Bloody fools that work alongside the light are clueless. It's typical of them to screw something up like this. They preach all day about being righteous and good but the moment something big comes up, they manage to make an absolute pig's ear of it." Damien scowled with fury.

"Oh, I'm a fuming boy. Honestly, but you know how these blundering idiots work. You were there from the very start!" Damien reminded Astrid, which caused Astrid to drift back to the time when he was just a young fellow, helplessly wandering around Spirisity, the very same day he met the famous Samuel Reynaldi.

~ One Hundred Years Ago ~

ASTRID HAD STRAYED from his home territory after finding himself feeling rather lost. He'd lost his mother and been separated from his brother, Silas. As a raven, it was natural instinct for him to form a close bond with his nearest and dearest. Alas, he was now alone and wandering around this deserted garden in the middle of nowhere.

Incandescent greenery dominated a picturesque grey castle that stood out among all the tiny violets and yellow crocuses that were spread out around the beautiful green grass. He didn't feel like going back to where he'd come from. Back home was different than this, and after everything was stolen away from him, going back didn't seem very comforting. So, he'd taken to hanging out here for a while; maybe he'd sit back, let the sun's rays warm his rings as he took in the scenery around him. Imagine his surprise when a shadow startled Astrid. It was such an internal shock that he spread his wings in panic.

"Now, now. Don't tremble. It's only me," the modest gentleman calmly announced.

He stood on airs in a tall black tailored suit jacket with matching suit trousers while he peeked down at Astrid with sky-blue eyes that emerged from silver half-moon spectacles. He also had slicked-back jet-black hair and a rather forlorn look about him like he too was troubled, just like Astrid. Astrid seemed to find this endearing as he stared up at the bewildering man before him.

"Oh, sorry. These are not my usual haunts. I was just taking a rest," Astrid excused himself guiltily. He didn't feel wholly comfortable about being caught unawares in this stranger's garden.

"Oh, don't be alarmed. No trouble at all. Tell me, are you far from here?" the gentleman piped up in a friendly voice. "I can't do much in terms of refreshment but I can offer you a warm chateau and some mead if that appeals to your fancy. Oh. How rude of me. My name is Samuel," he introduced himself warmly.

"I am partial to a few juicy earthworms. I'll pass on the mead though," Astrid interjected thoughtfully.

"Ah, I can't do much with that request. However, I imagine you'll find plenty of the buggers in the deep soil. Just don't go blundering around in my flower beds, though," Samuel said to Astrid carefully.

Astrid was about to turn away from Samuel to accept his gracious offer of finding himself a delicious snack when Samuel hastily wiped his brow, bending to sit next to Astrid on the warm grass. His head fell into his hands, looking as though he was weeping for a second.

"I am sorry you are anguished," Astrid motioned in a kind voice.

Samuel lifted his head apologetically. "It's nothing really, old chap. It's just there's a fated prophecy and, believe me, those are always fun, but this one is quite novel. A young female witch is set to wage the war on darkness in the next century. The details are very faint at present time but slowly things are emerging. I just have no idea who she is or what I am supposed to do to help. You see, being a light-bringer, I am the one they have in charge of rescuing these dark souls. I'm the one who is called upon to implore them back to the light. It's not always an easy task."

"I see," Astrid piped up, stopping for a moment. "I always knew the darkness was a sanctuary. Being a raven, well, I know nothing else. I've never heard of a methodology whereby we save those destined to go dark from their fate. That's most peculiar to me."

He perused amongst the soil to see what might appeal to him underneath all the earth.

"Well, it's the job, my boy. If I don't attempt to bring them back from the brink of their own destruction, who will?" Samuel asked coyly. "I see you don't have much experience in the light. I could do with a right-hand man, if you pardon the expression since you have feathers; someone that understands these tainted souls, that's if you are up to the challenge?" Samuel proposed with a wide-eyed stare.

ASTRID CAME BACK to reality with a thud. The realisation dawned on him that he'd been asked to join forces with Samuel from the very moment they had met but the most intriguing revelation of them all was Samuel had referred to Isra all those years ago. And Astrid had never connected the dots at the time because he didn't know who she was. But now it was starting to make sense.

He had been reigned in very early on and Isra was spoken about one hundred years before she was born. But how could this be? From an earthly perspective, it was nigh impossible, but then again, the mysteries of the "on high" was certainly an enigma. As was the equally eccentric Samuel.

Did Samuel somehow orchestrate it so that I was destined to be at his side? Was I planted as a pawn from the very near end because I was assigned to watch Isra? But she hadn't even blooming turned yet! I even questioned him as to how it was our domain as we only worked with those who switched to the dark side. Oh, hell. He'd been so elusive about it but realistically, he had known about her all along. What if he knew more about the prophecy than he detailed to me? What if Samuel knew that me and Isra were fated to be together and he ensured we were separated from the very start? If he planned to snatch her powers, well, it doesn't bear thinking about but one thing is for sure. He bloody knew who she was. You're damned right he knew! That snide, sneaky bastard! Astrid mumbled away, deep in a reverie.

He was unaware Damien was staring at him, nervously wondering why Astrid had slipped away from his consciousness.

"Astrid, may I beseech you that it's important to not dawdle now. You are sorely needed," Damien reprimanded formally.

"Yes, sorry. It's just I remember when I first met Samuel, he made references towards a girl who was destined to turn over to the dark side and how he had no idea what he was going to do in order to prevent that. I'm just trying to fathom in my mind how I ended up on the grounds of Spirisity that day when ravens shun any form of the light. It makes no sense to me," Astrid retorted in a befuddled tone.

"We can never really know how these things work. Magic isn't designed that way, old son. We could be one place one minute and the next, we could well be tittering over to oblivion. Nothing is guaranteed. I'm sorry to be brash, but you really must get on home now."

Damien scolded Astrid softly. He didn't want to be mean as he knew there was a great deal of pressure resting upon Astrid's shoulders but he didn't want Astrid to slack either.

"I guess I am just so thrown. I had everything figured out. Darkness was the raven's sanctuary. The light was our true enemy. We always knew that. I remembered what mother used to say while Silas and I were tiny hatchlings. *By nature, ravens are dark souls. We never dare touch the light. It sucks us dry.* So why would I ever have ended up with Samuel, by his side, almost destroying my one true love in the process?" Astrid questioned.

Damien didn't pay his inquiry much mind.

"I don't know, but it's not important at this time. You must go back to her. Reason with her. Convince her that letting Alan go is for the greater good. Please do this with extreme caution, Astrid, and explain how imperative it is that Alan Grimsbane returns to his base at Immortal Yonder without a scratch on him, or we are all in real perilous danger," Damien urged with immediate haste.

"He's been playing us all from the very beginning. Samuel being Isra's guardian as well is no coincidence. He's had access to her from a baby. Of course, he didn't extract her powers when he had the opportunity. He's simply been biding his time and none of us saw it coming!"

Astrid gasped. It had finally become clear to him what he was up against. Not only was Samuel Isra's very unlikely foe in the guise of a friend, but he was Astrid's too.

"Astrid, I have to cloak the area now because time is running out," Damien uttered as he quietly mumbled something under his breath. A flimsy white silvery sphere encircled him and Astrid, leaving no space for anything else to enter... or anyone, for that matter.

"All right, old chap, take her to Wretchenheart castle. If Isra has done something profoundly stupid, you can take her there, whereby she will be untouchable from the light. But be warned; it's not quite so closed off to the warring witch families. Wretchenheart is a place for tainted souls and it needs a new queen. Should Isra act irrationally, that's your best option. Now get on, old boy," Damien instructed coarsely, quickly dismantling the barrier surrounding them.

"Eh? That's where I took her innocence." Astrid chuckled. "As far as backup plans go, it's not unfathomable but keeping Isra out of the limelight may well be our only option," Astrid remarked with a thoughtful look on his face. "Still, it doesn't quite entirely unravel Samuel's obsession."

"You don't make much sense, old chap, but you best be getting a move on, eh? No time to waste," Damien reminded him casually.

"Yes, and now it's more precious than ever."

Astrid clicked his forefinger and thumb together, dissipating his essence from Damien in a flash.

19

"Be careful what you wish for," Isra hissed in Alan's direction. She laid back against the soft cushioning of her favourable red couch, drinking her beloved peppermint tea. It was invigorating and yet calming, something Isra desperately needed since Alan continued provoking her.

"Just end me!" Alan demanded again.

He was still laying on the cold stone floor in his silvery metaphysical cage. The silvery sparks forming the bars glinted ever so brightly as the shimmery new moon's brilliance crept through the open red velvet curtains.

"Argh. I am getting tired of your insolence. Why do you desire your death so much? Aren't you literally the youngest yet highest-ranking warlock set to topple them all? Why so glum, pet?" Isra mocked callously.

His pathetic whining was beginning to grate upon her but needless to say, she was doing her utmost to ignore his whimpering.

"There isn't much for me to live for right now. I came to you today in the hope you and I could rectify our impending situation," Alan muttered gravely.

Isra lifted herself from the couch, moving over to Alan. Scoffing nonchalantly, she said, "Oh, very good! You came to make amends yet you lied to me about having a past dalliance with my arch-nemesis, not to mention you broke up with me because of her! Why should I give you a moment's pardon, hmm?"

"I loved you. Not in the way you wanted, but I was in love with you. Part of me still is despite all you've done to castrate me," Alan bravely voiced through gritted teeth.

"Interesting," Isra remarked. "I am afraid my courtship with bewitching weasels is long past but please do enlighten me as to why you chose not to speak of your past with Everilda until I placated you in this predicament."

Isra sneered. Her tone was full of vengeful venom, caring not for his feeble excuses. Alan once again found himself reaching desperation. The fear of not being able to go back to Immortal Yonder ever again was too much to bear. If only he could reach Isra at her heart, maybe she'd be kind enough to release him from this magical prison.

"I wished I could take it back. I should have been upfront with you from the start but Everilda is greatly disturbed. I now stupidly realise you two ladies have yet another thing in common," Alan blurted out, much to Isra's revulsion.

She glared at him.

"Sure, you're not as obvious about it as Everilda but girl, you're just as emotionally scarred. Lacked a parental figure, did we? Goodness knows how many men you'll try shacking up with to fill that gap of emotional disillusion," Alan retorted.

Her eyes glowed blood-red with her impending rage. "How dare you mock me in such a manner, boy."

Alan did nothing but shrug as he said, "Well, it's true."

Isra stood inches away from Alan. Her hands were held out in position as the seething anger surged out of her. Bright lime-green lightning shot out of her hands, hitting Alan in all directions. The ferocity of the energy struck him at his heart's centre, causing him to jolt uncomfortably on the cold stone floor. The magic penetrated every blood vessel and cell imaginable as he lay completely rigid on the floor. His eyes stared up at her as he lay lifeless.

Isra stopped the lightning show, allowing her hands to drop. She stood to collect her thoughts for a moment. Astrid walked into the living area in a state of bemusement and glanced down at the cold stiff Alan lying dead on the grey stone floor. His blue eyes still emitted their perfectly soft sapphire colouring, looking as though he had become curious of Isra in his final moments.

"Well, this is quite a spectacle to see. I do believe I told you to leave the boy alone. But it seems that advice has fallen on deaf ears," Astrid chortled in a surprised tone and stared up at Isra with a worried look.

Isra hadn't realised that Alan had succumbed to mortality but suddenly looked down upon him. She had no feeling in her as she gushed, "Oh, my! Doesn't he look cute when he is sleeping?"

"You killed a warlock and exceeded all the light folks' expectations. We must act quickly. He will not be missed by his peers but he is loved by some. I have to get you out of here. Come on. I have a plan. I discussed this with Damien just in case you failed to heed my instructions," Astrid ordered Isra bluntly.

He snatched her hand into his own, clicking his index finger and thumb together before Isra could react or fathom where Astrid was taking her.

ISRA NERVOUSLY STOOD in her deep violet gown, watching herself in the gilded gold oval mirror set in front of her on the luminescent white wall. Astrid carefully affixed the solid gold crown laden with glinting green emeralds upon her head and he stepped back to admire his work.

"Well, I have to say, you really are quite something. Let us await your people, shall we?" he posed to her.

He led her along the dimly lit corridor where armed guards stood saluting Isra as she passed them by. A large archway beckoned with a narrow ruby-red carpet that led up to the most majestic throne ever seen, beautifully gilded in gold with lush deep violet cushioning on the seat and arms. Stunning amethysts were embedded on the sides and back of the chair. As Isra got closer, she saw the magnificent quartz points hanging down from the ceiling while diamond chandeliers showcased the entire room.

Astrid guided Isra to the elaborate throne, softly whispering, "Here you are. Welcome to your new humble abode."

Isra graciously sat upon the exquisite throne in anticipation. Astrid turned to face the growing crowd of onlookers assembled before them. Clearing his throat, he faced the bemused people that had gathered in droves for this regal ceremony. Looking upon them with his brown eyes with golden-yellow sheen, he looked extremely delighted to present them with their new ruler.

He reached for Isra's right hand, announcing proudly, "Citizens of Wretchenheart, I present to you your new queen! Lady Isra of the Dark, Queen of Wretchenheart. May she reign unto you for all eternity."

Astrid gasped as he looked on at Isra. She remained dignified, sitting upon her throne and looking towards all of her new subjects with much reservation.

She had been taken to the sacred realm of Wretchenheart once before by Astrid himself. But now, she was the Queen of Darkness.

The End.

INTRODUCING QUEEN OF DARKNESS

DARK SPELL SERIES BOOK 4

Just at the dead of midnight, Astrid watched quietly as Isra tossed Alan's decaying carcass onto the green grassy field. A murder of crows gathered around, preparing to feast on his flesh. Isra stood back in awe of her triumph from the balcony of her newly acquired castle that carried the same name as her beloved dominion. The castle sat empty for a good many years but Damien Daughtry told Astrid that Wretchenheart was unoccupied and in need of a new queen. So henceforth, Isra was to be that ruler.

Her coronation was short yet memorable and even she felt rather tired after the massive show that was put on for the over-eager citizens that had resided in this tainted dimension. Isra couldn't help but feel an emotional attachment as she watched Alan's cold body lying in a mass of green grassland. But by the same token, she didn't want his rotting corpse causing one heck of a stench. He had to go. However, she softly caught sight of all the crows preparing themselves to snack upon his lifeless body and felt it rather symbolic.

"It's sad he won't be remembered by many. It's a shame he'll only be regarded in disdain but when you consider all the heinous things he has done, well, it is to be expected, one supposes," she muttered as she wistfully caught Astrid looking upon her. "Have you been lurking there long, dear?" Isra asked in a friendly manner.

"Sorry. I couldn't help but admire you. You've become a marvellous creature. Far beyond anything any of us could have imagined. It is remarkable to witness," Astrid gushed apologetically.

"I'm still trying to make sense of all this. I was holed in a chateau for the longest time and now I am suddenly a queen of a forlorn nation. You whisked me away so quickly, it wasn't as though I had a choice," Isra commented as she perused the idea that Astrid knew more than he'd detailed to her.

This man is truly something else. His knowledge of the realms and how life manages to work itself out is overwhelming. He's so eccentrically regal that I can't help but think he was born for the role he's about to commence. That is if he'll accept my offer of becoming my king. I don't wish to have to utilise an alternative. I seldom trust men that are placed at my disposal but he has proved his loyalty to me so I'll accept no other, Isra thought as she watched the group of crows unceremoniously sink their beaks into Alan's soon to be rotting flesh. He'd only been in Wretchenheart for less than six hours but since they'd travelled so swiftly, he'd still been pretty fresh when they arrived.

All of this was so new to Isra. She'd been trapped in the fortress that was Shambre Fell and she knew it wasn't truly her idea. There were supernatural forces behind it, ensuring she was installed there. Isra was still rather hazy on the details but Astrid assured her it was the truth. She did wonder, however, if there was a way to snatch back her memories since she wanted to know all of the excellent accomplishments she had mastered in her short yet intriguing life.

"It doesn't bear any consequence. Be proud of all you've done! Alan is a means to an end but the reason we are here in Wretchenheart is that you took his precious life. You've accumulated a mass amount of enemies," Astrid carefully explained, though he was quick in changing the narrative when he reassured her, "But you are untouchable in Wretchenheart, and that's why I brought you here."

"It's unorthodox. I shall give it that," Isra responded coolly.

"Yes, and becoming queen at such a young age is no doubt a lot for you to get your head around, but I promise it only gets better from here on out," Astrid told her profoundly.

"If you do say so. I am just thrown by the whole shenanigan. So as you shipped me over here, you said I incurred the wrath of many. I was wondering if you might be so kind as to inform me who those may be," Isra asked sweetly. "It's no matter. I was just curious," she added, motioning a pause.

She hadn't known Astrid for very long but already Isra trusted him enough to take him up on his word. He'd whisked her to this deserted, demonic dimension the moment he realised she took her revenge scenario with Alan too far. Not only that, but Astrid held only Isra's best interests at heart when he'd made the major decision to bring her here out of the blue.

"And you had a choice in it. Of course, you did, but I knew after my conversation with Damien that you couldn't simply reside at Shambre Fell any longer. I wasn't sure if you'd simply come along if I asked so I acted on instinct," Astrid admitted in a strong stance. In any event, it will be dawn soon," Astrid reminded her. "That means Samuel will soon have full knowledge of your transgression."

My killing Alan will be seen as quite an enterprising feat. If Mr Reynaldi possesses a strong stomach, it may not be suited to his well-mannered tastes. But if Astrid proclaims him to be such a worldly leader, he will undoubtedly be prepared for such an occurrence as mine, Isra thought.

It went through her mind that Samuel's already piquing interest in her might be more than just a need to quell her existence from the realm.

"He has a lot of insight into what goes on within the realms, doesn't he?"

Isra pressed the issue gently with Astrid, knowing he was somewhat standoffish when it came to the subject of Samuel. But Astrid was more than happy to divulge his knowledge despite his bitter experiences with the light-bringer.

"That he does indeed. It's only a matter of hours before the intricate organisation 'on high' delivers the awe-inspiring blow that you've taken out a Grimsbane warlock. When you look at it in that context, it sure is a talking point," Astrid summarised.

In fact, I'll be very taken aback if he doesn't know already. Samuel is the great and powerful know-it-all of our magical lands. If he isn't abreast with it, then I don't know. Except for myself and Damien, who knew this would be a possibility that Isra would indeed take things beyond her means.

Astrid resigned to thinking that perhaps Samuel was already very much aware of their occurrence since he was drawn to all things unsightly.

Samuel shifted uncomfortably as he lay on the white silk sheets of his bed. His body rolled back and forth nervously and he endlessly grasped onto the equally soft white linen covers. The curtains in his bedroom were black, blocking out any light from the outside world. It was a bit of an odd colour for a light-bringer to choose but he was a light sleeper and easily stirred. Being in the position he was in, Samuel often had rather disturbing dreams and terrors invade his precious sleep. Tonight was no exception, considering it was just about to strike three o'clock in the morning.

There she is. Our femme fatale, bright as ever in her effervescent energy. Oh, but look, suddenly her shimmery golden hair doesn't quite contrast with the dark shadow in her eyes. And why is this?

Her eyes look duller. Almost as though they have been tainted. Yes, something has happened, but what is it?? Now our young enchantress has had quite the enthralling evening but I wonder if she'd be so kind to reveal just what sadness lies behind those normally glimmering green eyes.

From his dream state, Samuel came face to face with Lady Isra. She stood under the merciless blinding sun, looking flabbergasting in a serene white lacy gown ruched at the shoulders while the long sleeves were brilliantly matched with black roses embroidered on the ends. Samuel noticed that they were standing on lemon-yellow sand while calm, tranquil crystalline waves glimmered in the distance.

Samuel cleared his throat, preparing to speak with Isra in her etheric form. He knew there was something peculiar about the witch, for her stomach was bubbling ferociously. His eyes gently went upward to her heart, which was bulging out of her at the rapid rate it was vibrating inside her chest. The intensity of it caused Isra to clasp her chest hurriedly.

"Well, I guess here we are. I am not sure what you are doing in my dream?" Isra questioned. She was bewildered at seeing him here.

"I think it may be a case of you eavesdropping into mine, but it's no bother, girl. Tell me, why Nefaria Sands?" Samuel piped up. He knew his question was meaningless but still, he requested the reply as though she would thoughtfully give it.

"I guess this is where it all began," Isra mused, still grabbing her stomach. "Tell me, old man, why is it when things get rough in my life, I nearly always find you in the thick of it?" Isra probed tentatively.

"I don't know how to answer that. You mean to presume I am responsible for the unholy occurrence that has emerged in both of our subconscious?" Samuel asked in an eager tone.

"I guess, one way or the other, we are going to find out," Isra recited cryptically.

Oh, boy, is this getting irritating now. Something has gone down but our mysterious yet devilish enchantress has yet to detail to me just how delicious it is. I wonder if she somehow knows about Nefaria, otherwise, why bring me here? Samuel concurred in his thoughts. He was able to put his finger on the ideation that something had gone disastrously wrong.

"Something has happened, hasn't it, Isra? Come on now. Tell me. I might be able to help. Is it the Grimsbane chap? He let you down again, did he?"

Samuel gasped, exhilarated in Isra's presence; white illuminated sparks emitted off her as she stood erect in the dazzling mid-morning sun. The seas of Nefaria Sands had never looked so pristine as they did now in their stunning aquamarine colouring. The waves crashed against the seashore ever so violently, rushing in to keep up with the current.

Isra smiled at Samuel. She held a black rose in her dominant hand and lifted the rose to her lips, winking at Samuel as she stopped to smell its pungent scent.

"I suppose it has, but there's very little anyone can do now," Isra retorted quietly.

"What do you mean, girl? It's not too late. I know why you picked here of all locations. This is where I infamously disarmed you in front of Astrid's eyes. I know the experience must have been horrifically traumatic but believe me when I say I was doing what I believed to be right. If there's a situation unfolding with Grimsbane, just tell me. I am sure I can assist you with it. It's never too late to remedy something, even if we deem it to be impossible," Samuel implored.

His voice was so scratchy that he was almost begging her to let him know whatever it was that had happened. He *needed* to know. Samuel was a very desperate man at this moment in time but he was prepared to do anything to grasp whatever Isra had to relay unto him.

"That's just the trouble. No one can help Alan Grimsbane anymore," Isra remarked.

The jet-black rose fell to the ground at once as Isra's smile switched from sweet and friendly to a most mischievous glare whereby she remained triumphant, much to Samuel's perplexity as he couldn't comprehend her meaning.

"What do you mean, child? Of course, he can be helped, but my interest is you and only you," Samuel pressed.

Isra simply lowered her gaze before turning her back to Samuel. She looked out onto the beautiful, serene blue oceans of Nefaria Sands. "I am sure you believe wholly in your stratagem. Alas, I don't trust you, but since this is a dream, I know with absolute conviction that this was the scene whereby you stole a part of my life away from me. Since that time, I have felt completely beyond your 'help,' so don't pity me, old man. Worry about yourself."

Isra continued to have her back turned and Samuel's pleas went unheard.

Samuel uttered softly, "Please, Isra. Tell me. Tell me, girl."

Isra kept her smile firmly affixed as Samuel's urgent need to reason with her dissipated from her mind. Slowly, the image of Isra began to fade until Samuel's words were not even audible and blackness descended upon the two of them, obliterating everything into nothingness.

Samuel awoke in a cold sweat, clutching his bed covers. He felt the silk on his fingertips. Reaching over to his bedside table, he put on his half-moon spectacles and ran his hand over his slicked-back black hair. He pulled the bed covers off of him as he earnestly lifted himself upright, placing his feet onto the cold stone floor.

Tonight was not going to be a night where he'd attempt to sleep again anytime soon.

"One must busy themselves with something intellectual to stimulate the piquing interests of their mind," Samuel mused.

He proceeded to get out of his elaborate bed, taking care to put the silk bed coverings back in place as he made the bed. He stretched his tired muscles and walked quietly into his office, still wearing his jet-black silk shirt pyjamas. Samuel manoeuvred over to his well-kept bookcase, pulling a thick volume from the shelf before he strode over to his red velvet armchair, planting himself down onto the seat, and began perusing the pages of the large tome. Samuel's half-moon silver-framed spectacles kept his bewildering sky-blue eyes from wandering as he came to a distinct conclusion.

"I need to contact Damien Daughtry. If something is up with Isra, he's my best chance of finding the truth."

DARK SPELL SERIES READING ORDER

1. Her Dark Love
2. Kissing Darkness
3. Seducing Darkness
4. Queen of Darkness
5. Her Dark Soul
6. Her Dark Heart
7. Her Dark Rose
8. Darkness Reborn

ABOUT THE AUTHOR

USA Today Best Seller Isra Sravenheart resides in the UK. She is an avid reader, particularly in the fantasy and paranormal genres, and very much into all things fairytale and dark in nature. She is also a witty wordsmith.

Isra is known for being obsessed with coffee and very particular towards cats of which she owns four of the buggers.

You can follow Isra through her blog, or any of these social media platforms:

ALSO BY ISRA SRAVENHEART

The Dark Spell Series: Books 1 through 8

Heart of Oz

Tainted Siren

The Divine Spiritual Truth: A Twinflame Romance